LORD CARLTON'S KISS

"Oh, blast!" Roma exclaimed as she realized her elegantly arranged curls had managed to become entangled in the wooden archway.

"Hold still," Lord Carlton commanded, loosening his grip on her waist to inspect her tangled curls. "I fear you have made a devilish mess of this, my dear."

She sucked in a sharp breath, far too conscious of his nearness. "Could you please just untangle me?" she demanded.

"Patience, Roma," he murmured, gently pulling at her uncooperative locks.

"Surely it cannot be that difficult?"

He gave her a slow smile. "Actually, it is quite difficult. How am I to concentrate when I am being so thoroughly distracted by that enticing scent of honeysuckle?"

"My lord . . ."

"Giles," he corrected in low tones.

"Are you going to assist me or not?"

His breath sweetly brushed her cheek as he gave a last tug. "There. You are free."

Thoroughly unnerved, she waited for him to step back so that they could resume their circuit to the house. Annoyingly, he remained towering over her with that devilish amusement softening the angles of his magnificent countenance.

"We should retur~ to the house. Aunt Clara will be wondering what we are d~ ~uch a length of time."

"I am confide~ ~disposition will provide any num~ ~nger." A slender finger lig~ ~he moonlight, the scent ~ ~few stolen kisses."

"This is absurd," she brea~

"We really should not disappoint th~ ~t lady." His voice dropped to a husky pitch as his dark head angled downward . . .

CELEBRATE THE NEW YEAR
WITH ZEBRA REGENCY ROMANCE
AND THESE TALENTED NEW AUTHORS

December 1999
LORD ST. CLAIRE'S ANGEL, by Donna Simpson

January 2000
LORD CARLTON'S COURTSHIP, by Debbie Raleigh

February 2000
AFFECTIONATELY YOURS, by Kathryn June

March 2000
LORD STANHOPE'S PROPOSAL, by Jessica Benson

April 2000
LORD LANGDON'S KISS, by Elena Greene

LORD CARLTON'S COURTSHIP

Debbie Raleigh

Zebra Books
Kensington Publishing Corp.
http://www.zebrabooks.com

ZEBRA BOOKS are published by

Kensington Publishing Corp.
850 Third Avenue
New York, NY 10022

Zebra and the Z logo Reg. U.S. Pat. & TM Off.

First Printing: January, 2000
10 9 8 7 6 5 4 3 2 1

Printed in the United States of America

One

Gunshots pierced the chill night air, barely noticeable over the rumble of the approaching storm and the thunder of hooves as four desperate riders dodged through the well-prepared ambush. Lord Giles Carlton peered through the driving rain, urging his exhausted mount through the treacherous mud of the wide lane.

There was another round of shots and suddenly the horse closest to Giles's stumbled, and the slight figure upon it slumped forward. With a muttered curse, Giles leaned sideways to grasp the reins of the frightened horse, gritting his teeth at the effort needed to keep both nervous thoroughbreds under control.

The night had turned into an unmitigated disaster. In the comfort of his elegant London home, it had seemed a simple enough task. He and his cousin, Jack Howe, were to travel to the coast and at an isolated spot retrieve a packet of letters smuggled in from France. Although Giles had sold out his commission the year before, he had often carried out such delicate missions in a purely unofficial capacity.

Now, fleeing through the night with gunshots ringing in his ears and the cold rain drenching his rough wool clothing, he desperately wished he had outgrown his thirst for adventure and remained in his safe, warm house.

Of course, it was too late for regrets. He had accepted

the commission without hesitation, just as he had accepted all the other assignments over the past few years. He had always known that his luck might run out at some point.

Shoving aside these fruitless thoughts, he concentrated on his unfamiliar surroundings. Somehow he had to find shelter. Not only was he concerned with the condition of the silent youth at his side, but he realized it was suicidal to plunge through the darkness at such a speed.

Somewhere behind him, his cousin and the second man who had met them on the beach were attempting to avoid the gang of ruffians, but unable to relay any message, he could only trust in Jack's ability to fend for himself as he veered the two horses off the road and entered the small copse of trees.

Retreating a few feet into the sheltering darkness, he drew the horses to an abrupt halt. Then, barely daring to breathe, he listened intently to the angry shouts of his pursuers as they raced by. For a moment he could imagine he was close enough to smell the stench of their filthy clothing, to feel the spray of mud from their horses hooves. But, unbelievably, they never bothered to glance toward the trees where he hid.

Still, even when it was clear that he had momentarily given them the slip, he remained frozen to the spot, silently hoping they didn't have the sense to backtrack when they discovered they had lost their prey.

It wasn't until the lad at his side gave a low moan that he unclenched his taut muscles and turned to deal with his silent companion.

"I think we have managed to elude them for the moment," he whispered softly. "Are you hurt?"

"Yes, my shoulder." The voice was barely audible, and Giles moved his horse closer.

In the darkness the form appeared pathetically small, and Giles gave a sharp frown. When he and Jack had met the two couriers on the beach, he hadn't particularly noticed either of them. At the time he had been more intent on receiving the packet he'd been ordered to take to London, and only moments later they had been attacked. Now he wondered if the government had become desperate enough to recruit boys barely out of their short coats.

"Can you go on?" he demanded, his voice unconsciously harsh. "In time those brigades will realize that we are no longer ahead of them and come back to search the road."

"I know." There was a pause; then the soft voice continued. "There is a barn not far from here. Do you think we would be safe there?"

"A barn?" Giles thrust aside his irrational burst of anger. The child had suffered enough for one night. "Can you lead me there?"

"I think so."

With an obvious effort the young man regained control of his reins, then cautiously began to head deeper into the thicket. Giles followed close behind, silently cursing his predicament. For all he knew Jack was still being pursued by the bloodthirsty gang, and he was lost in the soggy darkness with a wounded child.

Once more his thoughts veered to London and the various invitations he had declined. Although the Season wasn't yet under way, there was always entertainment to be found. His hallway had been littered with various gilt-edged invitations, and he knew there would be several hopeful mamas fervently hoping he would make an appearance at their small gatherings.

He heaved a small sigh, deciding that perhaps his current troubles might not be so bad after all. Granted, he was human enough to appreciate the luxury and elegant ease of his life, but the price he paid was being forever hounded by suitable young women intent on capturing his wary heart.

There appeared to be no end to their feminine tricks and Giles had long ago given up hope of discovering a woman who could arouse more than a fleeting passion.

His father had warned him to live and love with honor—
words Giles had taken to heart. How could he possibly
honor a woman willing to sacrifice herself to the highest
bidder?

"There it is."

The muffled words diverted him from his dark
thoughts, and Giles peered through the darkness to see
the faint outlines of a large structure.

"Stay here," he commanded. "I will check to ensure
that it is safe."

Without giving the lad time to argue, Giles slowly made
his way to the edge of the trees. The storm was increasing
in intensity, and the brilliant flashes of lightning enabled
him to ascertain that the barn was well isolated and there
appeared to be no sign of life. Beneath him the horse
shied nervously at a loud clap of thunder, and with a
decisive nod of his head, Giles returned to his companion.

"I think we must risk the barn. At least until the storm
passes," he said. "Can you make it there?"

"I'll make it."

Giles smiled slightly. The child had spunk, he acknowledged as he turned and guided his wary horse to the
barn. Many men would have been complaining bitterly
at the miserable conditions and a no doubt painful
wound. And yet, this child had managed to find them
shelter without a word of complaint. He sincerely hoped
that meant the boy wasn't as badly injured as he'd first
feared. His doctoring skills were severely limited.

With his finely honed instincts on full alert, Giles cautiously approached the barn, pausing a moment before
slipping off his mount and tugging open one of the large
doors.

A pungent odor of dust and moldy straw instantly filled
the air, but Giles ignored the unpleasant scent. At the
moment the barn was as welcome as the finest home in
England. Leading his horse into the musty shadows, he
listened as his companion followed closely behind. Then,

jumping off his exhausted horse, Giles moved to search his bag for the candle and flint he had placed in it earlier. After considerable effort there was at last a soft glow of light. Turning he watched as the slender youth began to slowly dismount, but even as he moved forward to provide assistance, the small form abruptly crumpled into a heap on the hard dirt floor.

With a soft curse, Giles hurried forward, swiftly moving the horses to the far side of the barn. Tethering their reins to a pole, he returned to the frighteningly still child, and carefully reached down to move the fragile body onto a pile of nearby hay.

A stab of anger shot through his heart at feeling the slight weight in his arms. *For God's sake, the boy must be even younger than I imagined,* he thought in disbelief. *Who on earth would allow a mere child to be placed in such a dangerous position?*

It was something he was determined to discover as soon as possible. It was all very well for grown men to make the decision to risk their lives for the welfare of their country, but it was quite another to induce innocent children to do it.

With gentle care, he made the unconscious boy as comfortable as possible; then, turning, he cleared a space to set down the candle. In the feeble light he could make out the pale, almost delicate features of the lad, but attempting to ignore his disgust at a child's having been injured in such a manner, he forced his gaze to the thin woolen shirt that was stained an ugly shade of crimson.

Uncertain what he could do in the rough confines of the barn, Giles decided to at least inspect the wound. If nothing else he could reassure himself that the boy wasn't about to become a corpse.

Attempting to be as gentle as possible, considering his fingers were stiff with cold and the soggy fabric of the shirt refused to cooperate, Giles at last breathed a hiss of exasperation. The child might bleed to death at this rate, he acknowledged, and gritting his teeth, he grasped the material, about to give it a mighty yank.

Considering his recent run of luck, he wasn't particularly surprised when the shirt abruptly ripped from shoulder to waist. He could only hope the unfortunate lad possessed more than one set of clothing. Heaving a sigh, he grabbed the candle and leaned forward to survey the damage.

At first his sole concern was centered on the torn flesh from which a small amount of blood continued to seep. But, as he peered closer, he was deeply relieved to discover that there wasn't a serious injury. Clearly the bullet had merely clipped the top of the shoulder. A painful injury, no doubt, but not life threatening.

Satisfied the boy would survive, Giles was about to pull away when the candle flickered and instinctively his gaze followed the shadows dancing along pale skin. Abruptly his loud gasp filled the silent barn. For a horrified moment, Giles refused to accept what his eyes were telling him. It couldn't be possible. Or, at least, it shouldn't be possible. But even as he shook his head in denial, he knew it was the truth.

A woman. Hell and damnation, it was a woman.

Mesmerized by a combination of shock and utter disbelief, he stared wide-eyed at satin skin glowing with the rich luster of a pearl in the candlelight, and the unmistakable thrust of a rose-tipped breast exposed by the tattered shirt. Hardly aware of what he was doing, Giles reached out a hand and plucked the dark cap from her head, his breath rushing through his teeth as a cascade of deep auburn curls spread onto the hay.

Not just a woman, his bemused mind conceded, but an incredibly beautiful woman, despite the cheap male clothing and the dirt clinging to her delicately formed features. What color were her eyes? Green? With that hair it would be only natural . . .

A sudden wave of disgust rose through his body as he realized where his stunned thoughts were leading. With an almost violent movement, he was on his feet and striding angrily toward the neglected horses.

Had the government run completely mad, he seethed silently, searching for a brush to groom his weary steed. What could have possessed them to allow a woman to become entangled in such a dangerous liaison? Surely there had to be mistake? At least it had better be a mistake, he silently amended. Otherwise he would ensure that someone paid for this unforgivable act.

Consumed with anger, Giles devoted his time to caring for the horses, and taking a short walk around the barn to ensure that no one had noticed their arrival. Then, returning inside, he paused beside the slight figure stretched on the hay.

He had managed to work off his initial burst of fury, but at the sight of her lying so still and helpless, blood marring her white skin, he found his muscles once more tightening in anger. He wanted to confront whomever was responsible for the woman's presence on the beach, but unable to release his mounting frustration, Giles could do no more than carefully cover her limp frame with his heavy coat and retreat a few feet to settle his lithe frame uneasily on the lumpy hay.

He was thoroughly exhausted, but he had no thought of sleep. Someone would have to keep guard through the remainder of the night, and since it was clear that his companion was incapable of lending any aid, Giles resigned himself to a long, miserable night.

Unknowingly his gaze returned to the fragile profile of the mysterious woman, but rather than futilely ponder on where she might have come from or how she'd become involved in this current dilemma, he instead thought back to the moment when everything had gone wrong.

There had been nothing to warn him that they were being watched. He and Jack had set off from the Posting Inn at the appropriate time, and hadn't encountered a soul on their way to the secluded cove. Exactly as directed the two couriers had approached, using the correct pass-word before handing over the well-wrapped package.

It was at that moment a fatal flash of lightning had streaked through the darkness and they had heard the sound of a startled horse. Almost as one, the four on the beach had turned and headed inland, startling the wait-ing gang enough to pass by them before they could at-tack.

It was mere luck they had managed to escape at all. Giles had little doubt the men were under orders to kill all four of them, and he could only wonder who had set up the well-planned ambush.

His mind instantly dismissed the woman and her un-known partner. The thugs had fired randomly at the re-treating horsemen, obviously unconcerned as to whom they might hit. Besides, either of them could easily have killed him and Jack the moment they had approached.

No, it had to be someone else. Someone who had been intimately familiar with the details of the plan—and who wanted the packet, now safely stored in his bag, enough to kill for it.

Shivering slightly, Giles huddled deeper in the uncom-fortable hay. He was desperately worried about his im-petuously brave cousin. Had he somehow managed to escape the bloodthirsty gang? Would he have the sense to continue toward London or would he be foolhardy enough to return and risk his life in search of him?

Giles sighed, wishing he had left Jack safely in London. This wasn't the first adventure his cousin had accompa-nied him on, and normally he enjoyed Jack's ready hu-mor and enthusiasm. It wasn't until tonight that he fully realized the danger to which he had exposed the young man.

Sunk in dark thoughts as the night slowly passed and the storm eased, Giles eventually rose to stretch his knot-ted muscles. He was fairly confident the danger had passed, but his mind was far from easy.

There were still too many unanswered questions that

had to be settled. Starting with the woman still lying peacefully in the straw. Taking a step forward, he came to a sudden halt as she stirred slightly, her heavily fringed lids fluttering slowly open.

Absurdly Giles found himself holding his breath as her confused gaze traveled over his mud-splattered clothing and tousled raven hair. Hazel, he thought inanely, meeting her wide eyes with an unconscious frown. He had been almost certain they would be green.

"Where am I?"

The voice was weak, but Giles instantly sensed the fear in her low words. Moving forward, he knelt beside her on the hay.

"To be honest, I haven't the least notion. You led us to this barn after we managed to elude the gang chasing us."

Her lids briefly closed, then once more lifted, the vivid beauty of her eyes pronounced even in the dim shadows of the barn.

"I remember now. They surprised us on the beach . . . I was shot."

"Nothing serious," he swiftly reassured her. "You should be healed within the month."

She seemed to breathe a soft sigh. "I couldn't tell. It felt as if my shoulder were on fire. Do you think they are gone?"

"Yes, I imagine they gave up several hours ago. Such men might be willing to attack the unwary, but I doubt they possess the ambition to search for armed men in such miserable conditions as existed."

His brisk tone slightly eased the tension of her pale features, but his shrewd gaze didn't miss the flicker of unease that entered her large eyes.

"I suppose I should thank you. I have no doubt that you saved my life."

"Perhaps." Giles gave an indifferent shrug. "But you were the one who discovered this barn. Without it, we both would have suffered through a very unpleasant night."

"I am glad I remembered it was here." She displayed a small frown. "Do you know what happened to my . . . companion? I can barely remember what happened after I was shot."

Giles narrowed his gaze. The woman's voice was soft, but there was no mistaking the cultured tone.

"No, but I trust he and my cousin are fine. Jack is a good man to have along in an emergency."

She nodded her head, then flinched slightly as his heavy coat rubbed her tender wound. "I hope you are right."

"Are you in pain?" He reached out an instinctive hand to check her injury, only to be halted as she hastily sank deeper into the hay.

"No, I'm fine. Just a bit sore."

Giles arched a chiseled brow, the brilliant blue of his eyes filled with wry humor.

"I fear that it is a little too late for modesty. Unfortunately there was no one here but myself last night to see to your injury."

An unexpected flush bloomed beneath her pale cheeks. "I see."

His firmly sculptured lips twisted. "I did not, at least not until too late. I assumed that you were a young boy."

Her lids dropped in painful embarrassment. "I never expected . . . I did not think anyone would know."

"Clearly you were mistaken," he retorted firmly, ignoring the vulnerable image she made with her vibrant curls haloing that pale face and the full softness of lips trembling with emotion. He wanted an explanation for her outrageous behavior. "Now, I think it is time you told me exactly what you were doing in that cove last night."

Beguiled by her blushing confusion, he was caught off guard when her gaze abruptly lifted to stab him with a sparkling glare.

"I don't see why that is necessary. I am grateful for

your assistance, but I think it is best if we remain anonymous."

"Don't be absurd." Giles gave a disbelieving frown. "I can hardly escort you home without at least knowing your name. This situation is going to be difficult enough to explain as it is. I sincerely hope your father doesn't see fit to call me out."

"That's hardly likely, considering that he is dead," she retorted bluntly. "And there is no need for you to escort me anywhere. You have the letters you came for; you should be on your way to London."

Naturally he ignored her last foolish words. There would be no argument about his seeing her safely home, no matter what the damage to her reputation. But he did find himself curious about her family. What sort of people would allow this young innocent to roam through the night, disguised as a boy and interfering in matters she had no business knowing about?

"If you have no father, then who is your guardian?"

For a moment he thought she meant to ignore his question, but finally she gave a restless movement.

"My brother."

"I assume he has no knowledge of your adventure?"

She paused, an odd flash of pain rippling across her face. "No."

"I am relieved." He tilted his dark head to one side. "No doubt in the future he will be more diligent in his responsibilities. It was sheer insanity for you to enter into such a dangerous charade."

Once more the hazel eyes flashed. "And what of you?"

"Me?" His brow rose in surprise.

"Was it insanity for you to be at the cove last night?"

He experienced a flare of unexpected amusement at her sharp tone. The chit certainly had spirit.

"Perhaps, but at least I am capable of taking care of myself." He forced himself to lecture her severely. "Can you imagine what would have occurred if those ruffians had managed to waylay you? Trust me, you would have been pleading for death long before they eventually disposed of your body."

She gave a small shiver at his deliberately blunt words, and he felt a twinge of guilt at forcing her to contemplate such sordid thoughts. Still, he silently reassured himself, it was best she realized the extent of her folly. Perhaps the next time she would think twice before capering off on some madcap scheme.

"Please, I do not wish to discuss last night," she managed to murmur weakly. "My shoulder aches, and I am desperately thirsty. Could I have some water?"

He allowed himself to smile at her very feminine complaints. He'd been starting to wonder if she possessed any womanly qualities. At least in more than just the physical sense, he corrected, a sudden heat flickering through his lower body as he recalled the exposed beauty of her slender form. Almost instantly he was on his feet, disgruntled by his vivid memories.

"If I remember correctly there is a stream not too far away," he said rigidly, keeping his expression unreadable. "You rest here, and I will be back in a few moments."

"You are so very kind," she muttered, her lids drooping with a mixture of pain and exhaustion.

With a wry smile, he wondered if she would think him so kind if she knew precisely what thoughts had been burning in his mind; then, with a small shrug, he turned and headed for the bag he had left beside the horses.

Within moments he had extracted a fine silver flask, and with one last glance at the sleeping woman, he quietly made his way out of the barn, leaving the door wide open in case she should call for help.

It was a fine morning, he discovered, heading toward the line of trees they had traversed the night before. Overhead the early morning sun attempted to dry the lingering wetness of the tender spring grass, and the air was spiced with the pungent scent of wildflowers. A perfect day for a ride, he decided, feeling unexplainably lighthearted for a man in his position.

No doubt it was mere relief after the traumatic night, he concluded, halting beside the small stream. A natural reaction to a near-death experience.

Bending down, he was in the act of filling the flask with the chilled water when a sudden noise had him jumping to his feet.

Spinning about he rushed back toward the barn, his instincts on full alert. But despite his speed it took several moments to at last reach the edge of the thick woods, and even as he stepped clear of the trees a horse galloped past him, headed for the wide fields that surrounded the barn.

For long moments he stood in frozen amazement, watching the tiny woman disappear over a low hill. Then he gave a disgusted shake of his head.

"Damn."

For the first time in his life, Lord Giles Carlton had been neatly outwitted. And by a pint-sized chit with more courage than sense.

Two

The babble of conversation nearly drowned out the lively music playing in the corner of the large ballroom as the glittering guests swayed past.

"Smile, Roma. This is a party."

Slightly turning, Roma Allendyle favored her handsome young cousin with a condemning glare.

"That's easy for you to say, Claude. As a male you are free from the constant surveillance of those malicious tabbies in the corner. I am quite certain that they are impatiently awaiting for some excuse to rip me to shreds."

Claude Welford gave an appreciative chuckle at the frustrated edge in the young woman's voice. He easily remembered his first season in London and his terror of the grim dowagers. No doubt it was even more terrifying for Roma. Not only did she possess far more spirit than was proper for a young lady, but she had been raised in a haphazard style by her eccentric father. More often than not the Colonel forgot Roma was a young lady, treating her much the same as his oldest son, William. Now that she was being abruptly thrust into Polite Society, she must feel overtly aware of her lack of feminine polish.

"Ignore them," he commanded softly, drawing her slightly away from the large crowd filling the ballroom. "You are doing splendidly. I have overheard more than one old matron telling Mama how becoming they found your manners. I swear I nearly burst out laughing when one babbled on about your sweet nature and modest demeanor. I wondered what she would think if she could see you in your breeches, striding around Greystead Manor like a tyrant and frightening the poor estate manager with your riding whip."

The hazel eyes that Roma had kept properly subdued with stern determination abruptly flared to life.

"That poor estate manager was attempting to rob me blind, and with Father dead and William missing, I didn't have much choice but to take charge of the estate. Something impossible to do when everyone used my skirts as an excuse to ignore my every order."

"Don't fly into a pet, Roma." Claude flashed her an engaging grin, appearing boyishly handsome with his golden blond hair and elegant attire. Although not a dandy, he took inordinate pride in his Weston-tailored coat and elaborately arranged cravat. "You have my full respect for the way you have managed to keep Greystead on its feet. And I also appreciate the sacrifice you made in allowing Mama to drag you to London for your introduction to Society. I know quite well how much you detest behaving like a proper lady."

Roma attempted to send the taunting man a censorious glare, but the amused sparkle in his brown eyes was her undoing, and with a rueful sigh she glanced around the brightly lit room with its lavish decor and noble assembly. She knew most women at the advanced age of three and twenty would be overjoyed at making a long overdue entrance into the London *ton*. But while she did find many of the various entertainments diverting, she longed for the unrestricted freedom of her home. Only there could she feel truly comfortable and able to concentrate on matters far more interesting than the latest fashion or who had flirted with whom at the previous assembly.

Still, she had come to London with a purpose. It had been nearly three weeks since William had left Greystead on a covert mission for the government, and impatient with her futile attempts to discover his whereabouts locally, she had reluctantly given in to her aunt's insistent urging that she come to town—with the sole purpose of continuing her investigation. Now that she was here, however, she found herself uncertain about how to proceed. It wasn't as if she could simply begin asking each person she encountered if he or she knew where her brother might be. She had to somehow discover a means of being introduced to the few men who might have information.

"I will own that it has been difficult," she said softly. "In the week since we arrived I haven't had a moment's peace. Your mother has induced me to attend a dozen different gatherings, not to mention the visitations, the rides in the park and being outfitted with a completely new wardrobe."

"Yes, I applaud her efforts." With a languid movement designed to set his cousin's teeth on edge, Claude raised his quizzing glass to his eyes and slowly inspected her simple silk gown in a frothy sea green with jade ribbons that matched the velvet band in her vivid auburn curls. "You look quite different without your breeches, almost passable, in fact. But how did you manage to explain that bullet hole in your shoulder you are taking such pains to hide?"

Roma blushed. The wound, although nearly healed, was still shockingly red, and it had taken the modiste's considerable imagination to create gowns that satisfied the current fashion while hiding the disfiguring mark.

"I said that I had taken a fall while attempting to clear a hedge."

Claude gave a short burst of laughter. "Lord, that must have scratched at your pride. Everyone knows you have the best seat in the county. My mother must have windmills in her head to swallow such a Banbury tale."

"Please, Claude, I would rather not discuss that night," she said in a low tone. "It is something I am trying to forget."

"You never did tell me what happened to you." He tilted his head slightly. "All I know is that we were separated when those men attacked, and I spent one devil of a night waiting for you to return to Greystead."

She shivered slightly, unable to prevent the haunting image of a dark, aristocratic face and mocking blue eyes from rising to her mind. It was ludicrous that his potently handsome features should have troubled her during the last fortnight. He was just a man who had briefly passed in and out of her life, she told herself sternly. And if she hadn't met him under such traumatic circumstances, she doubted that she would have even taken note of him.

"Because there is nothing to tell," she forced herself to answer her cousin's subtle probing with a light tone. "Now why don't you go and flutter the hearts of the numerous young women who keep casting their lures in your direction? I wouldn't want to be accused of monopolizing one of England's most eligible bachelors."

Claude pulled a comical face. "I am not nearly deep enough in the pocket for that particular title. From all reports Lord Carlton is once more the season's prime catch."

"Carlton?" Roma wrinkled her brow. "I don't think we've been introduced."

"Trust me, you would remember if you had. According to most of the fairer sex, he is quite irresistible, not to mention as rich as a nabob," Claude informed her dryly.

Roma rolled her eyes. "You mean a shameless rake."

"Oh, I wouldn't go that far. He doesn't trifle with innocents, or anything of that sort. Of course, it is only natural that a man in his position would enjoy a few . . . pleasures in the petticoat line."

With a jaundiced eye, Roma watched her cousin blush. "Naturally."

"Dash it, Roma, I am constantly forgetting you are a woman and that I shouldn't talk of such things," he muttered.

"As if any woman were so noodle witted as not to know of demireps," she retorted in a chiding tone.

"Well . . . it is not proper."

She gave a small shrug. "Why should I care if this Lord Carlton has a dozen mistresses? He sounds like an odious man."

"Oh, no." Claude gave a shake of his head. "I only met him on one occasion, but he was a likable chap. Had a certain presence, if you know what I mean. And I can only wish I could have his reputation as a sportsman. He is a first-class Corinthian."

Thoroughly bored by Lord Carlton's seemingly endless list of accomplishments, she allowed her gaze to roam toward the dance floor now filled with colorful guests, all fully enjoying the music.

"How much longer need we stay?" she asked, her tone weary.

"Stay? We just arrived." Claude glanced at her in surprise. "Surely you would like to meet a few of the guests?"

Alerted to the odd edge in his voice, she abruptly returned her attention to the man at her side.

"Any guest in particular?" she asked in an ominous tone.

Thoroughly discomforted, Claude waved an embarrassed hand. "Just a few of my acquaintances."

"Oh, Claude, not you too," she cried, her expression annoyed. Claude was well aware that her presence in London had nothing to do with these devilishly dull parties or the various men dangled beneath her nose. It was bad enough to endure his mother's kindly, but relentless matchmaking without him adding to her trials. "You know I abhor starched-up dandies beyond all things."

Claude's fair skin reddened. "I'll have you know that my friends are not dandies, and if it wasn't for their continual badgering, I would never have agreed to introducing them to you. As it is, I can not imagine why they are so insistent. Granted you are not a bad-looking woman, but the fashion is for blond hair and blue eyes."

Roma's burst of anger instantly evaporated into a chuckle at Claude's sincere puzzlement. She, too, had been surprised by the attention she had attracted. As the daughter of a mere colonel with few female accomplishments to boast of, she had been quite prepared to find herself blithely ignored. But she hadn't counted on her determined aunt, who had complacently spoken of the Colonel's various acts of heroism, and of the Prince Regent's accommodation of his sacrifice for his country, or the fact that her mother came from a decidedly noble lineage. And she certainly hadn't counted on her unusually vivid coloring and deceptively frail form capturing the attention of men quite sated by the influx of insipid blond debutantes. Even her pointed lack of interest in their gallant attempts to engage her in light flirtations had only served to increase their pique. As a result she found herself in the uncomfortable position of being continually pursued, despite her best attempts to remain firmly in the shadows of the *ton*.

"Your compliments quite take my breath away, dear cousin."

He smiled sheepishly. "Well, I am more accustomed to seeing you astride a horse, with your face smudged and your hair hanging in your eyes. It is difficult to see you as a fine lady."

"Do not worry. I shall soon enough be back to my hoydenish ways," she reassured him, the light in her eyes dulled. "At least I hope so. So far my journey has been nothing more than a shocking waste of time."

Instantly sympathetic, Claude reached out a hand to lightly pat her forearm. "You must be patient, Roma. You can not hope—"

"Ah . . . Welford, isn't it? So good to meet up with you again."

Completely absorbed in their conversation, Claude and Roma gave a small start of surprise at the drawling voice interrupting their privacy. Strangely Roma felt a trickle of alarm inch down her spine as she reluctantly turned to regard the two men who were standing directly behind her.

A sharp stab of dismay held her spellbound as she

abruptly realized her instinctive recognition of the smoky voice. It was a voice she had heard far too often in her dreams. A voice that she had fiercely prayed she would never hear again. Now it was only with the most considerable effort that she forced herself to meet the mocking blue gaze of her rescuer.

Beside her, she felt Claude stiffen as well, but his next words proved that he failed to recognize the men who had shared their desperate flight for survival.

"Ah, Lord Carlton, this is a surprise. I thought you gave this sort of affair a wide berth."

Lord Carlton? Roma lifted her brows in silent surprise, recovering her shaken composure enough to notice the elegant knee breeches, the shimmering pale blue waistcoat and exquisitely molded coat. Every inch the refined gentleman, she acknowledged, remembering him in the muddy farmer's garments he had chosen for their first encounter. Of course, even when he was unshaven and in rough clothing, she had never taken him for anything but a gentleman. His completely natural air of command and the hint of arrogance etched in his handsome features had easily given him away. But . . . Lord Carlton? Rake, Corinthian, darling of society? It seemed preposterous.

As if he sensed her disbelief, a raven brow slowly rose, his finely molded lips quirking into a disturbing smile.

"I don't believe I've had the pleasure of making the young lady's acquaintance, Welford."

Completely rattled at being treated in such an intimate manner by the esteemed lord, Claude gave a nervous laugh.

"So sorry . . . My cousin, Miss Roma Allendyle. She is staying with my mother for the Season. Roma, may I present Lord Carlton and Mr. Howe?"

During the introduction, Roma took the opportunity to swiftly glance at the man standing next to Lord Carlton, instinctively sensing that the young, pleasant-faced fellow with the thatch of brown hair had also been on the beach that fateful night. She was certain, however, that he had no notion she had been involved. His glance was openly admiring, rather than filled with suspicion of a woman who would behave in such a reprehensible manner.

"Miss Allendyle, may I have the pleasure of the next dance?"

Unwillingly she returned her attention to the raven-haired man who seemed to tower unnervingly over her slight frame.

"Unfortunately I am recovering from a chill, Lord Carlton," she reeled off her well-practiced excuse. "My constitution is limited to merely watching the dancers."

Normally she added a charming smile to take any sting from her refusal, but battling her acute embarrassment and the unexplainable antagonism she had felt the moment she had met his cynical gaze, Roma found herself unable to do more than send him a stubborn glare.

The wicked amusement in the startlingly blue eyes only deepened. "How distressing, Miss Allendyle. We must ensure that you do not overly tire yourself and chance a relapse. Perhaps, Jack, you should go with Welford to procure some lemonade while I find a comfortable seat."

Caught off guard by his smooth manipulations, Roma could only blink in surprise. But clearly accustomed to his cousin's swift commands, Mr. Howe instantly rushed to assist.

"What? Oh, certainly, lemonade is most refreshing."

Grasping Claude's arm, he easily led the bemused man away, and Roma found herself abandoned to Lord Carlton's unwelcome company. Frowning, she turned to meet his narrowed gaze.

"That was completely unnecessary, my lord. I have no wish for lemonade, nor do I wish to sit down."

Her frosty tone had no effect on the man gazing at her with unnerving intensity, except perhaps to widen his sardonic smile.

"You must think of your health, Miss Allendyle. I remember how swiftly you can be overcome with fainting spells."

His tone was taunting, and Roma blushed as she realized he was referring to her behavior in the barn. Clearly it had rankled his pride to be outmaneuvered by a mere woman.

"I feel perfectly well, thank you."

"And I think you look a bit pale. Come along, like a good girl. You wouldn't want to create scene."

She opened her mouth to inform him that she couldn't care less, only to snap her lips closed when she noted the devilish glint in his eyes. No doubt his exalted position in Society would allow him to step well beyond the line of propriety with no more than a few raised brows, while she would be held up to condemning disgrace. A prospect that held little weight with her personal feelings, but at the moment she knew that she must think of her aunt and cousin. She couldn't deliberately harm them even if it meant succumbing to this odious man's manipulations.

"Very well, Lord Carlton," she gritted out lowly. "Since you are so insistent, I have little choice but to accept your kind offer."

He gave a low chuckle, reaching out to clasp her arm and draw her toward a small alcove that sported a loveseat and enough potted plants to ensure a discreet amount of privacy.

"Must you be so formal, Miss Allendyle?" he murmured, carefully placing her on the sofa before lowering his own disturbingly solid frame next to hers. "It is not as if we are complete strangers. In fact, I feel we are the most . . . intimate of acquaintances."

Thoroughly flustered, not only by Lord Carlton's deliberate taunts, but by the proximity of his very masculine form, Roma was hard pressed to meet his probing gaze with a steady composure.

"I had sincerely hoped you would be gentlemanly enough not to mention that unfortunate encounter, Lord Carlton."

"Oh? Is it a secret then?"

"Of course it is. No one but Claude knows I was there that evening."

"And me, of course," he reminded in a low tone.

"I assume that you are deliberately attempting to embarrass me?"

"Not at all," he retorted smoothly, quite unaffected by her icy demeanor. "I am simply delighted at the opportunity to become better acquainted. After you so rudely disappeared from the barn, I had resigned myself to the idea that I might never see you again."

"I am sure you must have been devastated," she retorted dryly. "As I recall, you considered me scandalously out of control and in need of more rigid supervision."

"Ah yes." His low laugh sent an odd flutter down the length of her spine. "At the time I was horrified at the thought you had placed yourself in such a dangerous position." The vivid blue gaze abruptly lowered to her unfashionably high neckline. "How is your shoulder?"

The gold flecks in her eyes were dangerously pronounced. "Healing."

"Good. Such delicate skin should not be so mistreated. You can not imagine how I longed to kiss it better."

She gave a small gasp. "Lord Carlton . . ."

"Giles."

"Lord Carlton," she repeated firmly, ignoring the way he managed to make her feel that he had actually stroked her shivering skin. "I refuse to proceed with this ridiculous conversation. If you have nothing more interesting to discuss, then I suggest we sit here in silence."

"Indeed? And what conversation would be more to your taste, dear Miss Allendyle? Lord Byron's latest poem? Turner's exhibition at the Royal Academy? Perhaps you prefer the more tantalizing rumors of Prinny's disfavor of Brummell?"

"I prefer the latest trend in tilling land, my lord, but I possess little hope you could supply such practical information. Like most London gentlemen, you are no doubt more intrigued with the cut of your coat and the sheen of your Hessians."

The prim words were specifically designed to strike at the arrogant man's pride, but rather than the anger she had expected, Lord Carlton merely tipped back his dark head to laugh with rich enjoyment.

"Well said, Miss Allendyle. I am relieved to discover your current transformation hasn't dulled your spirit." The blue eyes narrowed. "You know, I have thought of you quite often since our last encounter. You are a most fascinating young woman."

Roma had always taken great pride in her lack of feminine silliness. Unlike many of her contemporaries, she had never found pleasure in meaningless flattery or light flirtations. She had, in fact, found most men she encountered tedious, with their rigid expectations of how a young woman should conduct herself and of what mundane matters should occupy her mind.

In time she had considered herself thoroughly immune to masculine charm, but suddenly confronted by Lord Carlton's persistent attention, she discovered herself succumbing to an unfamiliar sense of flustered unease.

"I can not imagine why," she muttered, furiously wondering why it was taking Claude so long to return. Anyone would think he'd had to make the lemonade himself.

Lord Carlton studied her tense expression with languid ease. "Because I am curious about you, Miss Allendyle. You must admit that you are a most unusual young lady."

"Not at all," she instantly argued. "I am simply a mundane addition to this year's selection of debutantes. If you were to circulate you would discover far more interesting women ready to entertain you with their superior wit and charm."

"Ah, but I do not wish to be entertained by a bevy of insipid young debutantes," he countered smoothly. "You will soon learn, Miss Allendyle, that I have little patience for these types of affairs. Debutantes, managing mamas, and dowagers breathing fire in the corner are not my idea of a delightful evening."

She gave a sudden, triumphant smile as she rose swiftly to her feet.

"Why, Lord Carlton, you should have spoken sooner," she cried, her tone dangerously innocent. "I would never dream of keeping you here when it is so obvious you wish to take your leave."

"Not so quickly, Miss Allendyle." He rose to join her, his eyes sparkling with appreciation at her swift attack.

"But why? I should think you would wish to move on to the type of affair you find more to your taste."

"I was about to add that while I might find this gathering sadly flat, I am deeply relieved that Jack insisted we attend. Who knows how long you might have been in London without my being aware of your presence."

"Yes . . . What a stroke of luck." Her tone was singularly unenthusiastic.

He chuckled. "I fear you do not share my pleasure."

"I have little interest in Society, my lord, and unfortunately I make a tedious companion. You would be far better served to seek a more amiable partner."

"I am most qualified to determine which partner I prefer to seek, Miss Allendyle." He stepped closer, his gaze narrowing as he caught sight of Claude determinedly making his way through the crowd despite Mr. Howe's best attempt to distract his attention.

"We cannot converse here. I will call for you tomorrow afternoon, and we will go for a ride."

Her eyes widened at his authoritative tone. "I am quite sure I will be far too busy, Lord Carlton."

"I suggest you make time, Miss Allendyle." His indulgent humor remained intact, but there was no mistaking the edge of warning in his voice. "I fully intend to discover your reasons for being at that cove. I can do so in the relative privacy of my curricle, or in the presence of your family. Whichever you prefer."

"Is that a threat, my lord?"

"Most assuredly, Miss Allendyle."

Roma frowned in disbelief. She had attributed Lord Carlton's momentary interest in her to a means of enlivening a dull evening. Clearly he found her discomfort amusing. But she had never expected him to carry the joke to such extremes.

"Really, Lord Carlton, I think it is best if—"

"Ah, your escort has returned," Lord Carlton interrupted her as Claude and Mr. Howe joined them. Then, before Roma could guess his intention, he reached out to capture her hand and draw it to his mouth for a brief, but utterly unnerving kiss. For a moment her startled gaze was held by the mesmerizing blue of his eyes; then before she could even begin to protest, he was stepping back to nod distantly at the puzzled Claude. "Welford, a pleasure to see you. Shall we move on, Jack?"

With exquisite grace, Lord Carlton moved away, the crowd melting aside as he made his unhurried exit. Roma watched his departure in a haze of confusing emotions, not the least of which was the odd tingling across the back of her hand.

Claude, however, was unaffected by the strange spell that held Roma motionless, and he abruptly turned to eye her with baffled expectation.

"What the devil was that about?"

With a tiny shake, Roma forced herself to thrust aside her ridiculous sense of unreality. At the moment she didn't want to consider the disturbing encounter. Instead, she reached for the lemonade Claude still held in his hands.

"Do not inquire, Claude. Please, just do not inquire."

Three

Lord Carlton soon discovered that Claude Welford was not the only one who had noted his unusual interest in a young woman clearly in London for the Marriage Mart.

Only moments before he was preparing to leave for his appointment with Miss Allendyle, Jack Howe was shown into the long library, his face set into lines of open curiosity.

"Well, Giles, I hope you are aware you have the entire town chattering," he said, his gaze swiftly running over his cousin's elegant attire. As always Giles's tall, muscular frame managed to fill his superfine coat to perfection, and the black Hessians gleamed with a superior gloss. Even at his most casual he managed to cast others in the shade. "There are some saying that Lady Welford has somehow conduced you into making her niece the Toast of the Season."

With a lazy smile, Giles leaned against his massive walnut desk. "Considering that I have barely spoken a dozen words to Lady Welford, I would think that a remarkable task."

"My thoughts precisely," Jack retorted, moving to make himself comfortable in a wide leather chair. "So why don't you tell me the real reason you secluded yourself with Miss Allendyle for nearly a quarter of an hour?"

At two and thirty, Giles was five years older than his cousin, but that hadn't prevented them from forming a close friendship. Jack Howe was in fact one of the very few people who knew the man behind the elusive social charm, and the only one who was aware of Giles's secret connection to the government. But, for once, Giles felt no urge to confide his inner thoughts. The surprised delight he had felt upon seeing Roma Allendyle was something he planned to keep well hidden.

"My dear Jack, if you recall I was firmly against attending the affair in the first place," he drawled. "Who can blame me for attempting to relieve the boredom by chatting with a beautiful young lady?"

Jack frowned, clearly dissatisfied with the flippant response. "Certainly the Allendyle chit is attractive, but hardly your style, Giles."

Giles arched his brows in a lofty motion. "And what would you know of my . . . style?"

"I know enough to realize you normally give ambitious young debutantes a cold shoulder indeed," Jack retorted, his tone suspicious. "So why did you want me to drag poor Welford away so that you could be alone with the girl?"

"That is a question no gentleman should ask."

Jack gave an inelegant snort at his cousin's haughty tone. "Do not attempt to gammon me, Giles. You are up to something, and I think it is excessively unsporting of you not to include me."

Giles couldn't prevent a wry smile. It was obvious that Jack did not believe for a moment he could be interested in an innocent young woman, no matter how attractive she might be. And he couldn't honestly blame him for his disbelief. He had long shown a preference for the more experienced courtesans. Their beauty and pleasure could be easily acquired and just as easily dismissed, leaving his life uncomplicated. Besides, the price of a few jewels or even of maintaining a separate establishment was much easier to bear than the price young debutantes demanded.

And yet, for all his worldly sophistication, Giles couldn't

dismiss the knowledge that he had spent an inordinate amount of time wondering about the red-haired, hazel-eyed woman who had so annoyingly vanished into thin air. With great reluctance he had forced himself to concede he might never know her reasons for being at the cove, or why she had so rudely disappeared. That didn't, however, keep him from recalling her slender frame and bewitching eyes.

With an inward grin he recalled his surprise at sighting her vivid hair across the crowded room last evening. There had been no doubt it was his mystery woman, despite her transformation from grubby schoolboy to elegant woman of fashion. A completely unexpected flare of excitement had burned away his normal sense of ennui, and perhaps even more surprising was the realization that the brief, highly entertaining encounter had only served to increase his interest in the spirited chit.

He had half-expected to be severely disappointed by the meeting. After all, she was a real woman, and it was hardly fair to expect her to compete with the fantasies he had woven is his mind. But far from being disappointed, he had been even more intrigued and, with uncharacteristic determination, had resorted to blatant blackmail to achieve his goal of having her alone is his company.

With a mystified shake of his head, Giles returned his scattered thoughts back to his irritated guest.

"I assure you, Jack, I have no nefarious schemes up my sleeve," he replied, his tone deliberately bored. "I spent a few moments chatting with a charming young lady, nothing more."

"I don't believe you," Jack retorted bluntly, obviously piqued by his cousin's refusal to confess his thoughts.

With an amused laugh, Giles pushed himself away from the desk. "That is your option, of course, and to be honest I haven't the time to argue with you further. I have an appointment for which I dare not be late."

"An appointment?" Jack lifted his brows in surprise. "With whom?"

"Why, the charming Miss Allendyle. Who else?" He flashed his wicked smile, strolling toward the door. "You can see yourself out, Jack. Perhaps I will see you at the club later in the day."

Without awaiting an answer he strode firmly into the hall, pausing only long enough for his valet to help him slip into a caped driving coat before stepping out the door and easily vaulting into his well-sprung chaise.

As always the London streets were crowded, but keeping his spirited chestnuts firmly in check, he made his way to the quiet but fashionable square where the Welfords owned a modest home. He had been rather surprised to learn, through careful probing, that Miss Allendyle had lost both of her parents and that she was being sponsored by her aunt for the season. He seemed to recall her mentioning a brother and had assumed that she would reside with him and his wife. But, oddly, he had heard nothing of this brother.

With a small shrug, he dismissed the surge of curiosity and waited for his groom to sprint toward the team's head before climbing down. It was a perfect day for a ride, he noted with satisfaction, climbing up the steps and withdrawing a card as the butler opened the door.

"My lord." With a crisp bow the butler stepped aside, allowing Giles to enter the small but refreshingly uncluttered foyer. "If you would like to step into the library, I will announce you."

"That won't be necessary, Forbes." A light female voice floated through the air, and Giles glanced up to discover Roma Allendyle gracefully drifting down the wide staircase. "I believe Lord Carlton is here to see me."

"Very well."

The butler discreetly melted out of the foyer, leaving Giles alone to appreciate the sight of Roma dressed in a pale green muslin gown with a matching shawl.

A wood nymph, he thought inanely, his gaze lingering

on her brilliant curls and gold-flecked eyes. An elusive creature that could never be trapped by a mere human. Then, with a silent chastisement at his ridiculous flight of fancy, he stepped forward to meet his companion at the bottom of the staircase.

"Miss Allendyle, what a charming picture you make," he murmured. "The very embodiment of spring."

"Thank you, Lord Carlton."

Her tone was cool, but there was nothing cool about the resentment simmering in her clear eyes. Once again, Giles felt that unusual surge of excitement flickering through his veins. She was like an unbroken filly, wary of the slightest touch, and he knew that she represented a rare challenge.

"And most punctual. An unexpected quality in a woman."

"I do not recall that I was given much option," she returned sharply, her tiny chin tilted to an aggressive angle. "You made quite certain that I would accompany you today."

Giles flashed her a chiding grin. "Perhaps if you would be more susceptible to my irresistible charm I wouldn't need to rely on such unpleasant tactics."

"And perhaps your charm is not as irresistible as you presume," she replied with a toss of her head. "Shall we go?"

Momentarily startled by her swift thrust, he responded with a dazed blink before laughing softly in appreciation.

"By all means, Miss Allendyle. If my charm is not sufficient to impress you, maybe my skill with the ribbons will reach your distant heart."

With a roll of her eyes at his outrageous flirtation, Roma marched past him, scenting the air with a faint trace of honeysuckle. Giles inhaled deeply, discovering a decided preference for the pleasing aroma, before hurrying to open the door and politely escort her down the short flight of stairs.

Smiling slightly at her rigidly held body, he paused beside the curb, waiting to help her into the chaise, but with a small exclamation she abruptly moved forward, her frosty expression melting with unconscious delight.

"Oh . . . What a beautiful pair." She reached out to stroke the glossy coat of the nearest horse.

"Take care, Miss Allendyle," he warned. "These brutes are high spirited."

"Yes, I can see that," she murmured, obviously forgetting to whom she was speaking. "Such perfect form. They must have cost you a fortune."

"At least part of a fortune," he admitted, closely watching her distracted expression. Without her wary distrust, her small features were surprisingly soft, an unexpected hint of vulnerability about her full lips. "But well worth the investment."

"How lucky you are." She gave a small sigh. "Aunt Clara refuses to keep a stable in London. It isn't that she minds the expense, but she fears that Claude and I would spend more time with our horses than with the delights London supposedly has to offer."

He smiled at her unconsciously wistful tone. "Do you not find London all you expected?"

"Yes." She abruptly stepped away from the horses, turning to face him with a guarded expression. "It is precisely how I expected it. Shall we go?"

For a moment he silently gazed into her wide eyes, sensing that beneath her cool demeanor she was troubled. Quite unexpectedly he discovered an urge to ferret out her worry and help ease the strain darkening her beautiful eyes.

Not an easy task, he silently conceded. At the moment she considered him a most unwelcome intrusion into her life.

"Of course."

Giles moved to politely assist her into the chaise, remaining strategically silent as he climbed in beside her and directed his impatient team toward the park. As he expected on such a fine day, the streets were filled with assorted carriages, their fashionable occupants staring quite openly as Giles drove determinedly past curious gazes, heading for a less congested area before slowing his brisk pace.

"Now, Miss Allendyle, perhaps we can discuss the little . . . adventure that you seem so determined to keep a secret."

A covert glance revealed her staunch composure remained intact, although she couldn't disguise the tension in her slight frame.

"I fail to comprehend why I should explain anything to you, Lord Carlton. You have neither the claim of family nor acquaintanceship to press upon me."

"An unfortunate circumstance that I am attempting to rectify despite your obvious reluctance."

He barely heard her snort of disgust. "If you have realized your attentions are unwanted, then why do you continue to thrust them upon me? A true gentleman would graciously accept my feelings and be on his way."

"I assumed that we settled that argument last night," he retorted without apology. "We agreed that I was no gentleman."

"Well, you needn't take such odious pride in the fact," she snapped.

"And you needn't think to divert my thoughts, my little vixen," he drawled with evident amusement. "I am fully determined to discover your reasons for behaving in such a reckless fashion on the night in question."

She abruptly turned to face him, her eyes flashing. "And what of you, Lord Carlton? Are you prepared to confess your own reasons for being at the cove?"

He gave a small shrug. "Perhaps. However, at the moment we are discussing you, Miss Allendyle."

He heard her give a small hiss of frustration, but obviously believing that he intended to press the issue, she at last relented, sending him a furious scowl.

"Very well, Lord Carlton. I went to the cove in search of my brother."

The restless chestnuts gave a sudden surge as Giles momentarily loosened his tight hold on the reins. Swiftly regaining control of the nervous pair, he shot her a puzzled frown.

"Your brother? Was he with you?"

"No, that was Claude," she retorted shortly. "I haven't seen or heard from my brother in almost a month."

Belatedly realizing that he couldn't possibly concentrate on her confusing tale and keep an adequate check on his team, Giles pulled to an abrupt halt beneath a secluded tree, motioning the groom to jump down and tend to the animals. Then, shifting, he regarded her stony expression with shrewd curiosity.

"I think, Miss Allendyle, you had best start at the beginning. And I warn you, we will sit here all afternoon if need be."

The hazel eyes smoldered, but noting the stubborn set of his jaw, she reluctantly settled more comfortably on the cushioned seat.

"It's not a very interesting story, Lord Carlton," she said, the ice in her tone contrasting sharply with the hot flare of anger in her expressive eyes. "Perhaps you know my father, Colonel Allendyle, was killed while on duty almost five years ago. Since my mother died when I was just a child, my older brother, William, sold out his commission and returned to Greystead. Granted it was difficult for him to leave the military life and concentrate on the estate, as well as have the burdened of a young sister, but he never complained." She paused, her features softening as she spoke of her brother. "Still, I wasn't surprised when he occasionally disappeared from the estate and returned without a word of explanation. I knew that he must be working for the government in some secret capacity, although we never discussed the subject."

Giles swallowed an instinctive smile of disbelief. He had yet to meet a woman who could avoid asking a thousand questions when she sensed a secret. Clearly Roma Allendyle was even more rare than he had first suspected.

"And yet you are worried something has happened to him?" he inquired.

"Of course." She appeared startled by his question. "As a rule he is never gone more than a few hours, a day or two at the most. He would never be gone this length of time unless something terrible had occurred." She gave an unconscious shiver. "I try not to think the worse, but it is difficult."

Giles leaned back, slowly realizing that he might have bitten off more than he could comfortably chew. Sheer curiosity had led him to this confrontation, that and an unflattering sense of pique at her overt hostility, he admitted reluctantly. Only now did he acknowledge that by forcing her confession he was also embroiling himself in her troubles.

Still, he had gone too far to pull back now. And the faint edge of fear she tried so valiantly to hide all but sealed his doom.

"Why did you think he might be at the cove?" he questioned softly.

"Because of the letters," she replied simply. "I found them left in the library, along with a note describing the place and time at which they were to be handed over. I had no way of knowing if someone had placed them there for William, unaware that he was missing, or if they were there for me. In either case they were the only clue I possessed, and I was determined to go to the rendezvous, if only to alert someone that William is gone."

Giles frowned, carefully turning her words over in his mind. "There was no one in your family who could assist you?"

She grimaced. "Only Claude, and I regretted confiding in him when he insisted on accompanying me to the cove."

He bit back his instant desire to chastise her for even contemplating such a dangerous mission. Clearly she was determined to locate her brother, no matter what the cost to herself. And rather than indulge in futile arguments, he instead turned his thoughts to the vague unease nagging at the edge of his mind.

"You said that you confided your brother's disappearance to your cousin. Does anyone else know?"

She seemed puzzled by the question. "The servants, of course, although they have been with us too long to reveal such information to anyone."

He leaned forward, his face somber. "But did you question anyone about your brother?"

A faint flush touched her cheeks. "I did go to the inn where William was well known and speak with a few of his friends, but I was very discreet. I never actually said that William was gone."

"But if someone already knew that William was missing, then your questions might have been vexing, if not actually dangerous. It could be that this person hoped his disappearance would go unnoticed."

She frowned, but with an inward courage he could only admire, she faced him squarely.

"What are you implying?"

He paused, carefully considering his position. As a rule he would do everything in his power to protect a young lady from anything that might distress or upset her sensitive nature. But instinctively he realized that Roma would not thank him for his chivalry. What little he did know about her warned him she was not the type to submissively allow others to do what they thought best for her.

Thrusting aside his natural aversion, he met her probing gaze. "I find it odd that your brother should disappear and then a packet of letters mysteriously arrives, directing you to a meeting that ultimately ends in an ambush."

A small silence fell as she considered his words, but beyond a slight paling of her satin skin, she remained staunchly composed.

"You believe it was a trap for me?"

"I believe it is a possibility we should keep in mind," he conceded, his voice unconsciously grim. "It could be that someone has no wish for William Allendyle's disappearance to be investigated."

"I am not giving up," she instantly charged, a militant light of battle glowing in her eyes. "I don't care what it takes. I am going to find him."

Her brave words should have been ludicrous. Although his work with the government was on a casual basis, he had never underestimated the determination of the enemy. They would stop at nothing, including kidnapping a young man and ensuring this courageous but utterly innocent woman was kept from asking questions they did not want asked. And yet, there was something decidedly noble in her stark determination.

Besides, it would be futile to even hope he could somehow dissuade her from continuing her search. The most he could hope to do was keep her from plunging headlong into danger.

"And exactly what can you do?" he asked, not surprised at her instant anger.

"I came to London to discover who was William's contact with the government. At least then I will know where William went and whom he was supposed to meet. It will give me a place to start my search."

"You can not be serious?" he demanded, not bothering to hide his exasperation. "You may not gad throughout London asking questions about your brother."

"I am not gadding throughout London, Lord Carlton, and even if I were it would be none of your concern. You may have forced me to confess why I went to that cove, but you have no right to tell me what I can or can not do."

Unaccustomed to having his authority challenged in such a blatant manner, Giles discovered himself battling his own ready temper. Perverse minx. Could she not comprehend that he was simply attempting to protect her from her own foolish behavior? Then, with an effort, he reined in his flare of frustration. He wasn't about to indulge in a shouting match with this woman in the middle of the park. Society would be curious enough about his interest in the unknown Roma Allendyle without adding an unpleasant scene to the inevitable gossip.

"Perhaps not." He determinedly kept his voice calm. "But I can assure you that it will be nothing more than a waste of your time. The men who deal in espionage keep a very low profile, and discovering someone willing to admit he was in contact with William will be impossible. Especially considering you are a young woman with no political power."

Her face flushed at his blunt words, and he knew that he had managed to strike at her inner fear. Clearly she had already considered her tenuous ability to force information from an unwilling source.

"And what would you have me do, Lord Carlton? Return home and forget that my brother is in terrible danger?"

Giles abruptly pulled away, forcing his narrowed gaze from her delicate features and the wide eyes clouded with the harsh anxiety she tried so hard to hide.

Now was the time to pull away and assure her that he hadn't the least notion of what could be done for her brother. Certainly it was a heart-wrenching story, and she had his utmost sympathy, but as she kept insisting, her troubles were truly none of his concern.

The past few moments had satisfied his curiosity. He now understood why she had gone to such desperate measures and why a woman so obviously uninterested in Society would travel to London. The mystery cleared, it was time to turn his attention to a more stimulating form of entertainment.

But even as the thoughts passed through his mind, Giles had already dismissed them. He could not walk away from Roma Allendyle. He had no ready answer for his determination to involve himself in a complete stranger's life. It was, in fact, thoroughly out of character to thrust himself in where he was clearly not wanted.

But ignoring the tiny voice at the back of his mind that

warned him he was about to step into dangerous waters, he abruptly turned to capture her wary gaze.

"No, I want you to stay in London," he suddenly commanded. "But for the moment I want you to halt any attempts to find your brother."

"Why should I?" she demanded, her body tensing.

"Because you are doing nothing more than endangering your life, and perhaps the lives of your aunt and cousin," he retorted bluntly. "From now on any questions will be asked by me. Is that understood?"

Four

"What?" Roma blinked in startled disbelief, quite certain she had misunderstood the preemptive words. Not even this insufferable man was arrogant enough to presume he could blithely give commands to a woman he barely knew.

But, shockingly, his expression remained one of adamant determination.

"I want you to put an end to your efforts and leave matters in my hands," he retorted in firm tones.

"That is absurd. I will do no such thing."

"Come, Miss Allendyle. Even you must agree that it is for the best."

"I fail to comprehend why."

"Do you?" A hateful brow rose in mild reproach. "Unlike you, my dear, I do happen to possess the type of political power necessary to gain an interview with members of the War Department. But more importantly, I have contact with several gentlemen who can be trusted to make inquiries in a . . . discreet fashion."

"Even if that is true, Lord Carlton, I still fail to understand why you should insist on involving yourself in affairs that are not of your concern."

An odd smile tugged at his fine lips. "Let us say that while I am unacquainted with William I feel a sense of responsibility for his welfare. Not only did we both serve in the field of battle, but we have both chosen to continue our service to our country in a like manner. It is my duty."

Roma frowned. As the daughter of a military man, she understood the dictates of duty and honor to any soldier. Her father had drilled the meaning of them into both of his children since the day they were born. That didn't, however, ease her wary suspicion.

"That is very kind of you, my lord, but you have no duty to William. He is my brother and therefore my responsibility."

The blue eyes flashed. "You know, Miss Allendyle, for a lady who claims to be so determined to find her brother, you are remarkably reluctant to accept assistance," he drawled. "I can only wonder if it is all assistance you find so abhorrent or my own particular assistance."

As was becoming all too frequent in Lord Carlton's presence, Roma felt herself blush in confusion. He was right, of course. She should be delighted by his offer to help search for her brother. After all, he was far better qualified to approach those with knowledge of William's covert assignments. And certainly, she had accomplished little more than fluttering about London like a witless fool.

If only the mere thought of meekly conceding to his high-handed interference did not set her teeth on edge . . .

"I suppose I am simply accustomed to depending upon my own resources," she reluctantly conceded. "It is not easy to admit that I require help."

"Even for your brother's sake?"

A sharp, frustrated sigh hissed between her tight lips. "You are right, my lord," she forced herself to mutter. "I could use your assistance."

"There . . . That was not so difficult, was it, Miss Allendyle?" he questioned softly, his tone laced with amusement.

A ripple of exasperation crossed her expressive countenance before she managed to leash her emotions. Must he make the situation so intolerable? It was vile enough to admit she was in need of assistance without his annoying mockery.

"May I inquire what it is you intend to do?"

His shrug was nonchalant. "First I shall endeavor to discover who was in contact with William before his disappearance. There must be someone who kept track of his movements."

"And then?"

His lips tilted at her impatient words. "I will make that decision when the time comes, Miss Allendyle. For now I suggest that we make our way back to your aunt's. She is no doubt impatiently awaiting your return." His glance at her delicate features was wry. "I must not forget that you are a young debutante and that I must behave as a proper gentleman."

For no reason that she could imagine, her absurd color only deepened. "I care for nothing more than the safe return of my brother, Lord Carlton."

"Then you are a fool, Miss Allendyle," he chided in light tones, giving an imperious lift of his hand that brought his groom scurrying back to the carriage to return the reins to his long, slender fingers.

With a smoldering glare at his arrogant profile, Roma tossed herself back into the soft leather of the seat. Odious creature. Did he have to take such great delight in vexing her?

Barely noting the elegant duke who rode past on his notable white horse or the flamboyant courtesan who was attired in a most shockingly cut satin gown, Roma brooded on the ease with which her wings had been neatly trimmed. She had been so staunchly determined to rid herself of Lord Carlton's pesky presence. Why only this morning she had rehearsed the icily composed speech that would put an end to his interference. But rather than delivering the speech in a coolly composed manner, she had instead found herself conceding to his demands that he take control of the search for her brother. It was obvious she had at last encountered a will that matched her own. A rare occurrence for a headstrong young lady accustomed to having her own way.

Her dark thoughts were at last interrupted by a warm chuckle that returned her attention to the gentleman at her side.

"You realize, Miss Allendyle, that if you continue to sulk in that unpleasant fashion you will have my reputation in complete ruin?" he pointed out, favoring her with his roguish smile. "If it becomes known that a ride through the park induces nothing more than a fit of the blue devils in my companion, I shall never discover another maiden willing to bear me company."

Roma favored him with a glare, but she did settle her features into a less petulant expression.

"I have no doubt, my lord, that it would take more than a fit of the blue devils to convince most maidens you are an unsuitable companion. From all reports you are considered the catch of the Season."

His laugh was thoroughly spontaneous. "You needn't sound so disapproving, my dear. As I am sure you are aware my attractions have more to do with my estate than my dubious charm."

Roma would have liked to agree. After all, she was the last woman who wanted to admit that Lord Carlton had even a single desirable quality. But her innate sense of honesty could not be thoroughly suppressed.

How could she not acknowledge that he was remarkably handsome? she grudgingly allowed. He was the image of every young lady's dreams, with his finely chiseled features, his wide, intelligent brow, his astonishingly blue eyes and satiny dark hair. And no woman could possibly be indifferent to the muscular form set off to perfection in the tailored coat and pantaloons. But perhaps it was the hint of boyish amusement in his smile that was his most captivating feature.

Abruptly aware of the direction of her absurd thoughts, Roma laced her fingers tightly in her lap.

"I am sure you are mistaken, my lord," she forced herself to confess.

"My, my, Miss Allendyle, you shall quite turn my head," he teased. "Are you suggesting that I might possess more to attract an eligible maiden than a title and a vast estate?"

She caught her breath at his light words and frantically searched for some means of diverting the conversation. No doubt Lord Carlton was a master at such frivolous flirtations. She, however, was finding the banter increasingly unnerving.

"I . . . I believe your estate is in Kent, my lord?"

He regarded her for a long, amused moment before following her lead. "Yes, indeed. And while I am no doubt partial, I believe it is a fine house and set on some of the most beautiful countryside to be found in England."

Roma was rather taken back by the sincerity in his tone. She had somehow expected such a rake to be indifferent to the land that provided him such a life of ease. But it was obvious he felt a great attachment to his home.

"Do you spend much time there?"

"Not as much as I would like. My grandmother prefers to remain in London, and I dislike leaving her for any extended duration."

"I do not comprehend how anyone could prefer London," she muttered, glancing about the crowded park.

"Surely you have taken some enjoyment from you brief visit?"

"I will own that I have enjoyed the theater and our visit to the museum," she reluctantly conceded, "but I far prefer the comforts of Greystead."

His glance was quizzical. "You do not find it dull?"

An unconscious sparkle entered her eyes. "Not at all. I have my horses and garden to tend, as well as a household to manage. I also have a number of friends who keep me suitably entertained."

"And you want for nothing more stimulating?"

She ignored the tiny twinge in the vicinity of her heart. What did it matter if she had occasionally felt a wave of loneliness? Or that in more vulnerable moments she had wondered if her desire for independence was worth the cost of a husband and children? It was no concern of Lord Carlton.

"I am perfectly content," she said in tones perhaps a trifle more firm than necessary.

"You are a most uncommon young lady, Miss Allendyle."

She swiftly glanced at the dark profile, but it was impossible to determine if he meant the words as a compliment or an insult.

"Not so very uncommon, my lord," she denied.

A congestion of riders and carriages near the gate momentarily consumed Lord Carlton's attention, and it was not until they were free of the throng and headed down the street toward her aunt's home that he was able to resume their conversation. Turning to regard her pale profile, he allowed the wicked amusement to be replaced by a stern expression.

"Before I return you home, Miss Allendyle, I should make perfectly certain that we understand one another. Do I have your promise not to do anything foolish until I have contacted you?"

Roma instantly bristled at the condescending tone. "I have promised to allow you to do the questioning for now, my lord."

"And you will behave as a proper young debutante with nothing more on her mind than attracting a suitable husband?"

"That is absurd."

With a tug on the reins he brought the bays to a smooth halt in front of her door. "Your promise, Miss Allendyle," he said in stern tones, his narrowed gaze piercing deep into her affronted eyes.

"You have no right, sir."

"Perhaps not, but I will have your promise."

She glared at him for a long, silent moment; then, with grudging reluctance, she gave a tight nod of her head. What choice did she have if she wished to locate William?

"Very well, my lord, I promise to do my best to behave as any other debutante until you contact me."

"No dashing about London in male clothing or getting yourself shot?"

"I have given you my promise," she gritted out.

"Good girl. I knew I could depend upon you to see sense."

Roma resisted the urge to poke out her tongue in a childish fit of fury. Instead she rapidly rose to her feet and clambered out of the carriage before the groom or Lord Carlton could assist. One day, she silently promised herself, she would take great pleasure in knocking that smug smile from his handsome face. Until that day she would simply have to bite her tongue and pray that William would soon turn up.

She had almost reached the door when Lord Carlton managed to catch up with her, and reaching out a hand, he firmly grasped her fingers and lifted them to his warm lips.

"Thank you, Miss Allendyle, for a most delightful afternoon. Be assured that I will call on you very soon."

"My lord." She inclined her head in a stiff manner and then swept through the door being opened by the butler. Behind her, she could hear a soft chuckle floating through the air as Lord Carlton watched her rigid retreat.

Infuriated by the entire encounter, Roma wanted nothing more than to retire to her room and repair the damage to her composure. She could already feel the twinges of an oncoming headache. Unfortunately the door to the drawing room swept open just as she placed her foot on the bottom step, and her aunt bustled out to regard her in an odd manner.

"Ah . . . There you are, my dear. Would you be so good as to join me for a few moments?"

Surprised by the request, Roma allowed herself one last

longing glance up the stairs; then, drawing in a deep breath, she turned to make her way into the small but neatly furnished room. There was nothing for it but to hear her aunt out. Although a sweet, rather complacent woman, Lady Clara Welford could be decidedly tenacious when she chose. Some might claim it was a trait that ran in the family.

Crossing the daintily printed carpet Roma settled herself on a yellow brocade sofa. The scent of freshly cut flowers filled the room, reminding her that she had not even bothered to thank Lord Carlton for his bouquet of roses. Not that she regretted her oversight, she thought with a flare of annoyance. The man was a complete scoundrel.

With an effort, Roma gathered her scattered thoughts and turned to regard the plump, silver-haired woman who was standing beside the large marble fireplace.

"How was your shopping?" she inquired, recalling her aunt's remarks over breakfast.

"Quite vexing, I fear," she retorted in flustered tones, her round face uncommonly flushed.

Roma raised her brows in surprise. "Oh?"

"Yes, indeed." Lady Welford sniffed. "Colette promised quite distinctly that she would have my new morning gown finished today. Not only was it not completed, but she had sold that charming bonnet I had set my heart on purchasing."

"How unfortunate."

"Now I shall have nothing new to wear when we visit the Cadiz Memorial."

Roma swallowed a smile, knowing that her aunt was far more interested in parading her latest gown than in viewing the cannon captured from the French in Salamanca.

"Quite vexing indeed."

Clara gave a distracted tug at the modest neckline of her Pamona green gown. "And as if that were not trying enough I encountered Lady Powell while I was taking my tea."

Familiar with the large, overly opinionated Lady Powell, Roma gave an unconscious grimace. Although she had only met the woman on a handful of occasions, she had developed a swift dislike for her piercing voice and habit of presuming she had the right to meddle in other's affairs. Still, attempting to halt her interference was rather like attempting to halt a battleship in full sail.

"How is Lady Powell? In good health I trust?" she forced herself to inquire.

"Ha." Aunt Clara looked as if she had just eaten a sour grape. "That woman is an insufferable busybody. And how she dares to offer me advice on how to introduce a young lady to Society is beyond me."

Realizing that they had at last come to the reason for her aunt's distress, Roma slowly leaned forward.

"I presume she was referring to me?"

"Yes, indeed."

"What did she say?"

"She had the nerve to suggest that we were dangling after Lord Carlton," Clara stated in tones of outrage.

Roma's cheeks heated with color. "Lord Carlton?"

"Yes, have you ever heard such nonsense? As if I would throw an innocent young lady to the attentions of a known rake. Why, it is well known he can not abide debutantes who, as he says, 'still smell of the schoolroom and barley water.' Besides which, I am well aware that any man of Lord Carlton's rank is above our touch." She flashed Roma an apologetic smile at the younger woman's strangled a cough. "Not that we have any apology to make for our lineage, mind you, but I am no encroacher with an aim to push myself where I don't belong."

"No, of course not," Roma managed to choke out.

"But, unfortunately, we can not wholly discount Lady Powell's vicious tongue," the older woman grudgingly conceded. "It would not do to appear as if we were angling to entrap Lord Carlton."

Entrap? Dangle after? Roma gritted her teeth in frustration. If only they knew the truth.

"Do not worry, Aunt Clara. I assure you that I have no intention of dangling after Lord Carlton. Indeed, I have no intention of dangling after any man."

The steel in her tone brought an instant flare of regret to Clara's countenance. "Well, my dear, I did not mean to imply that we should not seek out the attentions of more suitable gentleman. After all, there are any number of charming parti to chose from."

Rising to her feet, Roma came to the decision that she had endured quite enough for one day. First to be practically kidnapped by the odious Lord Carlton, and then to be lectured on dangling after him—it was more than any reasonable woman should have to endure.

"No doubt. Now, if you will excuse me, I seem to have developed a most shocking headache."

"Let me call my maid." Clara was instantly concerned. "She has the most wonderful way with lavender water."

"No, thank you. I think a few hours of rest is what I need."

"Of course, my dear. I am sorry if I distressed you."

"Not at all." Roma smiled in weary fashion, then crossed the room and went toward the stairs.

What a vexing turn of events. It was bad enough to endure the knowledge that Lord Carlton had shrewdly managed to outwit her and had force her into making such a ridiculous promise. Now she was forced to realize that she was the subject of amused speculation among the tabbies. And it was all the fault of that . . . that man.

Virtually stomping up the long flight of stairs, Roma entered her room and closed the door with a decided bang.

Drat Lord Carlton, she silently seethed. *Drat, drat, drat.*

Five

"You understand Giles this is a very . . . delicate situation?"

"Of course." Taking a reluctant drink of the potent gin the barmaid had recently slapped onto the table, Giles gave a covert glance about the shadowed room. Although it was not yet five o'clock a loud, growingly boisterous crowd lined the tables and filled the air with laughter and an occasional off-key song. The scent of stale liquor and unwashed bodies assaulted Giles sensitive nose, and he barely prevented himself from shivering in distaste each time one of the locals drunkenly stumbled against him. But despite the unsavory surroundings, he realized that Lord Halcott had chosen the perfect location for their secret meeting. Not only would this gin house be the last place anyone would suspect two such prestigious aristocrats to willingly frequent, but there was enough noise and confusion to prevent anyone from taking an inordinate amount of interest in their private conversation. "You know I would not ask unless it was vitally important?"

Lord Halcott narrowed his shrewd brown eyes. Although he was well into his fifties, he maintained the strength and vigor of a man half his age and Giles knew that he claimed an unofficial, but highly powerful position in the government.

"The success of our various agents lies solely on the

fact that their identities are kept strictly confidential. Less than a handful of people know all the individuals who provide services for the government. It is the only way we can ensure that the enemy is unable to follow their movements, and more importantly, the best method to ensure their safety." He paused, strangely able to blend into his surroundings with remarkable ease. Both men were dressed shabbily, with a day's growth of beard and streaks of dirt to disfigure their strong bone structures. But while Giles unconsciously maintained his air of commanding power, Lord Halcott somehow seemed to disappear inside his oversized jacket and black cap. "If I answer any questions I might very well be endangering a number of people."

"I promise to keep my questions solely centered on William Allendyle," Giles said, leaning forward with a determined expression. "And whatever you tell me will be kept in the strictest confidence."

"It isn't that I don't trust you, Giles, but I need you to fully understand my position. There might very well be things I can not, or will not, be able to tell you. It is nothing personal."

"Of course." Giles shoved the harshly potent gin to one side, placing his elbows on the table. "Now, what can you tell me about Allendyle?"

A faint frown of curiosity tugged at Halcott's graying brows. "Actually, I think first you should tell me exactly what your interest in this young man is. As far as I'm aware he isn't any relation and is no particular friend of yours. Why would you care whether or not he works for the government?"

Giles hesitated. Absurdly, he felt almost embarrassed to confess that his interest stemmed solely from the momentary bewitchment of a stubborn redheaded woman with a fierce pride and pair of vulnerable hazel eyes. Over the past three days he had chastised himself endlessly for his noodle-witted insistence that Roma allow him to continue the search for her mysteriously missing brother. More than once he had considered forgetting he had ever heard the name William Allendyle. After all, a man in his position had no need to play the dandy for any lady, let alone one that had arrived in London days ago with nothing more to offer than a pretty face and an acceptable lineage. But oddly, Giles had been forced to admit that his offer had had nothing to do with gallantry or even a more self-serving desire to dazzle the lady with his noble deeds. He had only to think on the fragile young lady being hunted by cutthroat scoundrels as she futilely searched for evidence of her brother's whereabouts to make him awake sweating in the night. And the knowledge that she would go to any lengths, no matter how outlandish or downright dangerous, did nothing to relieve his troubled mind.

Perhaps he had inherited more of his father's stern belief in the old code of chivalry than he was willing to admit, he thought with wry humor. Or perhaps Miss Allendyle had managed to ignite more than a mere passing interest.

Whatever the reason, he had discovered himself unable to scrub the image of her frail features and deliciously honeysuckle-scented body from his mind.

"Actually I am attempting to aid a friend," he retorted evasively.

"A friend?" Halcott ran a finger down his shadowed jaw. "Your friend wouldn't be Allendyle's lovely sister, would it?"

Giles unconsciously stiffened. "Does it really matter?"

"Perhaps not." A mysterious smile hovered about the older man's mouth. "But I have heard that she recently arrived in town. I have also heard that she is quite an engaging child. In fact, my sister has already begun to moan that her precious son has developed an overwhelming *tendre* for the chit and that he refuses to pay the appropriate attention to the ladies already chosen for his prospective bride."

The jesting words were spoken in complete innocence.

It was the type of comment made a dozen times a day by a dozen different people. And yet, Giles was forced to stifle an angry urge to defend Roma. It annoyed him to think there were those who considered her unworthy to associate with the *haut ton*. As far as he was concerned, she possessed more spirit and courage than half of the Season's beauties lumped together. And certainly the Prince himself had often spoke, of Colonel Allendyle with a great measure of respect. Still, he knew that Roma was indifferent to the opinions of those like Halcott's lofty sister; it was ridiculous for him to feel so offended.

"I am . . . acquainted with Miss Allendyle."

"I see." Halcott tapped a finger on the edge of the table.

"Is she as lovely as everyone claims?"

"She is not perhaps lovely in the more traditional sense, but she certainly possesses her own style of beauty."

"And she is the reason you have developed an interest in Allendyle?"

There was an odd note in his voice that brought an unexpected flush to the prominent line of Giles's cheekbones.

"She is concerned about her brother, but more importantly she is bullheaded enough to turn the entire government upside down until she has discovered some evidence that he is well." He gave a shrug that he hoped was nonchalant. "I thought it would be in the country's best interest to stop her before she could cause too much damage."

"How very patriotic of you, Giles." Halcott appeared perfectly sincere, but there was a glint of humor deep in his brown eyes. "Perhaps you should start at the beginning. Tell me exactly what you do know and what has Miss Allendyle so upset."

Giles had an undeniable sensation that Lord Halcott found his interest in William Allendyle oddly amusing, but at the moment he was too relieved to know the powerful man was willing to help his investigation to question what Halcott could find humorous in the situation.

Leaning forward, Giles used a low voice to explain his unexpected encounter with Roma Allendyle at the cove and then the meeting with her in London and lastly her confession of why she had been behaving in such a madcap manner. He kept the story concise and easily skimmed over the more intimate details that had no bearing on the situation. He was, however, careful to emphasize his vague fears that Roma might very well be in danger and his knowledge that she would not be content to allow him to continue the search for her brother for long. After all, only through blatant emotional blackmail had he forced her to agree to his demand that she allow him to use his influence to find her brother. If he didn't come up with tangible clues to William's whereabouts quickly, then he had no doubt that she would stubbornly return to her original intention to find him on her own. Something that Giles was certain the government would be anxious to avoid.

The noise and the crowd flowed around the table, making the perfect cover for the two men intent on their private conversation. Lord Halcott listened in silence to Giles clipped words, his expression never changing. Then, once Giles had finished, he leaned back in his chair to thoroughly consider the unusual situation.

"Miss Allendyle is quite certain that her brother hasn't simply decided to spend a few weeks away from home?" he asked at last. "It would not be that unusual. Especially for a young man of his age."

Giles nodded. His first thought was that William had taken off with a few friends for a brief lark. Or perhaps that he had discovered a tantalizing mistress who had seduced him away from his responsibilities. But Roma had been so adamant, he had been forced to accept her assurances that William would never willingly leave his estate for such an extended length of time.

"From what little Miss Allendyle has told me about her

brother, he seems to be the traditional military man. His sense of duty and responsibility would overcome any passing fancy for his own pleasures."

"Not surprising." Halcott gave a rather reminiscent sigh. "I knew his father from the days when he first joined the military. A handsome man, I remember, with a completely natural ability to take command. Of course, there was a minor scandal when he married Carolyn Shefton. She was the Toast of the Season and expected to marry into the peerage. I believe two earls and at least one duke offered for her, but she turned them all aside for a lowly officer with very straitened circumstances." He paused, a smile suddenly lighting his features. "Still, Allendyle quickly proved to be a gifted tactician, and I believe he and Carolyn were very happy together. I didn't keep in close contact with him through the years, but I have no doubt that he raised his children with the same high standards and sense of pride that he expected from his soldiers."

Giles couldn't prevent a rueful laugh. "Yes, not to mention a streak of stubbornness as wide as the channel."

"That sounds like Allendyle," Halcott agreed. "He also had some rather odd notions about his children. Absolutely refused to send them away to school, and there was a rumor that his daughter could outride and outshoot the best of men. Of course, I dismiss such foolish nonsense as mere exaggeration. Since her arrival in London she has earned the reputation as a modest, thoroughly respectable young maiden."

Giles swallowed a grunt of disbelief. "Modest" and "respectable" were not the two words he associated in his mind with Roma Allendyle.

"She is also deeply concerned about her brother." Giles brought the conversation back to the problem at hand.

"To be honest, so am I," Halcott suddenly confessed. "If Miss Allendyle is correct, then her brother may be in serious danger, and he might not be the only one. I think

I should attempt to get to the bottom of this as swiftly as possible."

Knitting his raven brows together in a concerned frown, Giles clenched his hands on the table.

"What shall I do?"

For a long moment Halcott studied him in somber silence; then, narrowing his gaze, he tugged at the lobe of his ear.

"How close can you stay to Miss Allendyle?"

Giles gave a surprised blink. "Pardon me?"

Halcott laughed. "Oh, I am not proposing anything scandalous. I simply think it would be wise to have someone to keep a close eye on the young lady. As you have already guessed, her relationship to William makes her an obvious target."

"You think she might be in danger?" An odd stab of fear pierced Giles's heart as Halcott gave the question serious contemplation.

"I believe there is a potential for danger," he amended, "but I do not think we should alarm her. I would much rather have you remain near enough to prevent trouble and at the same time be in a position to know if she receives word from her brother."

It was certainly a logical request, but Giles found himself hesitating. He had already involved himself far more than he had ever intended in Roma's life. It was quite simply absurd that he devote any more effort on the situation. But even as a firm voice at the back of his mind urged him to tell Lord Halcott that he would have to request someone else to be Miss Allendyle's guardian angel, he discovered himself readily nodding in agreement. He knew deep down he would never trust Roma's safety to anyone else.

"I will certainly do my best. Of course, you should be aware that I am not precisely in Miss Allendyle's best graces. Indeed she has made it painfully clear that she considers me a blackhearted scoundrel who should never darken her threshold again."

"Really?" Once again the speculative amusement glowed deep in the brown eyes. "You must find that a unique reaction. Is there any specific reason you can not charm her into accepting your company?"

"I have discovered that Miss Allendyle is completely immune to whatever charm I might possess, but thankfully she is devoted to her brother. She will tolerate my presence if I convince her that it is in his best interest."

Lord Halcott let out a small chuckle, clearly finding humor in Giles peevish tone.

"I really must meet this Miss Allendyle. She sounds like a fascinating woman."

"Yes"—Giles gave him a rueful smile—"she is also annoyingly independent, thoroughly unyielding and given to using her sharp little tongue like a saber. I would advise you to seek the company of the numerous young maidens with less volatile temperaments."

"Ah . . . but men like ourselves could never be truly content with a life or love without a bit of spice, eh, Giles?" Quite surprisingly Halcott flashed the younger man a knowing grin; then, rising to his feet, he dropped a few coins on the table. "For now I must be on my way. Shall we meet here in say . . . four days? That should give me time to question a few of my friends. Unless of course either one of us happens to discover any pertinent information. In that case we will use the usual code, and we will meet as quickly as possible."

Giles lifted himself to his feet. "What should I tell Miss Allendyle?"

"Nothing for the moment," Halcott responded decisively. "I wouldn't want to raise her hopes too soon, and more importantly I do not want to reveal we have taken an interest in William Allendyle. His safety just might depend on the fact that no one has raised the alarm about his disappearance."

"Of course." Giles reached out a hand to briefly squeeze the older man's shoulder. "Thank you, John."

Halcott smiled. "Remember, back here in four days, and keep an eye on Miss Allendyle."

With a final nod, Lord Halcott managed to melt into the ever-growing crowd and Giles nonchalantly shuffled his way toward the door. He felt decidedly better since revealing Roma's dilemma to the older man. If there were some danger lurking about, then Halcott would undoubtedly uncover the truth, and more importantly the people involved. Strangely, he wasn't even annoyed by Lord Halcott's command that he remain close to Roma.

Slipping through the door into the refreshingly brisk spring breeze, Giles made his way down the crowded street, his mind centered on the vivacious red-haired Roma rather than the noise and confusion of his surroundings. Surely he should be thoroughly dismayed at the thought of trailing behind a young debutante straight from the country? After all, he was well known for his aversion for twittering young girls. And the mere notion of being forced to attend one insipid social event after another would normally be enough to send him rushing for his country estate as if the devil himself were on his heels.

But rather than battling an ungentlemanly urge to rush as far away from Roma Allendyle as possible, Giles instead discovered himself regretting the knowledge that even if he were to hurry home he could not change in time to call upon the Welford house before they left for their evening of entertainment. He wanted an opportunity to speak with Roma as quickly as possible to reassure her that he was doing everything in his power to locate her missing brother.

But then, perhaps if he were to allow her to stew for a few days, she might be somewhat more eager to see him, he suddenly realized. He was well aware that she would be expecting him to seek her out. She was no doubt preparing at this moment an icy set-down to punish him for his interference. Maybe he would be better served to pretend a bland indifference until she developed a proper appreciation for his generous determination to help her. He did, after all, have her promise not to do anything absurd until he sought her out. A day or two of punishment would not harm anyone.

An unconscious gleam of anticipation suddenly glowed deep in the vivid blue eyes, contrasting sharply with his shabby clothing and the air of depression that clung tenaciously to the downtrodden surroundings. Ignoring the curious stares of the various people who crowded the street, he pushed his way down the block. He had ordered his groom to wait several blocks away and to be on the safe side he took a roundabout route and even leaned against a dilapidated building for several long moments to ensure he wasn't being followed. At last satisfied, he swiftly dodged across the street and hopped into the unmarked carriage. He had barely closed the door behind him when his groom gave a sharp whistle and the anxious team of grays took off down the street at a rapid clip.

Alone in the shadowed carriage, Giles gratefully shrugged off the heavy coat and rough cotton shirt. The smell of smoke and raw gin, not to mention several unwashed bodies, lingered in the coarse material with a tenacity that caused Giles's stomach to roll with disapproval. But with his usual foresight his groom, Jameson, had placed several wet cloths in a container on the floor as well as a clean shirt and coat. He could at least rid himself of the most offensive fumes, and by the time they arrived at his elegant town house, he felt almost his old self.

As the carriage came to a halt he waited for a footman to open the door, and shoving the dirty bundle of clothing into the young man's reluctant arms, he sprinted up the long flight of stairs with athletic ease. There was an unfamiliar sense of urgency coursing through his blood as he stepped into the vast foyer to be greeted by his properly impassive butler.

"Hello, Murdock." He ran a self-conscious hand over his unshaven jaw. "I need a brandy, a bath, a shave and my evening clothes laid out . . . in that order."

"Of course, my lord."

"And tell Jameson I will want the new pair sent over by Tattersall's brought around in an hour. Oh . . . and I want to have a note with some flowers hand-delivered as quickly as possible."

"Very well."

On the point of heading toward the wide flight of stairs, Giles was startled when Murdock gently cleared his throat, a subtle indication that there was something on his mind. Coming to an abrupt halt, he turned to eye the small, utterly dignified man with a raised brow.

"Is there a problem, Murdock?"

"Not exactly a problem, my lord, but you did receive this note several hours ago. The messenger stressed that it was of the utmost urgency."

He held out a heavy, sealed envelope, and with a curious frown Giles stepped forward to glance at his name elaborately scrolled across the front. Recognition of the handwriting, along with the all-too-familiar scent of a cloying feminine perfume, had him taking a sharp step backward.

"Have it burned, Murdock," he said with a forbidding frown. "And in the future you are to refuse any correspondence from Lady Hoyet."

If the butler was surprised by his abrupt decision to end all contact with his long-term mistress he was far too well trained to reveal more than a respectful nod of agreement.

"Certainly, my lord."

Feeling ridiculously disturbed by the incident, Giles turned to head up the wide steps. It wasn't the first time he had suddenly decided to end an intimate relationship with a beautiful woman. In fact, there had been times over the past month when he had found himself becoming more and more restless in Lavania's company. But while he could logically tell himself that the end had been written in the cards for weeks, and that her ill-timed message had only precipitated the inevitable, he couldn't completely dismiss the knowledge that it had been the unexpected image of a heart-shaped face dominated by a pair of hazel eyes that had created his abrupt aversion to the insatiable, utterly sensual charms of Lavania Hoyet.

At the moment, he absolutely refused to contemplate the dangerous thought. He had quite enough on his mind without adding unnecessary problems.

Six

"Egads. Do my eyes deceive me or is that Freddie Scowfield in the corner?"

With a surprised gesture Claude raised his quizzing glass to peer across the crowded room. At his side, Roma turned with mild interest, quite certain her cousin was mistaken. The Scowfield estate bordered Greystead Manor, and she had known Freddie since he was in short coats. Certainly he would never leave the pleasure of the country for London. And even if he should have some business in town, he would never be induced to attend such a dreary assembly. But even as she opened her mouth to inform Claude that Freddie would preferably be dragged to the gallows as to this affair, her gaze suddenly caught sight of the familiar dark-haired man.

"How exceedingly odd," she breathed out. "What could possibly have induced Freddie to make an appearance in London?"

"Who knows? Perhaps he has grown weary of playing the grand signor over the village maidens and has decided to see if his rather stale charm has any effect on the more sophisticated ladies."

"Claude." Startled by the edge of contempt in her cousin's voice, Roma turned to gaze at him in astonishment.

He dropped his quizzing glass with a rather embarrassed shrug. "I never could abide the fellow."

Roma gave a slight shake of her head. "But why? I have always found him quite amiable. Indeed, I could not hope for a more civil neighbor."

"Perhaps because you are a woman. He has always possessed an annoying fascination for the fairer sex. Although I can't think why."

"He can be quite charming. But surely that is not what bothers you?"

"In truth it is nothing I can actually put my finger on," Claude confessed. "The man has simply always put my back up with his stiff-rumped manner and habit of tossing about his fortune."

"Why, Claude, that is ridiculous." Roma laughed with surprised disbelief "I believe you are jealous of Freddie."

Her cousin's face darkened with an angry scowl. "Don't be absurd. Why should I be jealous of that noodle-witted peacock?"

Roma tilted her head to the side, thoroughly confused by Claude's attitude. Certainly Freddie had never been a member of her intimate circle of friends, but she had never suspected that Claude actually disliked the man.

"I can not imagine. As far as I am concerned Freddie has always been a perfect gentleman. And to be honest, it is a relief to see a familiar face among so many strangers."

With uncharacteristic tenacity, Claude continued to regard the elegantly clad man with open distaste.

"Do you not find it odd that he should choose to come to London at the same time as yourself?" he asked, his tone suspicious. "As you said, he rarely leaves his estate unless it is to visit his relatives on the Continent."

"For goodness' sake, Claude, what is the matter with you?" Roma demanded in exasperation. "The man has every right to come to London if he chooses, and he certainly need not ask our permission."

"I would still like to know what the deuce he is doing here," Claude muttered.

"Well, you can ask him," Roma breathed in a low voice. "I believe he is walking in our direction."

Feeling Claude stiffen at her side, Roma covertly watched as Freddie determinedly threaded his way through the throng. Although he was a rather small man, he managed to appear quite dapper in his satin pantaloons and well-molded jacket. And there was no denying that his thin, almost delicate features were very attractive. More than one pair of female eyes watched his steady progress across the floor, and Roma found herself wondering what Claude could possibly dislike about the man.

"Roma . . . what an unexpected delight. Have you at last succumbed to the lure of the London Season?"

Roma smiled as Freddie gallantly bowed over her hand, his dark eyes running an appreciative glance over the thin gauze of her pale yellow gown.

"Actually Claude and I were just saying the same thing about you, Freddie. I didn't realize you ever enjoyed a Season in town."

"Only under duress," he confessed with a charming grimace. "I have a great dragon of an aunt who bullies me into visiting her every few months. She refuses to accept that I am not enthralled by these insipid gatherings and insists that I accompany her from one tedious event to another. And since I am utterly terrified of her, I unwillingly play the role of the dutiful chaperon."

"Poor Freddie," Roma teased lightly.

"Yes, indeed. I would far prefer to be at home training my latest hunter." He suddenly smiled. "Until now, of course. Somehow the evening has taken a decided turn for the better. I must say you are looking inordinately beautiful, Roma."

Rather taken off guard by his flirtatious manner, Roma slowly withdrew her hand from his lingering grasp.

"Thank you, Freddie," she murmured, still uncomfortable with such unexpected compliments.

"And I have no doubt that you have already taken London by storm," he continued, smiling slightly at her blushing confusion. "Such beauty and charm must have caused quite a stir when you arrived in town."

Beside her, Roma heard Claude mutter beneath his breath. Something about Freddie's unusual admiration for someone other than himself and Roma's ridiculous susceptibility to such blatant flattery.

"How long are you staying in London, Scowfield?" Claude at last demanded, his tone a shade away from insolence.

Raising his brows, Freddie slowly turned to confront Claude. "A few weeks. Why do you ask?"

Claude shrugged "Simple curiosity. As Roma said, it is a surprise to see you here."

A rather taunting smile suddenly played about Freddie's thin lips. "A pleasant surprise I hope?"

"But of course," Claude graciously agreed, his own smile not quite reaching his eyes. "It is always nice to meet up with old friends."

"Yes." The dark head dipped. "And now that we are all staying in London we must endeavor to spend some time together. Perhaps we could ride tomorrow . . ."

"I fear that my mother did not open the stables this year, Scowfield," Claude interrupted with a regretful shrug. "And besides, Roma is obliged to speak with Mama before accepting invitations. A young lady being introduced into Polite Society must be very careful about whom she is seen with in public."

Roma gave a small gasp at the blunt insult, not surprised when an angry flush crawled beneath Freddie's pale skin.

"What the devil do you mean by that?"

"Simply that I would prefer Roma to seek a more . . . respectable companion."

"Now see here, Welford, I have no intention of allowing you to provoke me into an ill-bred scene." The thin face tightened with dangerous anger. "If you are still upset about that lovely barmaid that gave you the shrug, we

can take this to a more private setting and have it out
once and for—"

"Gentlemen, please," Roma hurriedly interrupted, her
own hazel eyes flashing signs of warning. "Isn't it enough
I have to endure being here at all without the added
burden of having you two squabbling like a pair of foolish
schoolboys? Claude, I am surprised at you. Are you not
the one constantly reminding me that one misstep could
be enough to spell disaster?"

Although he possessed enough sense to blush at his
cousin's chiding words, Claude remained annoyingly antagonistic.

"I was simply reminding Scowfield that we are no
longer in the country where less formal manners are accepted, Roma. It would not be wise to been seen constantly in each other's company despite the fact we are
all old friends."

About to demand whether or not her social schedule
would have to revolve around those men who had not
managed to seduce away his favorite barmaid, Roma suddenly froze as she felt a distinct tingle of awareness inch
down her spine. Ignoring the two men who remained
bristling at her side, she slowly turned her head to encounter a pair of vivid blue eyes, closely monitoring her
from across the room.

A sharp, oddly exciting jolt of alarm pierced through
her as her startled gaze ran swiftly over the black satin
jacket and matching pantaloons that somehow managed
to make Lord Carlton stand out from the gaudy concoc-
tions around him.

Although it had been three days since she had last seen
him, a growingly familiar surge of tension instantly flowed
through her stiff body. Detestable man, she thought silently, attempting to convince herself that the flare of tingling electricity that raced through her blood was no
more than righteous indignation. After all, he had ruthlessly coerced her into agreeing to his ridiculous demand
that he take over the search for her brother. And then,

when he must realize how anxious she was to hear some word of encouragement, he had simply disappeared.

It was little wonder her heart was pounding against her chest, and that her cheeks were warm with self-conscious color. She couldn't recall ever encountering a more annoying man.

Unaware of the vibrant animation that had suddenly lit her face, Roma watched in breathless silence as Lord Carlton lazily strolled in her direction, pausing to speak with the guests who managed to capture his attention, and yet never allowing his gaze to stray from her darkened eyes.

"Did you hear me, Roma?"

A hand impatiently touched her arm, and with a determined wrench, Roma forced her attention back to the two men eyeing her with varying degrees of curiosity.

"I am sorry, Freddie. What did you say?"

A flash of irritation seemed to glow deep in his dark eyes, but his smile remained as charming as ever.

"I was hoping to convince you to join me for a ride tomorrow in the park," he said, ignoring Claude's snort of disapproval. "Lady Welford can hardly object to such a harmless request, and it will give us an opportunity to catch up on the neighborhood gossip."

Roma wasn't sure what her answer to the unexpected invitation might have been; in the end it didn't matter as a dark, utterly masculine voice arrogantly took command of the conversation.

"Unfortunately, Miss Allendyle has already promised tomorrow's ride to me," Lord Carlton lied blatantly, a wicked smile playing about his mouth as he firmly grasped her slender fingers and raised them to his warm lips. "And I have no intention of releasing her from her pledge."

"Really?" Tilting his chin, Freddie eyed the larger man with a hint of anger. "You should allow Miss Allendyle to chose her escort for herself."

"And risk being cut out by another? Do not be ab-

surd." There was a decided edge of mockery in the dark
voice. "As the daughter of a military man, Miss Allendyle,
I am quite sure, appreciates the philosophy of an offense
being the very best sort of defense. And with that in mind
you will have to excuse us. I have promised our hostess
that I would ensure Miss Allendyle tasted her champagne
punch. Come along, Miss Allendyle."

With a smooth bow toward a suddenly smiling Claude,
Lord Carlton boldly placed a hand on Roma's arm to
firmly lead her away from the chattering crowd. Instantly
offended by his smooth arrogance, she felt her skin
prickle beneath his possessive touch, but strangely she
discovered herself following his lead.

"I sincerely hope, Lord Carlton, that you have a compelling excuse for so rudely interrupting my conversation
with Lord Scowfield."

"Scowfield?" He deliberately feigned confusion.
"Ah . . . the weasel-faced gentleman who was so urgently
attempting to press his invitation for a ride tomorrow."

"Freddie does not have a weasel face," she angrily de-
fended her friend. "Most women find him very handsome."

"Do you include yourself in that group, Miss Allendyle?"

"That is none of your concern, Lord Carlton." She
flashed him a chastising frown. "Surely you did not drag
me away to discuss my taste in men?"

"Perhaps not, but it certainly presents a fascinating
source of conversation." His amused gaze drifted over
her stiff features, lingering a tantalizing moment on the
innocent fullness of her mouth. "Do you for instance
have a preference for dark-haired men? Do you enjoy the
normal flirtations, or do you like a gentleman who speaks
his mind? And what about passion? Do you prefer a man
to use a slow seduction or are the impatient type who—"

"Lord Carlton, that is quite enough," Roma interrupted in a low tone, her eyes darting wildly about to
ensure that no one had overheard the outrageous con-

versation. "I assume you are attempting once more to embarrass me?"

"Not at all." He leaned close enough for her to catch the clean scent of his skin. "I am most sincerely interested in your opinion."

Roma wished she possessed the nerve to give the sinfully handsome man the set-down that he deserved. She had no doubt that he considered her a naive fool ripe for his particular brand of teasing, but while she trembled with an angry urge to slap his mocking features, her father's rigid discipline kept her firmly in check. Creating an embarrassing scene would harm no one but herself. All she could do was give back a portion of his own medicine.

"Very well, Lord Carlton." She determinedly tilted her chin to meet his amused gaze. "In my opinion, men are far more trouble than they are worth. Dark or fair, flirtatious or honest, romantic or notorious, they all demand that a woman conform to a certain standard of behavior, while they are free to make their own rules for their lives. Thankfully I am in a rare position to inherit a comfortable legacy without the burden of marriage. I fully intend to enjoy my independence without a man to interfere with my happiness."

The raven brows arched in genuine surprise. "Surely you must jest, Miss Allendyle? I presumed that all young maidens were dazzled by the notion of capturing a suitable husband to care for them."

"I assure you that I am in complete earnest. I can think of nothing more repugnant than being required to sacrifice my freedom for the heavy bonds of matrimony."

"You speak so prosaically. What of love?"

She shrugged. "Love is for children and poets, Lord Carlton."

He gave a snort of disbelief. "So you do not secretly long to be swept off your feet, Miss Allendyle?"

With an effort, she forced herself to meet the piercing

blue gaze. "There is not a gentleman in all of England capable of sweeping me off my feet."

The disturbing fingers tightened on her arm, and without warning, Lord Carlton tugged her into a shallow alcove, using the tall plants to shield them from the passing crowd.

"I can not decide, Miss Allendyle, whether you are shockingly innocent or simply far more clever than any woman I have ever encountered."

The genuine note of pique in his voice had Roma glancing upward in surprise.

"What?"

The blue gaze narrowed as he studied the clear depths of her eyes.

"Do you deliberately attempt to challenge me, Roma, or is it a completely unconscious provocation?"

She should have been angered by his easy familiarity and arrogant assumption that he could speak to her in such an intimate manner, but instead she experienced that odd sense of panic that made it impossible to think in a coherent manner.

"I do not know what you mean."

"No?"

"What do you want from me?"

The blue eyes darkened and the large masculine body seemed to stiffen as he unconsciously drew her small frame closer. Feeling the uncomfortable tension that had so unexpectedly filled the air between them, Roma shivered. A building excitement lodged deep in the pit of her stomach, a sense of anticipation that was as unexplainable as it was unfamiliar. But while the electric sensations tingling through her weren't exactly unpleasant, Roma abruptly pulled away as a stab of fear pierced her rapidly beating heart.

"I should get back to Claude—he'll be wondering what has happened to us."

Almost instantly the darkly handsome face was resuming its normal expression of mocking amusement and the odd flame in the blue eyes was deliberately dampened.

"Your cousin is currently absorbed with a very charming brunette. I doubt that he will concern himself with your whereabouts for some time to come."

A swift glance over her shoulder revealed that Claude was indeed making sheep eyes at a pretty brunette who simpered in obvious appreciation. Traitor, she thought silently. He had behaved like an overprotective mother hen with Freddie Scowfield, a man she had known and liked most of her life. And yet, when Lord Carlton had blatantly kidnapped her beneath his very nose, he'd acted as if he did not have a concern in the world.

"I still think we should return," she retorted stubbornly. "My aunt has already hinted that people are beginning to gossip."

There was a faint edge of distaste in her voice that brought a smile to his face.

"Really? And what are they saying, Roma?"

"Does it really matter?" she hedged.

"I suppose they are suggesting I am too old to be pursuing a debutante fresh from the country?"

"Of course not." She blushed, her eyes sparkling with anger. "They are saying that I am dangling after you in the most shameless manner."

The dark head tilted backward as Lord Carlton gave a short laugh. "That must have rubbed at your prickly pride."

"It is not amusing."

"If only they knew the truth, eh, Roma? No wonder you treat me as if I am carrying a contagious disease. Would you like me to inform the gossiping tabbies that you have repeatedly rejected my pursuits and that I find myself in the uncomfortable position of worshiping you from afar?"

His gentle teasing darkened her confused color, and Roma struggled to maintain at least a semblance of her usual composure.

"Certainly not. It would be far better if you would simply leave me alone."

"I can hardly do that if we are to work together to discover what has happened to your brother."

"Have you discovered something?" she demanded, instantly forgetting her irritation. If he managed to find William alive and well, then she silently promised that she would willingly kiss the ground he walked on. She would do anything to save her brother. "Do you know where he is?"

"No." He shook his head, his voice gentle. "I am afraid not. But I am quite sure that we will have some news very soon."

The sharp flare of hope faded back to the dull ache that had haunted her for the past month.

"And I am just expected to wait?" she demanded, unreasonably blaming this man for the frustration seething in her heart.

"What else can you do, Roma?" he asked, his expression somber. "For the time being we must be patient."

"That is easy for you to say. It isn't your brother who is missing, perhaps hurt and in need of help," she accused. Despite the logical part of her mind warning her that Lord Carlton could be her greatest ally, she couldn't prevent herself from striking out in annoyance. It was that or throw herself into his arms and sob her troubles onto his broad shoulders, she acknowledged with a flash of insight. She wasn't nearly as strong as she pretended to be. "William would certainly be doing everything possible to search for me if the situations were reversed. Why am I supposed to be content to simply wait for you to tell me what I can or can not do?"

"Because the world is a very unfair place," he retorted, tapping a finger on the end of her nose. "And because I have already done everything possible for the moment. As difficult as it might be, you must trust me, Roma."

Strangely enough Roma knew that deep down she did trust him. No matter how he might disturb her, there was something very solid and dependable about his large frame and classic features. Still, she wasn't about to reveal such an unexpected failing to the arrogant man.

"I'd as soon trust a snake, Lord Carlton," she informed him in a haughty tone.

His chuckle sent a tingle of excitement down her spine and without warning, he took hold of her hand.

"You truly are an enchanting creature, my dear. Until tomorrow." He gave an elegant bow, bringing her fingers to his lips in a slow motion. "I look forward to our ride with great anticipation."

Quite determined to inform him that she had no intention of riding with him tomorrow or any other day, Roma gave a toss of her head, but even as she prepared to give him a proper set-down, he flashed a wicked grin and, with one smooth motion, deserted her in the small alcove.

Dragging in an angry breath, she ignored the lingering scent of warm male skin and enticing cologne. Somehow she had been outmaneuvered again by this devious man. She had no doubt that tomorrow afternoon he would arrive at the house, fully expecting her to meekly concede to his wishes.

A sudden, highly dangerous glint entered her eyes as she watched him make his slow exit from the room. Her father had perhaps been one of the greatest tacticians the military had ever known, and she wasn't his daughter for nothing.

If Lord Carlton wished to interfere in her life for his own amusement, he would soon learn he had chosen the wrong woman for such a game. She could do some maneuvering on her own, and she couldn't wait to see how he enjoyed being treated with such careless arrogance.

Seven

"The devil take you, Giles; you know I can not abide parading up and down the park like some peacock on display," Jack Howe grumbled, wondering if it was the vast amount of burgundy he had drunk the night before or the vile remedy for a hangover his unsympathetic valet had insisted he swallow that was causing the dull ache behind his eyes. "I can only assume you lost a wager with some fool at White's last evening and now must pay the penalty."

A portion of Lord Carlton's normal humor was distinctly absent as he scanned the numerous carriages that clogged the street. With a strained control, he kept his frisky bays in check, inwardly sympathizing with their restless need for urgency. He felt the same desire to thrust his way though the slow-moving vehicles. Dash it all, how was he supposed to catch up to Roma and that Scowfield cad if he was forced to go at this snail's pace?

"Must you rattle on in such a manner, Jack?" he asked in exasperation. "It is tedious enough to be trapped in this traffic with meddling dowagers and empty-headed debutantes without being subjected to your endless stream of complaints."

More than a little offended, Jack threw himself back in his well-padded seat with a wounded sniff.

"You needn't fly into a pet, Giles. I can not imagine what has gotten into you lately."

Giles swallowed a self-derisive smile. He knew exactly what had gotten into him. A five foot nothing of a chit with a pair of hazel eyes and an irritating ability to intrude into his thoughts on a regular basis. That, however, was not something he would admit to anyone.

"I haven't the least notion what you are bleating about, Jack," he retorted in an offhand manner.

"No?" Jack carefully turned his aching head to study the finely chiseled profile beside him. Although Giles appeared as elegantly turned out as ever, Jack sensed an edge of distraction about the handsome features, one he had never noticed before. It was as if he had run headlong into a brick wall and was still reeling from the impact. "After years of treating Polite Society with barely concealed contempt, you suddenly appear at a variety of functions, more often than not singling out Miss Allendyle for your attention, before disappearing without a word to anyone else. And now you've even taken to parading through the park like a veritable dandy. I just do not understand what is going on."

The irrepressible twinkle returned to Giles's eyes as a peevish note entered Jack's tone. He was well aware that his cousin faithfully attempted to pattern his life in the same mold as his own. It was a knowledge that had more than once kept him from any outrageous exploits. Now he couldn't help but find humor in the notion that his impressionable cousin was offended by his current behavior.

"I did not appear at a variety of functions, Jack," he corrected in mild tones. "I appeared at precisely two and behaved with the utmost decorum."

Jack let out a loud, very ungentlemanly snort. "Do not attempt to fob me off, Giles. There is something distinctly odd about your sudden interest in Miss Allendyle."

"I can not imagine why. She is a remarkably beautiful woman."

"And clearly dangling after you like a hundred other

debutantes," Jack burst out in frustration. "Normally you give such obvious lures a wide berth."

Giles laughed, remembering Roma's angry accusations of the night before.

"Any notion that Miss Allendyle is attempting to lure me into marriage is quite ridiculous. I will admit there have been moments when I suspected she was clever enough to pretend an indifference in an effort to capture my interest, but I have come to the conclusion that her fervent dislike toward me is completely genuine."

His amused, rather meditative tone had Jack regarding him with open puzzlement.

"Do you mean to say this Miss Allendyle has not tossed her heart at your feet?"

Giles smiled with blithe unconcern. "She thoroughly detests me."

"Do not gammon me, Giles. Debutantes have gone into transports since you left Oxford and took your place in London Society. I refuses to believe Miss Allendyle can be any different." Jack frowned, clearly disturbed by the implication in his cousin's words.

"I assure you, Jack, Miss Allendyle considers me boorishly overbearing and arrogant to a fault."

Glancing at his young cousin's face, Giles was suddenly reminded of a puppy he had once raised that could never quite comprehend what had happened when he pretended to throw a stick and instead hid it behind his back. Obviously Jack found it difficult to accept that any woman could remain immune to the potent allure of his idol, but before Giles could assure the young man that he had all the normal faults and failings of every other male, he abruptly caught sight of deep auburn curls shimmering like tongues of flame in the afternoon sunlight.

The brief glimpse of humor rapidly fled from his face, leaving it harshly masculine as he watched the approaching carriage. Roma looked extraordinarily lovely in a white carriage dress trimmed with silk ribbons, a gay straw hat perched at an impudent angle on her tousled curls.

But it was the slight flush on her creamy skin and the decided glint in the hazel eyes that captured his attention. She seemed to be thoroughly enjoying her ride with the weasel-faced man at her side. Instantly a deep frown marred his face as he deliberately angled his chaise so that Scowfield was forced to stop or risk locking wheels.

"I say . . ." With an effort, Scowfield brought his hired hack to an abrupt halt, his narrowed gaze stabbing Giles with a glare of dislike. "Can't you keep a greater grip on the ribbon, man? You nearly ran us off the road."

Jack nearly choked at the angry accusation, his mouth opening to inform the rude man that Lord Giles Carlton was not only a member of the Four-in-Hand Club, but considered the finest whip in all of London. Before the words could tumble past his tight lips, however, Giles was performing an elegant half-bow toward the coolly indifferent Miss Allendyle, seemingly unaware that he had just been deeply insulted.

"Miss Allendyle, what an unexpected pleasure." He summoned his most charming smile, his shrewd gaze not missing the flicker of unease that flashed through her hazel eyes before Roma could erect her well-rehearsed air of staunch composure. "And what a charming hat. I have no doubt that within the week every envious female in London will be sporting just such a gay concoction."

It was the type of frivolous exchange that was expected from a notorious flirt, but Roma shot him a suspicious frown.

"Thank you, Lord Carlton."

"Of course, not one of them could hope to compete with your own particular style," he continued, blithely ignoring Jack's puzzled stare and Lord Scowfield's dark frown. "I have it on the best authority that several women have begun to add a dash of henna to their hair in the hope of capturing the radiant beauty of your lovely curls, but of course they have managed to do no more than become a pale imitation of the Incomparable original."

Despite her clear intention to treat him with a cool

civility, Roma couldn't entirely prevent the warm flush of embarrassment that rose to her cheeks at his lavish praise.

"I am quite sure you are greatly exaggerating, Lord Carlton."

"Not at all," he returned swiftly. "How unfortunate for me that I arrived too late to escort you today. I am quite sure your companion is the envy of every male in the vicinity."

His subtle taunt deepened Roma's blush, but with the spirit he could not help but admire, she met his mocking gaze with a defiant tilt of her square chin.

"Lord Scowfield and I are neighbors as well as old friends. Naturally when I discovered he had arrived in London I was eager to hear all the latest gossip from home."

Giles allowed a patently unconvinced smile to tilt his full lips. "Naturally."

The hazel eyes flashed. "And, of course, he was kind enough to extend his invitation for a drive last evening."

"Yes, I remember," Giles retorted blandly. "It is a pity, however, that you have a previous engagement today. I most particularly wanted to speak with you."

Giles felt no remorse in using his only weapon to strike past Roma Allendyle's impervious wall of indifference. It bothered him more than he cared to admit to see her seated beside the unknown man, and not even the knowledge that she was simply attempting to punish him for his careless assumption that she should fall in with his own plans could ease the simmering anger. Old friend or not, he had a distinct urge to plant a facer on the smugly smiling Lord Scowfield.

Just for a moment, Roma wavered between wary suspicion and reluctant interest.

"Was it anything . . . important, Lord Carlton?" she at last inquired, her prickly composure cracking enough to reveal a glimpse of the fragile woman beneath.

A flare of warmth shot through his heart, and for no reason he could explain, he was abruptly reminded of the awareness he had experienced in the secluded alcove the night before. It was more than mere physical attraction, he silently acknowledged. The feelings racing through his body certainly held more than a trace of sensual attraction, but it was almost overshadowed by the odd desire to snatch her into his arms and protect her from the world.

"Nothing that can not wait," he amended with a certain reluctance, wanting to punish her for daring to spend her time with another man and yet reluctant to upset her unnecessarily. "Perhaps we can speak tomorrow?"

"Yes, of course." She bit her lower lip, clearly regretting her decision to punish the only man who could help in her search for her brother.

A wave of unfamiliar guilt began to twinge at his heart as he met her darkened gaze, but before the admirable emotion could induce him to confess he had no news that could not wait, Lord Scowfield made an untimely attempt to assert his own influence over the suddenly confused woman.

"It may have passed your notice, but for the moment Miss Allendyle is my companion," he said, his tone filled with a lofty superiority that instantly set Giles's teeth on edge. "And since I did promise her a drive through the park, I would appreciate having you move your cattle out of the way."

For a crazed moment, Giles measured the distance between him and the obnoxious Scowfield, knowing one swift punch would ensure his long, aquiline nose would remain swollen and painful for the better part of a week. Then, realizing Roma was quite contrary enough to sympathize with the much smaller man and blame him for the entire incident, he instead conjured up a sardonic smile.

"But of course. Although I do feel I should point out that you should always warn a lady before dragging her off in a hired hack, Scowfield. You'll discover in time they prefer to wear something that can be disposed of without undue upset. The seats you know are never quite clean, and the smell tends to linger no matter how much effort the maid might give. It truly is a pity for Miss Allendyle to have ruined such a beautiful gown." His smile widened. "Still, you can always hope that your company is adequate compensation for the loss of a dress, no matter how expensive."

With a small dip of his dark head, Giles raised his whip to execute an uncomplicated, but extremely difficult maneuver, easily steering his pair away from the hired carriage. He did have the satisfaction of seeing Scowfield flush with anger and what appeared to be a renegade flash of humor in Roma's wide eyes before he moved away, but any comfort he might have felt at the knowledge he had struck a blow to the annoying man's pride was offset by the realization he was behaving in a most peculiar manner.

What the devil was he doing riding through a crowded park when there were dozens of other pleasurable pursuits he could be enjoying? Surely it could not be for the simple need to see Roma Allendyle, if only at a distance?

Clearly Jack's thoughts paralleled his own, and as they once more entered the slow-moving traffic he sent his cousin a worried frown.

"Did you know Miss Allendyle would be here today?"

"As a matter of fact I did."

Jack frowned. "And that was the reason you insisted I accompany you?"

Giles turned his pair off the main thoroughfare, ready to be away from the annoying crowd.

"That and the fact I find your company thoroughly delightful."

"That is a bag of moonshine," Jack retorted with a roll of his eyes. "If I didn't know better, I would almost dare to say that you are attempting to make a cake of yourself over the lovely Miss Allendyle."

"But of course, you do know better than that," Giles mocked, a self-derisive smile tugging at the edges of his mouth. "A man with my reputation would never trail after a woman for the mere pleasure of seeing her smile."

Although Jack was blessed with more than an average intelligence, he seemed to possess a remarkable blind spot when it came to his cousin's unexplainable behavior, and it was with an obvious sense of relief that he eagerly accepted the cynical words at face value.

"No, by Jove, that's true enough. Not when the entire *ton* knows you have your pick of London's most beautiful women."

A brief, unwanted image of Lavania's glittering black eyes and pouting red lips rose to Giles's mind. With a tiny shudder of distaste he abruptly thrust the thought away, feeling unexplainably displeased by the memories of the passionate relationship. In retrospect it was easy to see just how shallow and greedy the beautiful woman was at heart. And worse, he had to acknowledge that his own motives had been entirely selfish. For some reason the realization left a lingering unease in his mind. In an effort to put an end to the unwanted self-analysis, Giles determinedly turned his attention to more pressing matters.

"What do you know of Scowfield?"

'Scowfield?" Jack frowned, his forehead furrowing in concentration. "Not a great deal. I don't believe he comes to London very often, prefers the life of the country gentleman. I believe there was some trouble a few years back, damn what was . . . Ah, I remember." Jack suddenly snapped his fingers. "There was a rumor floating around that he played fast and loose with a young debutante. The girl was sent home and quietly married to some local merchant. I don't think anything was ever proven, but there was quite a bit of talk, and a few hostesses refused to invite him to their homes. In the end he returned home, and to my knowledge he never dared return until now."

Giles absorbed the words in thoughtful silence. Quite ridiculously, he was forced to suppress a smile of satisfaction at Jack's condemning words, as if he was happy to have his instinctive dislike for the man reinforced, if only by an outdated scandal. It helped to ease the strange suspicion that his bristling antagonism had anything to do with Roma Allendyle.

"I wonder what brings him back to London?" he mused.

Jack shrugged "Perhaps he hopes that people have forgotten his past . . . indiscretions. After all, it can't be much fun to rattle around a dreary estate when everyone is in London for the Season."

"Spoken like a true man of the town," Giles teased, aware of his cousin's total lack of interest in his own family estate. "Still, I think I will keep a close eye on Lord Scowfield. I am not nearly so certain that a desire to reenter polite society has driven him to London. It seems much too convenient that his visit should come at the same time as Miss Allendyle's, and that he should show such a determined interest in her since his arrival."

"I don't see why," Jack retorted bluntly. "As she pointed out herself, they are neighbors. What could be more natural than for the two of them to seek out each other's company?"

For an answer Giles once more cracked his whip, able to pick up the pace as the traffic slowly thinned. Certainly Jack had a point. Roma knew few people in London, and it would perfectly understandable if Lord Scowfield was in the same position that the two would gravitate toward each other. But while he could remind himself not to jump to conclusions, Giles already knew that he had decided to discover everything possible about the mysterious man. And much more importantly, he was determined to keep him far away from Roma Allendyle until her brother returned home safe and sound.

Eight

Roma paced restlessly across the formal sitting room, her fingers unconsciously tugging at the full skirt of her muslin gown. For a woman who had supposedly achieved her goal, she felt remarkably frustrated. And, of course, the full blame for her seething dissatisfaction could be laid at the door of Lord Carlton.

Her decision to ride in the park yesterday with Freddie Scowfield had been a deliberate attempt to prove she was thoroughly indifferent to Lord Carlton's arrogant demands. He had no right to blithely expect her to fall in with his slightest whim as if she were one of the innumerable foolish women susceptible to his potent charm. She was an independent woman who made her own decisions, and just to prove her point she had bravely flaunted his subtle demand that she agree to his lie that they'd had a prior arrangement to ride through the park and had instead chosen to be escorted by Freddie.

It was a decision that she had been quite proud of, even after Freddie had arrived and they had set off for the park. But any sense of smug self-confidence had come to an abrupt end the moment she had caught sight of Lord Carlton's heart-stopping smile and vivid blue gaze. All at once she had poignantly regretted her stubborn resistance. As ludicrous as it might seem, she couldn't deny a flare of desire to be seated at his side, exchanging bantering words and using her sharp intelligence in an attempt to remain a step ahead of him.

I must be going soft in the noodle, she silently chastised herself, realizing where her traitorous thoughts were leading. She didn't want to spend time with Lord Carlton. He was just another arrogant, self-absorbed male who was concerned with nothing more than his own pleasure. And only because he had hinted that he might possess news of her brother had she suddenly wished she had chosen to ride with him.

That was also the reason she had feigned a headache that morning and sent her aunt and cousin off on their round of calls without her. If Lord Carlton did have information, then she was certain he would attempt to contact her as quickly as possible.

Yes, that had to be the reason for her unexplainable emotions, she thought with a rush of relief. It was all quite simple once she thought it out in a logical manner.

Her supreme logic did not, however, ease the lingering restlessness that had plagued her all morning, and for what seemed to be the hundredth time, she paced back across the carpet. If only she weren't in London, she thought with a sigh of frustration. At home she would be free to work off her nervous energy with a wild gallop, or even a stormy encounter with her notoriously lazy bailiff. And certainly there would be enough problems related to the estate to keep her from perpetually dwelling on her missing brother.

But more or less stuck in London, she found herself bound by the strict rules of Society. A proper lady did not don breeches and ride like a hellion across open fields, nor did she manage an estate with a shrewd eye on the account book and the threat of a riding whip if her orders were not carried through. Instead she was expected to sit meekly in a house and hope that Lord Carlton and his mysterious contacts were doing everything possible to locate her brother. It was little wonder her nerves were twisted into tight knots of unease.

With an unconscious toss of her head, Roma once more turned on her heel, about to retrace her steps across the floor, when she abruptly caught sight of a dark form poised at the edge of the wide French windows. Instantly alarmed, she cautiously moved toward the center of the room, attempting to ascertain that there was indeed someone skulking beside the window without alerting the intruder that she was aware of their presence.

Her heart was racing with a surge of adrenaline, but it never entered her mind to run from the room or even to call for help. It was a decision she was destined to appreciate as the French door was unexpectedly pushed open and a shockingly familiar male figure stepped into the room.

Pressing a hand to her jolting heart, Roma gazed with wide-eyed amazement at the dark, aquiline face and bewitching blue eyes.

"Lord Carlton . . ." she breathed out unsteadily.

The wicked grin that had haunted more than one of her dreams was very much in evidence as be lifted his hands in a casual apology.

"I am sorry if I startled you, Miss Allendyle, but I wanted to speak with you in private. And since I happened to note your aunt and cousin leaving, I took the chance I would find you in here alone."

A proper lady would no doubt have been deeply insulted by Lord Carlton's forward manner. After all, a gentleman would never treat a woman of good breeding with anything but rigid respect, and such continuous transgressions of the normal code of behaviour could only imply he considered her less than well bred.

Today, however, Roma had little interest in proper manners. She had waited all morning for this moment, and rather than being offended by the unexpected intrusion, she instead rushed across the room, experiencing a wild surge of hope.

"Have you found William?" she demanded, her voice eager.

Reaching out his hands, he grasped her shoulders, his gaze searing her flushed features and anxious eyes.

"No, Roma, I haven't found him, but I do have some information."

"Information?" A wave of disappointment rushed over her. "What information?"

"I received a note yesterday morning from an acquaintance who happens to know your brother."

"What did it say?"

"According to him, the last time William made contact with the government was nearly a month ago. Since then they have attempted several times to reach him by the usual method, but with no luck. You are not the only one to worry about his sudden absence."

"I knew it." The dull ache in her heart was becoming more pronounced. "I knew there was something wrong. William would never disappear unless something terrible had happened . . ."

His grip tightened on her shoulders. "Do not jump to conclusions, Roma. At the moment he is simply missing."

"But he would not be missing unless something was keeping him away."

"No good can come from assuming the worse. We must take a positive outlook."

Oddly his firm grip and authoritative tone instantly quelled the wave of panic that threatened to sweep over her. Meeting the blue eyes that probed deeply into her wide gaze, she forced herself to drag in a steadying breath.

"You are right, of course. I have to believe that we are going to find him and that everything will soon be back to normal."

A small smile tugged at his lips. "That is the spirit."

"Did the note say anything else?"

There was a brief pause, almost as if he were considering whether or not to reveal what else the missive had contained. Something in the determined set of her features, however, must have convinced him that she would be satisfied with nothing less than the full truth, and he at last gave a small shrug.

"Actually he has arranged for me to meet with an associate of your brother's."

"An associate? Did he say who it was?"

"No. I have very few details."

Roma frowned. "I wonder if it is someone I would know?"

"It is possible, but highly doubtful. You have pointed out yourself, you know few people in London."

"Yes, I suppose. Why does he wish to see you?"

"So that we can discuss the situation. Hopefully, together we can come up with a few ideas on where to begin to search for your brother."

"That is an excellent idea." Roma unconsciously raised her hands to lay them against the smooth fabric of his dark blue jacket. At the moment her disturbing awareness of his potent masculinity was overshadowed by a vast sense of relief that he truly intended to help her locate William. "Where are we supposed to meet him?"

She sensed more than she actually felt Lord Carlton stiffen at her eager words.

"Roma . . . This is a highly secretive meeting, not a social gathering," he pointed out in a gentle, but firm voice.

"I realize that."

"There can be no question of your attending."

"Why not?" she demanded, her ready temper sparking to life. "It is my brother you will be discussing. Certainly no one knows more about him than myself."

The impossibly handsome features tightened as he gazed down at her militant expression.

"That may be so, but I can hardly drag you unescorted to a secluded spot and then return you here without creating a major scandal. You must use some sense, Roma."

The hazel eyes flared at the patronizing note in his voice, and with a toss of her head, she glared at him in the precise manner her father had used to quell a troop of rowdy infantry men.

"Do not talk to me as if I am a complete simpleton, Lord Carlton," she snapped angrily. "I am well aware that I can not simply disappear with you. I may have lived most of my life in the country, but I do know the proper behavior for a young woman."

Lord Carlton's features remained set in stern lines, but Roma suspected that the glint deep in the dark blue eyes was one of amusement.

"And so you understand that you must allow me to deal with this situation? At least for the moment?"

"I understand that Roma Allendyle can not accompany you," she corrected, "but if she were to take to her bed to nurse a lingering headache, there is no reason you could not take along a young groom to help with your horse."

Just for a moment he gazed at her blankly, as if he didn't completely understand her meaning. Then the hands on her shoulders abruptly tightened, and he gave her a slight shake.

"It is absolutely out of the question."

"Why?"

"Why?" He glared at her in exasperation. "Not only would you risk exposing both of us to a shocking scandal, but more importantly there is a very real possibility that this meeting might hold an element of danger. I will not allow you to put yourself in such peril."

Roma's chin jutted out in a stubborn gesture. It seemed impossible that just a few moments ago she was waiting with nervous anticipation for some word from this man. She had even wondered if perhaps she wasn't beginning to think of him a bit too much. Now she could only remember how truly annoying he was.

"I am quite capable of deciding whether or not to put myself at risk, Lord Carton. You might have insisted on helping me with my search for my brother, but you have no right to tell me where I can or can not go."

There was a dangerous edge in her voice. It would have warned the people who knew her best that now was not the time to openly challenge her independence. Unfortunately Lord Carlton possessed his own share of mulish pride, and he wasn't about to back away from his rigid stance.

"Perhaps not, but I do have the ability to keep the whereabouts of tonight's meeting a secret. If you wish to get yourself killed out of some stubborn notion that it will help your brother, you will have to do so without my help."

"Why, you . . ." Literally shaking with fury, she glared into his harshly handsome face. "You have no right to keep me away. You know quite well that I could contribute details about my brother and his movements before his disappearance. They might very well be of importance. By keeping me away, you are more than likely putting my brother in serious danger."

Her accusing words fell on deaf ears. If anything the dark, aquiline features hardened with arrogant determination.

"You have heard my decision, Roma. I apologize if you consider it unfair, but I will not change my mind. I do, however, promise to keep you informed of everything that is discussed tonight."

"How very generous of you!" she snapped.

"Would you prefer that I not tell you anything?"

"I would prefer that you had never intruded into my life."

The blue eyes darkened with frustration, and without warning Roma felt herself being jerked against the solid warmth of his tall frame.

"Roma, there are times when . . ." The muttered words slowly drifted away as Lord Carlton began to realize just how intimately he was holding her.

Roma eyed him warily, finding it strangely difficult to breathe as she waited for him to release his tight grasp. But surprisingly the lean fingers continued to press into the sensitive skin of her shoulders, while his narrowed gaze swept over her startled features, halting on the full curve of her mouth. Her heart actually seemed to flip over as he carefully scrutinized the trembling lips that had never known a man's touch, but even as she frantically considered the notion that he was about to kiss her, his body abruptly stiffened and with a firm movement he stepped away.

Confused as much by the unfamiliar strain that marred Lord Carlton's features, as by the unexplainable excitement fluttering through her stomach, Roma struggled for the angry composure that she had somehow lost in the last few seconds.

"I am greatly disappointed in you, Lord Carlton," she forced herself to say. "I thought perhaps you were different from the others."

"Different?"

"I thought perhaps you understood me."

Something flashed deep in his eyes. "I understand that I will do nothing that might lead you into danger," he retorted, his voice unusually husky. "Why can you not accept that I am only doing what I think is best for you?"

Feeling the nearly overwhelming force in his magnetic gaze, Roma abruptly turned away. She wasn't about to be coerced into once more agreeing to his demands. He was wrong to keep her away from a man who might very well have information about William. And it only made it worse to know that his reason for keeping her away from the meeting was solely because she was a woman.

It was thoroughly unfair, she told herself grimly. And if he was determined to treat her like a helpless fool who was incapable of taking care of herself, then he had no one to blame but himself if she chose to act on her own.

Unconsciously squaring her shoulders, she turned back to meet his wary gaze.

"It seems I have little choice but to accept your decision, Lord Carlton. I can hardly force you to reveal the location of your meeting."

The blue eyes narrowed, almost as if he sensed she was hiding something behind her stiff mask of indifference.

"And I can trust you not to rush about London asking those you encounter whether or not they have plans to meet with me this evening?"

Her chin tilted to an indignant angle. "I have no intention of speaking of this with anyone. Whatever I might think of you and your underhanded methods of manipulating people, Lord Carlton, I am deeply concerned about my brother. I would never do anything that might put him in even greater danger."

A silence fell as Lord Carlton carefully inspected her stiff expression. Roma was well aware that he remained suspicious of her abrupt capitulation, and with a determined effort she forced herself to meet his probing gaze with a steady indifference.

After a long moment he gave a small shrug, seeming to realize there was little he could do to ensure that she stay out of trouble.

"Will you come for a drive tomorrow so that we can discuss what has been decided?"

She gave him a meaningless smile. "Of course."

"Roma . . ." He stepped forward, a frown marring his wide brow. "What are you thinking?"

"Thinking, my lord?" She swallowed an angry retort and instead batted her eyes in an innocent motion. "Why I was just wondering if my new gown will be delivered in time for the Blanton ball tonight. It truly is the most charming concoction, and Aunt Clara has promised to loan me her emeralds for the occasion. It is a pity you will not be there to see me."

His suspicious frown deepened at her fluttering words. "Are you attempting to bamboozle me?"

"Not at all." Her tone abruptly hardened. "I was simply practicing my role as the proper debutante. What else could I possibly have on my mind but how utterly ravishing I am going to appear tonight?"

"Roma . . ." With a frustrated sigh he took a step forward, but she quickly backed away, her expression grim.

"I think you should be leaving, Lord Carlton. You claim to be concerned for my reputation—it would hardly do me much good for you to be discovered here."

For a moment she thought he was going to argue with her stiff logic, but with an irritated shake of his head, he obviously decided that she was in no mood to be reasonable.

"I will call on you tomorrow."

"Very well. Good day, Lord Carlton."

With one last glance, he turned on his heel and disappeared through the open French door. With a small smile she watched as he covertly dodged his way to the high hedge, knowing all the while she had no intention of leaving her brother's fate in the hands of strangers. Dangerous or not, she was going to be at that meeting. Now, all she had to do was come up with a plan to accompany Lord Carlton without his being aware of her presence.

Not an easy task.

Nine

Annoying, aggravating, utterly unreasonable woman. Seething with a sense of wounded injustice, Giles threw himself into the waiting Tilbury, condemning women in general and Roma Allendyle in particular.

She was completely beyond the pale, he told himself fiercely. Did she actually expect him to aid and abet a scheme to sneak her from her aunt's home and escort her to an isolated, perhaps even dangerous, location dressed as a groom? It was ludicrous.

Hadn't he already risked his good name by sneaking into the house so he could explain in person the latest change in the search for her brother? And didn't she appreciate the trouble and danger he was risking in an effort to discover the whereabouts of a young whelp he had never even met?

The answer to that was a resounding no, he thought with a burst of frustration, making his groom frown in alarm as he gave a crack of the whip and set the restless bays off at a brisk pace.

If he had the least amount of sense he would wash his hands of the entire situation. After all, he had dozens and dozens of invitations to occupy his time. But even as he visualized the pleasure he would receive by informing the ungrateful woman that he was finished attempting to please her and that she could find a less gullible fool to

make a cod of himself, he was woefully aware that he
would do no such thing.

He might not be able to explain his uncharacteristic
behavior, but he was wise enough to realize there was no
point in fighting the inevitable. His fate had been sealed
on the never-to-be-forgotten evening when Roma had so
bravely led him to the deserted barn. And while he had
no clear notion of where the bizarre relationship might
lead, he did know that for once in his life he was in
control of emotions he had never even suspected he
might possess.

Of course, his rational explanation of his highly irrational behavior did little to ease his dark mood. Despite
all logic, Roma had managed to make him feel guilty for
his refusal to allow her to attend the meeting that evening. It was an unfamiliar emotion for a man accustomed
to having his decisions treated with respectful compliance
and one he angrily attempted to thrust from his churning
mind. He was doing what was best for her whether she
was willing to admit it or not. It was ludicrous to allow a
pair of wounded hazel eyes make him feel like an insen-
sitive devil.

Dwelling on his confused thoughts, Giles was barely
aware of his surroundings, and it was as much luck as
skill that kept the Tilbury on the road and out of a nasty
accident. Eventually, however, the thickening traffic
forced him to slow his pace, much to the relief of
Jameson, who was deeply disturbed by his employer's uncharacteristic lack of concentration. The groom had been
with Lord Carlton since he had left Oxford, and he had
never known him to drive with anything less than perfect
control. Of course, Jameson was forced to acknowledge,
the usually levelheaded man had been behaving in a peculiar manner for the past several weeks.

Unaware that he had created such unease in his stony-
faced groom, Giles reluctantly pulled in the bays, firmly
ignoring the various waves and nods from the other carriages. He had enough on his mind without attempting

to indulge in meaningless chitchat with distant acquaintances. But it was his sheer disinterest that made him vulnerable to danger. Not until too late did he notice the
delicate phaeton in a royal blue with a cream interior. It
was bearing down in a determined manner, and cursing
beneath his breath at his witless lack of attention, Giles
grudgingly pulled to a halt.

With the flamboyance that had made her one of the
most celebrated beauties in all of England, Lady Lavania
Hoyet had her phaeton pulled close beside the Tilbury,
the near black eyes that perfectly matched her glossy curls
glittering with a dangerous light.

"Ah . . . the elusive Lord Carlton. What a pleasant surprise!"

Giles swallowed a grimace at her overtly sweet tone. He
had no doubt that she was utterly furious at his recent
neglect. After all, she possessed enough beauty and fortune to chose her lovers with fastidious care. It wouldn't
have surprised him to discover that he was the first man
to have ever cast her aside.

"Lady Hoyet." He gave a perfunctory bow. "May I say
you look as ravishing as ever?"

"How absolutely divine of you to say so," she purred,
her gaze as sharp as a cutthroat's dagger. "Especially considering your taste seems to run toward buxom country
girls lately."

Giles stiffened, his blue eyes freezing at the deliberate
thrust. Just for a moment he allowed his gaze to roam
over the perfect oval face, the creamy skin and curva-
ceous form revealed rather than concealed by the flimsy
gauze gown. At one time she had seemed to be an embodiment of his deepest fantasies. A woman with a heated
passion that could rival his own. Now he could only see
the insatiable greed that smoldered deep in the black
eyes and the self-indulgent droop of her full mouth. A
sudden shudder racked his body.

"You really shouldn't refine too much on idle chatter,
my lady. It is notoriously inaccurate."

"Indeed?" Her smile held a hint of cruelty. "Then it isn't true that Miss Allendyle has managed to tame you into a biddable slave, ready to dance attendance upon her every whim?"

The taunting words were designed to strike at his pride as well as arouse his temper, but Giles ignored the bitter thrust.

"I have no intention of accepting or denying any such claims." He gave a negligent shrug. "People are free to think what they will."

The black eyes abruptly narrowed, as if she were caught off guard by his nonchalance.

"Then it doesn't matter that the entire *ton* is laughing at the manner in which you are mooning over that inconsequential chit?" she demanded, a shrill edge entering her voice. "I assure you there is a vast amount of amusement at the thought of you behaving like an infatuated schoolboy."

"I am delighted that I can provide such entertainment for society." The dark features gave nothing away. "After all, the Season can be so tedious without a few expected *on-dits.*"

The black eyes flashed with a wave of fury. "I do not believe you, Giles," she hissed, her pricked vanity obviously making her forget they were in full view of the public. "What could you possibly see in a naive country miss? From all accounts she possesses no fortune and only passable looks. There must be some nefarious reason you have taken such an interest in her."

If she had been genuinely hurt by the abrupt end to their relationship, then Giles might have felt a measure of remorse for her anger. But he was fully aware that her emotions stemmed solely from a need to revenge her damaged pride, and he felt no compassion as he met her venomous glare.

"My reasons, nefarious or not, have nothing to do with you, Lady Hoyet."

She flinched at his icy tone. "How can you say that

after all we have meant to one another?" she demanded, her voice throbbing with barely controlled passion. "Surely you can not have forgotten the times we have—"

"Lady Hoyet, this is hardly the time or the place for such a conversation," he interrupted, his brows lowering in a warning motion. "In fact, as far as I am concerned we have said all that needs to be said between us."

"No." She shook her dark head, her usually seductive mouth thinning to an ugly line. "I refuse to believe you prefer that . . . that absurd child to me. There has to be some reason you are behaving in such a preposterous manner."

"You are free to think what you like of course."

"Trust me, Giles. I will never stop searching until I discover the reason. No one treats me in the manner you have and gets away without payment. Eventually I will make you regret what you have done."

With a stern effort, Giles kept his expression bland. He had no doubt that Lavania would dearly love to wound Roma as well as himself if she could find some means to do so. It was vital that he warn her away before she could even attempt to bother Roma.

"I would be careful if I were you, my dear. There is nothing the *ton* finds more amusing than a scorned woman desperately seeking revenge." His smile mocked the sudden uncertainty that rippled across her lovely face. "I have no doubt that several of your rivals would dearly love to hold you up to ridicule. Why would you wish to make it so simple for them?"

Her full bosom heaved as she reluctantly allowed his sardonic words to override her burning need to hurt him. It was clear that she did indeed fear being seen as a woman tossed aside for a mere debutante, and he could already see her mind turning with desperate thoughts of how to avert such a tragedy.

"I wish you in Hades, Giles Carlton," she at last hissed, giving a toss of her dark head before abruptly motioning to her driver to be off.

Giles swallowed a self-derisive smile. He was quite certain that Lavania was busily constructing some means of ensuring that society believed she had ended her relationship with him long before his attention had wandered toward another woman.

It would be no easy task, especially since she possessed more than a few enemies who would be anxious to laugh at her unexpected position. Giles was indifferent to any excuse she might concoct, as long as it kept her far away from Roma Allendyle.

With his temper even more strained than before, he drove the last few streets to his house, barely giving Jameson time to grab the reins before he was leaping off the Tilbury and storming up the steps to his house. He was undecided as to whether to spend the rest of the day drinking himself into insensibility or packing for an extended rest at his country estate. Anything to take his mind off women and the trouble they always seemed to bring with them.

In the end he did neither. Instead he soothed his ruffled nerves with a very fine luncheon followed by a relaxing discussion of the benefits of crop rotation with several cronies at his club. He even managed a session with his tailor before carefully preparing for his arranged meeting.

Then, dressing in the tattered clothes and heavy overcoat that served as his usual disguise, he was careful to sneak out a side door and into the stable where Jameson had the carriage prepared for their departure. With a few brief words, they were headed toward the outskirts of London.

Slumped in the corner of the shadowed carriage, Giles reviewed the brief message he had received from Lord Halcott early yesterday morning. The older man had only stated that William was indeed missing and that he wanted Giles to meet with a Thomas Slater who presumably had information concerning the disappearance of Allendyle. He had also given directions to a deserted house set well outside of the city. Giles had experienced a completely unexpected flare of excitement at the note, almost as if he had a personal connection with the unknown man. And then, of course, he had been annoyed beyond reason when he had discovered that Roma had chosen to ride with Scowfield and had denied him the opportunity to reveal the information he had gained. That hadn't however, prevented him from using the pitiful excuse to rush over to the Welford house that morning, going so far as to actually creep into the sitting room for a private word with the exasperating Roma.

He had told himself that the message would bolster her courage and assure her he was doing everything possible to locate her brother. Unfortunately, he now realized it was a crackbrained scheme from the start. He should have suspected that she would be ridiculous enough to suggest she come to the meeting.

With a shake of his head, Giles attempted to push his dark thoughts away. He needed his mind clear to concentrate on what might have happened to William Allendyle. He would have plenty of time later to dwell on Roma's various character flaws.

The carriage rumbled over the uneven roads for nearly an hour before it mercifully pulled to a halt behind a tall, unmanicured hedge. Ensuring his small pistol was loaded and tucked into the hidden pocket sewn in the lining of his coat, Giles cautiously stepped into the overgrown grass. Nearly hidden from the road, he took a long moment to study the dilapidated cottage. It looked as if a strong breeze might send it tumbling to the ground, but Giles knew better than to let appearances fool him. He was quite certain he was at the right location, he just had to reassure his edgy nerves that he wasn't about to walk into a trap.

With a small nod toward Jameson, Giles began to edge his way around the house, his narrowed gaze studying his surroundings with careful attention. Most importantly he ensured that there were no hidden assassins or thugs wait-

ing to attack the moment he let down his guard. He had
learned his lesson well.

The soft coo of a nearby dove was the only sound to
break the silence as Giles slowly counted to one hundred,
his gaze carefully scrutinizing every clump of brush and
blade of grass. But when he was on the point of actually
approaching the open door to the cottage, he was
abruptly halted by the warning sound of his groom's short
whistle. With a concerned frown, Giles swiftly made his
way back to the carriage, finding Jameson peering
through the hedge.

"What is it?" he asked, his voice a low whisper.

Jameson turned, his voice as soft as his employer's. "I
seen something across the road. I think someone is watching the house."

"You stay here. I'll circle around."

Ignoring the trickle of alarm that inched down his
spine, Giles slowly made a wide detour around the hedge,
darting across the road and diving into the heavy bushes
on the opposite side. He lay there for a long moment,
listening for any unusual sounds. Then, assuming his less
than graceful approach had gone unnoticed, he raised
himself to his feet and slowly began to make his way
through the thick overgrowth.

At a painfully slow pace, he inched his way toward the
spot Jameson had pointed out, his senses on full alert.
Although he could see or hear nothing, he had enough
confidence in his groom to know Jameson wasn't the type
to overreact or to jump at mere shadows. If he suspected
someone was lurking in the bushes, then Giles had no
doubt there was indeed an uninvited intruder. The trick
was finding him without actually stumbling over him.

Hardly daring to breathe, he crept forward; then the
faint sound of a snapping twig brought him to an abrupt
halt. Crouching low to the ground he peered through a
clump of tall grass, closely inspecting the shadowed figure
that was poised only a few feet in front of him. Just for
a moment he considered pulling the gun from his coat

pocket; then he gave a decisive shake of his head. If the unknown man was not alone, he had no intention of warning the others that he was on to their scheme.

Instead, he determinedly tensed his muscles and drawing a deep breath, he suddenly leaped forward and tackled the stranger with enough force to send them both rolling across the ground.

Expecting a vicious fight, Giles clamped his arms tightly around the surprisingly tiny form, his blood freezing as a startled, wholly feminine scream pierced the heavy silence.

With a final twist he pushed himself on top of the oddly limp body, his heart coming to a painful halt as a horrible suspicion rushed over him.

Narrowing his gaze, he swiftly reached up a hand to pull off the heavy hat that effectively hid the small face. Somehow he wasn't even surprised when a heavy mane of auburn curls spilled onto the crushed grass.

"Good Lord . . ." He slowly shook his head, not sure whether to laugh or be furious at her unbelievable tenacity. "I should have known. Let me give you a bit of advice, Miss Allendyle: The next time you attempt to get yourself killed, I would appreciate it if you would chose to do so somewhere far away from me. I am frankly tired of saving you from your own stubborn stupidity."

Ten

Aching from the unexpected impact of Lord Carlton's attack, Roma glared furiously into the darkly grim features that hovered far too close for comfort.

"I hardly consider being thrown to the ground an attempt to save me," she hissed, potently aware of the solid weight of the muscular frame pressed intimately against her lower body. "In fact, I was doing quite well until you decided to leap on me like a . . . a wild animal."

"You're lucky I didn't put a bullet through your heart," he growled with a flare of anger. "It is no less than you deserve, sneaking about in these bushes."

Roma flinched, but as usual her strange antagonism toward this man refused to allow her to back away from her rigid stance.

"I have as much right to be here as you," she argued. "More, in fact, considering that you came here to discuss my brother."

His raven head shook back and forth, his expression one of exasperated disbelief. "I should have suspected you would attempt some crazy scheme," he muttered, his gaze lowering to her tattered shirt and breeches. "The only way to ensure that you will behave is to lock you in a room and throw away the key."

"What choice did you give me? If you had simply agreed to bring me along, then none of this would have been necessary."

"You can not possibly mean to imply your absurd behavior is now my fault?"

She met his glare with staunch courage. "If you would avoid treating me like a bird-witted fool then we could have found a less . . . absurd method of my coming this evening."

"And if you would act like a proper lady, then I wouldn't have to worry about you harrying about London dressed like a chimney sweep."

She curled her lips in a scornful motion. "I have no desire to act like a proper lady. All I want is to find my brother so that we can return to Greystead Manor and continue with our lives."

He stiffened, almost as if her words had caught him off guard.

"And then what, Roma?" he asked, his eyes oddly watchful. "Do you intend to bury yourself in the country forever?"

It was a question that she hadn't considered. She had been too consumed with the need to find William to even think of the future. And much to her surprise, she found herself hesitating. A month ago she would have easily accepted the idea of spending the rest of her life at Greystead Manor, content with her friends and her freedom. But now she wasn't quite so confident that she could accept such an undemanding life. Her recent adventure had added an undeniable spice to her existence, and she knew that she would find her world rather dull after it had all been settled.

Perhaps she had inherited more of her father's spirited nature than she had suspected, she thought with a quiver of alarm. Certainly there could be no other reason for her to regret the thought of leaving London.

She carefully eluded a direct answer. "I can give no thought to the future until my brother is safely home."

His expression tightened with displeasure, although Roma had no notion what he found so annoying about her ambiguous statement.

"There will be no future for either one of us unless you put a halt to these dangerous antics," he charged, his eyes abruptly narrowing. "And now perhaps you will explain just how you managed to discover my destination. I know for certain that I told no one where I was going."

She attempted to shrug, then regretted the sudden movement as he shifted to press her more firmly against the hard ground.

"It wasn't difficult," she answered, desperately attempting to ignore the odd tremors racing through her taut form. "I simply waited outside your house, and when I saw you come from your stables, I followed a short distance behind."

She didn't mention the fact she had been forced to hide in the hedge outside his house for nearly three hours or that the horse she had hired had proven to be a stubborn nag that had forcibly reminded her of the man currently glaring at her with open disbelief. Both were obstinate, provoking and in dire need for a proper set-down.

"Truly? And you expect me to believe that Jameson never noticed we were being followed?" He gave a sharp shake of his head. "You are obviously unfamiliar with my groom, Roma, or you would never suggest such a thing. His ability to sense danger is uncanny. He has saved my life on more than one occasion."

"And no mere woman could hope to outwit him?" She easily interpreted his blatant insinuation. "You obviously overestimate your groom's skill. Of course, I suppose he can be forgiven. Like most men, he assumes that danger can only come in the form of another man. What interest would he have in a ragged child trailing behind him?"

The blue eyes flared as her smooth thrust slid home, and his lips thinned to an annoyed line.

"Very well, I take your point. Clearly Jameson is no more immune than myself to the treachery of a desperate woman."

"And what would you do if a member of your family

were missing, Lord Carlton?" she demanded. "Would you be content to remain at home and allow others to search? Or would you insist on being involved?"

"The situation would hardly be the same," he retorted with a deep frown.

"Why?"

He heaved an irritated sigh. "Because, Roma, as difficult as it might be to accept, beneath those tattered clothes and that stubborn independence, you are a woman, while I am very much a man."

A completely ridiculous heat rose to her cheeks. "I am well aware of the differences in our gender, Lord Carlton."

"Are you?" A sudden, thoroughly alarming flare of heat darkened his eyes. "There are times when I wonder, Roma."

"And what do you mean by that?"

His unnerving gaze drifted over her pale features and the tangled cloud of auburn curls; then Roma felt her heart give a sharp jerk as it slowly lowered to the swells of her breasts clearly outlined by the thin shirt.

"Do you understand what it is to be a woman, Roma?" he asked, his voice thick with emotion. "Have you ever experienced the need to be loved by a man?"

"Please, Lord Carlton . . ." Frightened as much by the sudden surge of heat that flickered through her racing blood as by the unfamiliar edge that had entered his voice, Roma lifted her hands to press them against his firm chest. "You must let me up."

"Must I?" His eyes darkened. "Why?"

It seemed ridiculously difficult to think of a coherent reason. In fact, everything seemed difficult, from taking a normal breath to slowing the frantic beat of her heart.

"I . . . the meeting . . ."

"Roma." He sucked in a harsh breath, a slender hand raising to twine in the vibrant silk of her hair. "Do you know how many nights I have lain awake, torturing myself with the memory of your body? I remember every perfect detail.''

She shivered, too startled by the compelling sensations tingling through her to summon the outrage she knew she should feel.

"Please do not remind me of that night, Lord Carlton," she pleaded.

"Why should I not?" he demanded, an odd fire burning deep in his eyes. "Once again we are alone. Only this time you are uninjured and I am free to do what I wanted to do that first evening."

Her eyes widened at the determined note in his husky voice, and instinctively she pushed her hands against the firm muscles of his chest. But her feeble effort barely checked his slow, relentless downward movement and with a sense of suspended unreality she watched the raven head approach. A deep shudder ran through her, but surprisingly she found her muscles unwilling to fight against his overt physical dominance. It was almost as if she had been waiting for this moment since she had first caught sight of this impossibly handsome man.

Seeming to sense her peculiar lethargy, Lord Carlton paused to study the darkened confusion of her hazel eyes and the unconscious invitation of her parted lips. She felt his body stiffen and, for a brief moment, thought that common sense would prevail; then an unfamiliar expression of longing rippled across the lean features and the dark head swooped downward to claim her mouth in a kiss that sent her world spinning.

She had never actually considered what it might feel like to be held in a man's arms. And she certainly hadn't dreamed she would ever truly enjoy the feel of a man exploring her mouth with his lips and even the tip of his tongue. But contrary to all her long-held beliefs, Roma discovered that such intimate actions were far from repulsive. In fact, the tiny tremors that seemed to radiate from the very center of her being were startlingly pleasant, and unaware of the unconscious invitation in her

compliant lips or the fingers that curled into the rough
fabric of his shirt, Roma allowed the exquisite sensations
to sweep away her rigid defenses. Somewhere at the back
of her mind a tiny voice whispered that she should be
terrified by the potent heat racing through her blood,
but she felt no fear as he gently cupped her face to
deepen the possessive kiss. No matter how tumultuous
their strange relationship might be, she had always felt
as if she could trust him with her very life.

With a leashed hunger, he drank of her innocent offering, plundering her willing lips before restlessly moving to trail a path of liquid heat over her cheeks, her
temple, the vulnerable curve of her jaw and then, with a
harsh groan, to bury his face in the soft cloud of her
hair.

"Honeysuckle . . ." he rasped, his·body tense with the
effort to control his emotions.

Still caught in the new and wondrous sensations that
rippled through her trembling limbs, Roma reluctantly
lifted her heavy lids.

"What?"

"You smell of honeysuckle," he explained, raising his
head to meet her bemused gaze. "It is a scent that has
haunted me for weeks."

"Lord Carlton . . ."

"Giles," he interrupted firmly.

"Giles," she consented, more out of a sense of despera-
tion than any desire to conform to his demands, "please
let me go."

"Am I frightening you?" he asked, his fingers tenderly
stroking the tingling skin of her neck before moving to
absently play with a stray auburn curl.

She trembled, but not from fear. It was absurd, she
thought with a sudden flare of disbelief. She claimed to
hate this man, but there was no way to deny that she had
responded to his touch with a wanton eagerness that was
frankly shocking. Too late she abruptly attempted to res-
urrect the barriers he had so easily swept aside.

"Of course I am not frightened," she retorted, her voice sharp with the effort to control the emotions still thundering through her heart. "I am furious that you would . . . would take shameless advantage of a helpless woman."

"A helpless woman? You?" His brooding sensuality swiftly changed to mocking amusement. "My dear Roma, you are about as helpless as a snake poised to strike."

Ridiculously his words induced a twinge of pain. "There is no need to be insulting."

"It is pure self-defense, I assure you," he muttered; then with a jerky movement, he rolled away from her trembling body and pushed himself to his feet. With a guarded expression he gazed down at her pale features and at lips still reddened from his kisses. "I have never encountered a more dangerous woman, and if I had any sense I would flee from you with as much haste as possible."

"You are free to leave if you wish."

"Am I?" He gave a short laugh. "If you believe that, then you are even more innocent than I first suspected."

Roma frowned. "Must you speak in riddles?"

He slowly shook his head, a resigned expression crossing his aquiline features. "Come, Roma, now is not the time for such a discussion. It will take more than a kiss to teach you the meaning of being a woman, and to be honest, I am not sure I possess the patience to be your tutor."

Ignoring the hand that he stretched out, Roma hastily scrambled to her feet. She had no notion of what he was speaking, but she was quite certain it was far from flattering. Despite the fact that he had seemed to take considerable enjoyment in holding her in his arms, she had no doubt he maintained his previous opinion that her want of delicacy made her quite below reproach.

"I ache all over," she complained, dusting off the clinging leaves and dust in an effort to hide her embarrassment. "Did you have to be so rough?"

"You are lucky to be alive," he retorted, clearly unrepentant. "If you had listened to me and remained at your aunt's home, then none of this would have occurred."

"And if you had brought me along as I requested, then I wouldn't have been forced to trail behind and hide in these bushes," she pointed out, refusing to accept responsibility for his reprehensible behavior.

"Do you truly—" He abruptly cut off his angry words, clenching his fists as he battled to maintain control of his composure. "Not again. This is a futile argument. The question now is what to do with you."

With an effort, Roma thrust aside the emotions that clouded her mind. Later she could regret the vulnerability that had been exposed by his disturbing kiss, but at the moment nothing mattered but that she meet with the man who might have some information concerning her brother.

"You will do nothing with me," she informed him with a defiant toss of her head. "I came to attend this meeting, and that is exactly what I intend to do."

"That is my decision to make." His voice was filled with an arrogance that instantly set her teeth on edge. "And I am very tempted to bundle you into my carriage and have you returned to London where you belong."

Her eyes flashed a warning. "I would only return as soon as I was able."

"Then perhaps I should tie you to a tree until I am ready to leave. At least then I would know you were out of trouble."

In spite of her best intentions, she took a backward step. "You wouldn't dare."

A raven brow flicked upward "Wouldn't I?"

She eyed him warily. At the moment he looked every inch the aristocratic Lord Carlton, even with his rough clothes and tousled hair. The dark features were stamped with a masculine authority that warned her he was quite capable of doing what he deemed necessary to protect her from herself.

With a determined effort, she forced herself to swallow her pride. Surely she had learned by now that there was little use in meeting this man head-on? Perhaps it was time she attempted to use a more subtle approach.

Conjuring up what she hoped was an appealing glance, she met his glittering gaze.

"What harm can there be in my meeting with this man?" she asked, tempering her voice to a soft plea. "I promise not to interfere. I simply want to be here to answer any questions that might lead us to William."

A sudden stillness settled over him as he slowly took in the unconscious enchantment of her softened expression. She felt her heart give an unnerving jerk as a tender smile drifted at the edges of his firm mouth, erasing his insolent expression.

"And you promise to sit meekly in the corner and allow me to handle the meeting without your meddling?"

She paused, biting the fullness of her lower lip. Could she make such a promise in good conscience? She, better than anyone, knew her impulsive tendency to speak and act without thinking. Could she curb her natural instincts for the good of her brother?

Straightening her shoulders, she gave a decisive nod of her head.

"If that is necessary, then yes, I promise."

"Let us hope that this promise is worth more than your previous promise," he muttered.

"That isn't fair," she cried. "You forced me into that promise."

"Ah, Roma . . ." He heaved a small sigh. "What am I to do with you?"

The blue eyes probed deep into her wide gaze as she waited breathlessly for his answer. Strangely, it seemed vitally important that he understand her need to be a part of this search for her brother. It was almost as if his agreement would prove that he was one of the few men capable of appreciating her for her unique style.

Silence reigned for several long moments as he clearly

battled his ingrained sense of chivalry and the reluctant acceptance that she was no normal woman who preferred to be coddled and protected.

At long last he breathed out an irritated sigh, his expression almost grim as he threw her a warning glance.

"Very well, Roma. Against my better judgment, I will take you along. Please do not make me regret this decision."

Eleven

Inwardly cursing his uncharacteristic burst of compassion, Giles reached out to grasp the exasperating woman by the upper arm and lead her from the thick bushes. He already regretted the momentary weakness that had allowed her pleading hazel gaze to overcome his better judgment, but he knew he wouldn't go back on his decision. As difficult as it might be to admit, he knew that deep down he respected the unwavering loyalty and absolute courage Roma had displayed by following him to this isolated spot.

What other woman would have possessed such nerve? he silently questioned as he led her across the deserted road. Precious few would even have thought up such a scheme, let alone have carried it through, he had to admit. And even fewer would have done so with such success.

Not that he approved of her outrageous behavior, he thought, swiftly checking the renegade glow of admiration. As much as he disliked delicate females that could faint on will or fly into vapors at the least hint of trouble, he couldn't help but wish that Roma possessed a bit more decorum. She simply had no notion of how very dangerous her impulsive behavior could be.

Suppressing a tiny shudder, he covertly studied the classic perfection of her profile. Even now he experienced the sharp pang of terror he had known when he had realized the fragile form he had just attacked was Roma. It was sheer luck that had prevented him from breaking one of her bones when he had jumped onto her back, but worse was the knowledge that he had come very close to pulling out his gun.

Could she not comprehend that he wanted to protect her from such danger? he silently wondered. That it tortured his mind to realize another man might have discovered her in those bushes and taken much more than a kiss . . .

With a sharp breath, he abruptly cut off the unbearable thought. No one would be allowed to harm Roma if he had to be at her side twenty-four hours a day, seven days a week. He knew that if anything were to happen to her, his life would not be worth living.

A rueful smile lightened his grim expression as he allowed the truth he had kept locked away to rise to the surface of his mind. On some level he had known from the moment he had glanced into those clear hazel eyes that she was the one woman who could stir not only his passions, but the deeper emotions that made him long to sweep her into his arms and carry her to a magical place where she would never be hurt or afraid again. And feeling her pressed so intimately against him had only reinforced the sense that he had found the woman he had only dreamed existed.

She had felt so small, so utterly fragile in his arms, yet she had trembled with an instinctive desire that had rivaled his own. Her generous nature would make her the perfect lover, and he had been torn between a very masculine need to brand her as his woman and a new, unfamiliar urge to protect the innocence that shimmered like a beacon in the depths of her eyes.

The knowledge that he needed much more than a fleeting physical encounter had brought sanity crashing through his smoldering passion. This was the woman to whom he intended to devote the rest of his life, but first he had to somehow convince her that he wasn't her worst enemy.

Still holding her arm, he pushed open a section of the hedge that lined the road and helped her to step through. Instantly Jameson was at his side, his startled gaze roaming over the very feminine captive in his employer's grasp.

"I was about to come in search for you," he chided with the familiarity of a longtime servant.

"Sorry, it took longer than I expected to subdue our uninvited guest. Have you been able to peer into the cottage?"

"Yes, it is empty except for a Mr. Slater who is waiting in the first room to your right."

"Mr. Slater?" For the first time since she had made her reluctant promise, Roma broke her unnatural silence. "Thomas Slater?"

With a frown, Giles turned to send her a sharp glance. "Do you know him?"

"Yes, he has stayed at Greystead Manor on a number of occasions." She gave a puzzled shrug. "I believe he served in my brother's regiment, but I haven't seen him for several months. What would he be doing here?"

"That is what we are going to discover," Giles answered; then he gave a nod toward his groom. "Jameson, I want you to stay here and watch the road. Give the signal if you sense anything unusual."

"Are you sure?" The groom frowned, his pug face creased with lines of concern. "Perhaps it would be best if I go in with you, at least for a time." His eyes darted in a meaningful manner toward Roma. "Just in case this proves to be a trap."

Giles felt Roma stiffen at the less than subtle insinuation, and he flashed her a taunting smile.

"I do not believe that will be necessary, Jameson; however, I do want you to keep plenty of rope within reach. If this rather annoying young woman retracts her promise to keep her sharp tongue firmly silent, then I have every intention of having her tied to the nearest tree."

Roma gave an audible gasp, and with a distinct twinkle in his eye, Jameson gravely nodded his head.

"Very good, my lord."

Suppressing a chuckle at the fury he could feel trembling through Roma, Giles headed toward the cottage, his sideways glance lingering on the determined thrust of her stubborn chin.

"Tell me about this Thomas Slater."

Her look could have slain a dragon at ten paces.

"And risk being bound to a tree by your groom? No, thank you, my lord."

His lips trembled, but he kept his tone arrogant enough to rub against her already sensitive nerves.

"I give you leave to speak for the moment. I find it highly curious that you should be acquainted with this man."

Always unpredictable, she swallowed her anger and gave a mocking toss of her head.

"Perhaps Jameson was correct to worry, my lord. This might very well be an elaborate scheme concocted to lure you into a diabolical trap."

Giles arched a raven brow. "And what is your role in this elaborate scheme? The damsel in distress or the seductress?"

With great anticipation, Giles watched as an endearing blush flooded her cheeks.

"Obviously the damsel in distress," she snapped.

"A pity." He heaved a rueful sigh. "If I am to be lured into a diabolical trap it seems the least you could do is satisfy—"

"Lord Carlton, I have no wish to continue this ridiculous conversation."

"Coward," he breathed out, then relented with a small chuckle. "Very well, Roma, but on the condition that you answer my questions in a reasonable manner and that you remember, at least in private, that my name is Giles. Is that a deal?"

She paused, clearly resenting the fact that he momentarily held the upper hand; then with an audible hiss she gave a sharp nod of her head.

"Very well . . . Giles."

An unexpected surge of pleasure entered his heart at the sound of his name on her lips, and convinced that love had completely addled his brain, he attempted to turn his thoughts to the serious matter at hand.

"Now, what do you know about Thomas Slater?"

"Really no more than I have already told you." She wrinkled her brow as she attempted to remember. "He and William seemed fairly close in age, and as I said, I was under the impression they served in the same regiment. He was quiet, polite and always the perfect guest. When William first returned to Greystead Manor, Mr. Slater would visit on a regular basis, but I haven't seen him for some time."

Giles absorbed her words in thoughtful silence. He had already suspected that William Allendyle was more involved with covert government operations than his sister had thought, and now he was even more certain.

"Let us hope he has some information that will aid in our search," he said softly.

Still holding her arm, Giles led Roma into the shadowed cottage, his instincts on full alert despite Jameson's assurances that it was safe. Pausing until his eyes adjusted to the gloom, he was surprised to discover the interior of the small house was in considerably better repair than the outside. No doubt it was a deliberate ploy to convince a casual observer the place was unoccupied and of little use, he acknowledged, having some experience with the government's delight in creating false images. With a cautious step he moved across the foyer, entering the room on his right, which proved to be empty but for a heavy desk and two battered armchairs.

At their entrance a slender man with a long face and

a rumpled thatch of blond hair rose to his feet, a pair of shrewd blue eyes abruptly narrowing at the sight of Roma.

"Good God, Miss Allendyle. What the devil are you doing here?"

"I am searching for William," she said, her voice husky with emotion. "And I am desperately hoping you might have some information to help me."

Surprisingly unaffected by the sight of a well-bred lady dressed in breeches and presumably alone in the company of two unrelated men, Thomas Slater sent her a compassionate smile that was far too familiar for Giles's peace of mind.

"I wish that I did, Miss Allendyle. Like you, I am deeply concerned about his welfare."

With a frown, Giles stepped forward, not liking the feeling that the two had forgotten his presence.

"Perhaps we could make ourselves comfortable before we begin this discussion, Mr. Slater? It has been a rather . . . eventful day thus far."

"Of course." With a wry smile, the younger man ran a distracted hand through his tangled hair. "I am afraid the amenities are not the best, but I did bring along a fine bottle of brandy."

"I will forgo the brandy for now." Giles carefully seated Roma in one of the armchairs before taking the one next to her. His protective manner was quite deliberate, and he was pleased that Thomas Slater carefully noted his possessive attitude. "I think we should first share all our information and then decide what is best to be done."

Slater gave a slow nod of his head and sank back into his chair.

"Very well. Halcott assured me that I could trust you fully with any information that might be considered classified by our government, and of course, I know that Miss Allendyle is trustworthy." He sent the silent woman an encouraging smile. "William often rued the fact that you were born a woman. He claimed the military lost a great soldier when you were unable to buy a pair of colors."

Roma blushed, but it was obvious she was pleased by his words. A ridiculous stab of irritation shot through Giles's heart.

"Perhaps you should start by telling us exactly what your relationship with William Allendyle is," he said, his sharp tone bringing a surprised glance from Roma and a curious frown from Slater.

"Certainly," the younger man agreed, his own tone mild. "We met when we both joined the regiment. We arrived on the same day which, I suppose, helped to begin our friendship, since we were both forced to endure the torture of being raw recruits and were usually thrown together to complete whatever vile task needed to be done. Over time we developed a strong trust that can only be forged between people who depend on one another for their very lives. We watched out for one another and helped to keep each other sane after the fire of battle. When William sold out his commission, I was determined to keep in contact with him. We were like brothers, perhaps even closer than most brothers."

Giles unconsciously nodded his head. His own time spent in the military had revealed the extraordinary bonds forged between men in battle. The hardships of war had the ability to strip aside social status, lineage and prejudices. Soldiers were just men, most of them scared and homesick, attempting to stay alive. And the only thing important was that you could trust the man guarding your back.

"Were you the one to approach William about working for the government?"

"Yes, not long after William sold out, I took a bullet through the leg. Nothing serious, but enough to put me back in London. Lord Halcott contacted me and asked that I . . . run a few errands for the government. Since I was close to Greystead Manor, I took the opportunity to spend time with William, and he quickly guessed my reasons for being in the vicinity and volunteered to help."

Giles stretched out his legs, templing his slender fingers beneath his bluntly chiseled chin.

"Can you tell us precisely what he was doing?"

Slater gave a small shrug. "Usually it was passing information from one courier to the next."

"To you?"

"Not usually." Slater opened one of the desk drawers to pull out a bottle of brandy and a glass, setting them both on the desk. "There was another agent in the area. That was his usual contact."

"Really?" Giles was surprised by the information. "Do you know who it was?"

"No. The government is careful that each person is only privy to a small amount of information." He waved a hand in a rueful motion. "I was in fact hoping that you or perhaps even Miss Allendyle might have some notion who it might be."

"Me?" Roma blinked in surprise. "No, he never said a word to me."

Slater heaved a sigh. "That is a pity."

"Why do you say that?" Giles demanded, unconsciously reaching over to grasp Roma's hand in a reassuring motion.

The younger man paused, pouring himself a large shot of the brandy before breaking the tense silence.

"The last time I spoke with William he seemed worried. It took some time, but I at last convinced him to confess what was troubling him." He took a swift drink of the brandy, sending the apprehensive Roma a concerned glance. "He said he suspected someone was selling information to the French."

Giles heard Roma gasp in dismay, and his hand tightened in reaction to her response.

"That is a serious charge," he said. "Did he say who it was he suspected?"

"Unfortunately, no." Slater shook his head, his youthful face lined with an expression of deep concern. "All I know is he was determined to find some proof of his suspicions. That was nearly six weeks ago. I haven't heard a word from him since."

A shaft of cold pierced Giles's heart. Treason. No crime carried a heavier penalty, and few such criminals would not sink to any level to protect their own skins. If William had been foolish enough to attempt to corner such a man on his own, there was a good chance that he had indeed stumbled into a hornet's nest.

Still, Giles knew it was important that he keep such dark thoughts to himself. One glance at Roma's white face was enough to prove she fully understood the danger in which her brother had placed himself. What she needed at the moment was a measure of hope that her brother would be found and returned home safe and sound.

"Did he mention where he intended to search?"

Slater gave a vague shrug. "Why, London of course."

Giles frowned, not completely satisfied with the answer. "Is there anything else that might help us?"

"No, not really."

Another silence fell, and Giles slowly rose to his feet. There was little point in remaining and simply going over the same information. Besides, he knew that he needed to get Roma back to her aunt before she was missed.

"I assume you will contact us if you do hear from William?" he asked.

"But of course." Slater rose to his feet, rounding the desk so he could cross to help Roma from her chair. "And Miss Allendyle, I want you to know that I am doing everything possible to find William. If I hear anything, anything at all, you will be the first to know."

She flashed him a weak smile. "Thank you, Mr. Slater."

"Thomas," he corrected in a kind voice.

"All right . . . Thomas."

Giles broke into the conversation, recapturing her hand in a firm grip. "Come, Roma, we must go." He found the easy familiarity between Roma and this man extremely annoying. In fact, he had a completely ridiculous urge to wipe the boyish smile from Slater's overly handsome face. Instead, he pulled the startled Roma close to his side, his entire body bristling with a very masculine possessiveness. "You can contact me through Halcott if you need anything."

"Very well."

Without giving the man any further opportunity to speak with Roma, Giles determinedly led her from the cottage, using her distracted inattention to herd her toward his waiting carriage. It was only as she actually climbed into the dark interior that she abruptly became aware of her surroundings.

"My horse—"

"Jameson is collecting the beast as we speak," he reassured her, half-pushing her into the far corner of the carriage before climbing in to join her. "Although if someone happens to notice such a nag trailing behind my carriage, my reputation will be in shreds."

"What? Oh . . . yes." She smiled, but it was clear that her thoughts were faraway.

With a frown Giles leaned forward, his expression concerned. "Roma, you can not give up hope," he reminded her in a stern voice.

She gave a small sigh, her hazel eyes much too large in her somber face.

"Actually, I haven't. As absurd as it might seem, I truly believe I would know if something . . . terrible had happened to him."

"There's nothing absurd about that at all." He sent her an encouraging smile. "And we now have Mr. Slater helping us in our search."

She gave a vague nod. "Yes."

"Roma"—he abruptly narrowed his gaze, sensing trouble in the air—"what scheme have you come up with now?"

She reacted with a small start, as if surprised by his perceptive question, but for a pleasant change, she confided her inner thoughts without a protracted argument.

"I was thinking about Thomas's words," she said, un-aware of Giles's deep frown at her casual use of another man's name. "If my brother was just a courier who worked close to Greystead Manor, then whoever he sus-pected would have to be in the area as well."

Giles raised his brows at the logic in her hesitant words.

"True enough," he agreed.

"And if he was searching for proof, it would make no sense to come to London." She wrinkled her brow, clearly attempting to reason out her growing dissatisfaction. "It would be much more logical to remain at Greystead and do his investigation from there."

"You are right." He took in a sharp breath, realizing that she had managed to expose his own inner puzzle-ment. Clearly William Allendyle would have remained close to home if he'd suspected there was a dangerous criminal in the area. "And the chances are that any clues to his whereabouts are there as well."

"I have to go home," she cried, her tiny frame taut with apprehension. "I should never have left."

"Easy, Roma," he said in a soothing tone. "You did what you thought best at the time. But I agree. We do need to return to Greystead. The only question is how we can accomplish the trip without causing any unneces-sary attention."

She opened her mouth as if to declare that she couldn't care less about causing needless chatter, but the realization that her actions might very well endanger her brother had her grudgingly swallowing her angry words.

"You can not expect me to wait until Aunt Clara is ready to return home? That might be weeks," she com-plained in frustration.

He paused; then a slow smile tugged at his mouth. On one level he knew the idea that had so abruptly popped into his mind was utterly reprehensible. It also revealed just how desperate his newfound emotions had made him, but any sense of right or wrong seemed to be over-shadowed by his need to bind this woman to his life.

"I believe I have a plan that can allow us to return to Greystead Manor without anyone questioning our motives."

"Really?" Her sudden expression of relief was almost his undoing. "What is it?"

Closing his mind to the vague voice at the back of his mind that warned him he was behaving in a less than honorable manner, Giles settled back in his seat with an enigmatic smile.

"I have a few details yet to work out. Tomorrow, however, I promise that I will have everything set in motion. You should be home by the end of the week."

Twelve

Roma was up early the next morning after a restless night, thankful that she nad managed to return to her room the evening before without anyone realizing that she hadn't spent the entire day in bed with a migraine. But while she was grateful to Giles for his assistance in returning her to London without creating a scandal, she did resent his refusal to discuss his mysterious plan that would allow her to return to Greystead Manor.

It wasn't like the arrogant man to give a decision such careful thought, she acknowledged with a flare of impatience. He was the type who decided a course of action and forged ahead with complete confidence that he had chosen the correct path. But as he had helped her to slip into her room last evening, he had momentarily grabbed her fingers, his expression unnaturally somber as he had gazed deeply into her wide eyes.

"Do you trust me, Roma?" he had asked softly.

Bemused by the unexpected question, she had nodded her head without thought. "Of course."

The blue eyes had darkened with an unreadable emotion, and his grip had tightened on her fingers.

"Then, whatever I decide to do tomorrow, you must believe that I am acting in your own best interest. Remember that, Roma."

With one last lingering glance, he had disappeared into

the shadows surrounding the house, leaving behind a very suspicious young lady.

Did she trust Lord Giles Carlton? That question, along with the memories of her shameful reaction to his kiss, had kept her awake most of the night. It simply made no sense. How could she supposedly detest a man, yet know deep in her heart that he was the only man she would depend upon in a time of trouble—and even more frightening, the only man who had made her understand the poignant pleasure of being a woman?

He instilled in her such a maze of confusing emotions that she barely knew what she was feeling from one moment to the next. The only thing she was certain of was the knowledge that he had turned her sane and normal world upside down.

Sighing at her ridiculous thoughts, Roma determinedly focused her concentration on more important matters, namely her brother and his unexplainable disappearance.

Her initial reaction to Thomas Slater's information had been panic. If William was indeed attempting to capture a man willing to betray his own country, then anything might have happened to him. Horrible visions of him being brutally tortured or smuggled to France and tossed into a dark prison had rushed though her mind. But with a determined effort she had thrust aside the hysterical thoughts and had attempted to view the situation in a reasonable manner.

There were still a thousand unanswered questions, but Roma had been nearly overwhelmed by the abrupt need to return home. She had accomplished what she had wanted in London by alerting the government to the fact that William was missing and by discovering that he had no reason to leave Greystead Manor. Now she was anxious to return to the estate so she could continue her search. She was certain there must be some method of tracing his movements.

But she had to reluctantly concede that Giles had a legitimate point. She couldn't simply leave London without offending her aunt and, worse, creating unwanted gossip throughout town. She didn't want people speculating on her reason for returning home, especially the person or persons, responsible for William's disappearance. But what possible excuse could she give for leaving?

With a small shake of her head, Roma absently finished pinning her auburn curls into a manageable knot. The maid who had been assigned to her when she had first arrived at her aunt's home had long ago reconciled herself to the fact that Roma refused to behave like most young ladies in her position. Roma far preferred to see to her own needs, and only when she was forced to wear a gown that was ridiculously designed so that she was unable to dress herself did she allow Mary to help with her toilet. Now she barely noted the fresh muslin gown in a pale cinnamon shade or the tiny tendrils of auburn curls that stubbornly strayed from the severe chignon to rest against her ivory skin. Her beauty was completely natural and unstudied, but she cared only for the fact that she was presentable to make her appearance downstairs.

With a last glance to ensure her expression did not reveal the anxious impatience that simmered just below the surface, Roma left the privacy of her bedroom and made her way down the long flight of stairs. Without thinking, she turned toward the long hall that would lead her to the breakfast room. Quite unfashionably, the family made a habit of sharing an early morning meal rather than lying in bed until noon and taking trays in their rooms. But even as she absently began to cross the marble floor, the door to the formal salon was abruptly thrown open and her aunt appeared with an expression on her round face that sent a strange tingle of apprehension down Roma's spine.

"My dear," she gushed, practically glowing with an excitement that made Roma halt in wary puzzlement, "why did you not tell me?"

"Tell you?"

"You could at least have dropped some hint in which direction the wind blew."

"What?"

"It is so sudden . . . so unexpected . . . I can scarcely think of what to say."

"Aunt Clara, is everything all right?" she asked, cautiously moving toward the older woman.

"All right?" Clara gave a twittering laugh, her blue eyes gleaming with open pleasure. "Things could not be better. You realize, of course, that you have pulled off the social coup of the Season, and that I shall be the envy of every matchmaking mama in town. I can not wait to spread the news, especially to that overly superior Lady Powell. Just to think that she had the nerve to suggest you were dangling after Lord Carlton, not to mention she was so certain that milk-and-toast miss of hers would be the toast of the Season. Between you and me the poor girl hasn't had so much as an offer. This should take her down a peg or two . . ."

Shaking her head with indulgent confusion, Roma broke into the unintelligible chatter with a firm voice, "Aunt Clara, what in heaven's name are you talking about?"

"As if you didn't know." She reached out to lightly tap Roma with her fan. "Such a sly young woman. Here I was worried that you might ruin your chances at a proper match by revealing such a lack of interest in your suitors, when all along you were capturing the elusive affections of Lord Carlton. What a tremendous stroke of fortune."

Suddenly concerned that her aunt had taken a serious injury to the head or perhaps been afflicted with an unexpected mental illness, Roma carefully considered the best method to approach the deranged woman.

"Maybe you should go upstairs and lie down for a little while, Aunt Clara," she suggested softly. "You appear a bit flushed."

"Nonsense, I feel fine." Clara gave an airy toss of her silver head. "And what woman worth her salt would not be flushed at the realization that she had managed to launch her debutante and within a few weeks land Lord Carlton, the top catch of the Season as a groom?"

Roma blinked; then, without warning, the floor seemed to shift beneath her feet, her mind spinning with bewilderment at the outrageous words. She wanted to laugh at the ludicrous misunderstanding, but even as she opened her mouth to protest, a dark shape suddenly appeared behind the portly woman and she found herself meeting a warning blue gaze.

"Good morning, Roma," Lord Carlton said, looking as superbly handsome as ever in his superfine jacket of pale blue and buff pantaloons. Not even his strangely watchful expression could mar the dark beauty that had begun to consume her thoughts in a manner she refused to contemplate. "I apologize for calling at such an unreasonable hour."

"Lord Carlton—"

"Giles."

She sucked in a sharp breath, overtly conscious of her aunt's avid curiosity.

"Giles, what are you doing here?"

"I did say that I would call, my dear," he answered with an engaging grin. "And I am afraid my eagerness to speak with your aunt led me to arrive on the doorstep unfashionably early."

"So romantic"—Clara sighed, clearly missing the stunned puzzlement in her niece's eyes—"but come, let us make ourselves comfortable. We have a great deal to discuss."

"Yes, but I don't suppose"—Giles paused, sending her susceptible aunt a glance that had melted the hearts of women since the day he was born—"Roma and I could have just a few moments alone?"

Clara hesitated, torn between her rigid sense of propriety and her purely feminine love of romance. At last it was Lord Carlton's irresistible charm that swayed the balance, and with a teasingly stern glance at Giles, she gave a reluctant nod of her head.

"Very well, but mind, only a few moments and remember that Roma is still under the protection of her brother and not yet your fiancée. I may have acquired gray hair and a few years since I was a wide-eyed debutante, but I clearly remember the impatience of a man in love and I will not have you stepping over the line."

"You have my word as a gentleman."

Clara smiled. "I shall go order us tea. You have precisely five minutes."

"Thank you."

With a small chuckle, Clara turned to walk out of the room, firmly closing the door behind her retreating form. Roma, however, barely noted her exit. Instead, her horrified gaze was attached to the man calmly eying her with a suspiciously bland expression.

"Fiancée?" she breathed out, the vague apprehensions forming into a solid lump of unease in the pit of her stomach. "You told my aunt that I was your fiancée?"

He carefully studied her shocked expression before giving a small shrug. "I told her that I wanted to ask for your hand in marriage."

The floor once more did its crazy tilt. "Have you taken leave of your senses?"

A small, unexpected spark of amusement entered the vivid blue eyes.

"It is a definite concern," he murmured. "However, at the moment I am simply attempting to fulfill the promise I made to you yesterday."

She raised a hand to her thundering heart. "What promise?"

"I said that I would find a way for us to return to your home without creating unnecessary gossip."

"And this is your solution?" She gave a disbelieving shake of her head. "As far as I can see it will only create a flurry of gossip without getting us one step closer to Greystead Manor. It is a completely preposterous idea."

His lips twisted to a mocking smile. "Thank God I have an arrogant belief in my own self-worth, Miss Allendyle, a lesser man would have already crawled away in the certain knowledge that he was a thoroughly worthless creature in your esteem."

She possessed the grace to blush at his taunt, but remained determined to stand her ground. There was something deeply disturbing in the mere thought of becoming this man's fiancée.

"I did not intend to insult you, Lord . . . Giles, but you must realize that even the rumor of our engagement would send tongues wagging all over England. You have eluded the Marriage Mart too long not to cause a sensation when you abruptly decide to take a fiancée. Especially when your intended is an unknown, the daughter of an obscure family with no assets and a young woman with no claim to beauty."

His humor only deepened at her dry words. "And what does any of that have to do with love, my dear?"

"Would you please be serious?" she snapped, irrationally annoyed by his ability to laugh at such a situation.

"But I am," he retorted smoothly, "and if you would calm down and allow me to explain, then you would realize that I have come up with a perfect solution."

"Calm down?" She gave him a smoldering glare. "I wake up to what I assume is another normal day and come downstairs to discover that I am newly engaged to London's most eligible bachelor, and you expect me to be calm?"

Without warning he gave a sudden laugh, moving to place an arm about her shoulders.

"Come and sit down, Roma. I promise that I can fully explain my madness."

This time she was on the receiving end of that melting smile, and Roma abruptly understood why her aunt had found it so disarming. Almost unconsciously she allowed herself to be led to the loveseat and carefully arranged on the hard cushions, her hands being held in his slender fingers as he took a seat close beside her.

Belatedly realizing that she had somehow lost control of the confrontation, she squared her shoulders in a determined manner.

"All right, Giles, explain exactly how this absurd plan can possibly help me find my brother."

He paused, as if considering the best approach to use in the face of her less than enthusiastic attitude.

"Well, to start with, we need a viable reason to return to Greystead Manor," he began, his expression unreadable, "and since your aunt brought you to London with the express purpose of finding you a husband, it occurred to me that if you were to supposedly locate a prospective groom there would be no more reason for you to remain in town, especially since it would only be natural that I approach your brother as your legal guardian to ask for his permission. What better excuse to return to Greystead Manor?"

She frowned, attempting to push aside her jumbled emotions and consider his words in a logical manner.

"But my brother is not there."

"Yes. No one is aware of his disappearance, however," he said slowly, as if speaking to a rather dim-witted child. "At least, no one that will spread the news. All we need say is that he is currently visiting a friend in the north, and as an anxious suitor waiting to officially claim you as my fiancée, it will seem quite natural for me to put up in the neighborhood and await his return."

She silently absorbed his words, reluctantly conceding this wasn't as crazy a scheme as she had initially thought.

"But that won't prevent people from speculating on our relationship," she pointed out.

"What will they say?" he asked, lifting his shoulders in a negligent motion. "That they are surprised by our engagement? What does it matter as long as they do not suspect we have any other reason for leaving London? In fact, the more people discuss our swift engagement, the less time there will be to question our movements and the fact that your brother is absent."

She bit her lip, feeling the fiery indignation slowly slipping away. A part of her grudgingly conceded that she had overreacted. After all, this man had no reason to go to such lengths to help a complete stranger, beyond the fact that he had given his word to aid her in her search. And certainly he was making a considerable sacrifice, not only to leave London at the height of the Season, but to also lumber himself with an unwanted fiancée.

But while she knew she should feel a portion of guilt for her ingratitude, she couldn't prevent herself from shying away from the outrageous scheme. Somehow the notion made her nerves coil into a tight ball of unease that refused to be dismissed.

"Must we say that we are engaged?"

His brows drew together as if annoyed by her resistance. "Do you have a better suggestion?"

"I . . ." She heaved a small sigh. "No, I suppose I do not."

"You needn't fall into such a dismal state, Roma," he protested, an exasperated smile tugging at the edge of his mouth. "Surely there are worse things than being engaged to me?"

"I—"

"All right, you two lovebirds, that is enough time alone for the moment." Without warning, Clara bustled back into the room, her smile widening at the sight of them seated together so intimately. "We have a simply appalling amount of work ahead of us. There will be plenty of time to be alone after the wedding."

Roma felt a warming blush rise to her cheeks, and it was almost a comfort to have Giles give her hand a reassuring squeeze before firmly taking control of the situation.

"To be honest, Lady Welford—"

"Oh, my dear boy, you must call me Aunt Clara, you are about to become a part of the family, after all."

"Aunt Clara"—Giles gracefully slipped into his role—
"I have never been a notoriously patient man, and since
I am quite anxious to make Roma my bride, I intend to
leave for Greystead Manor almost immediately."

Clara blinked in surprise. "Well, of course you will have
to speak with William," she agreed reluctantly, "but did
you not say he was currently away from the estate, Roma?"

"Yes, but I expect him back before the end of the
month."

"I see." Clara frowned, clearly not seeing at all. "I do
not suppose you could convince him to come to London?"

"Oh, no." Roma firmly shook her head. "He will no
doubt be very busy getting the estate back in order."

Clara sighed. "Then there is nothing for it but to return home. Until we have William's blessing we can not
very well announce the engagement."

Her disappointment was so obvious that Roma could
not help but try to cheer her up.

"There is no need for you to leave, Aunt Clara. I know
how much you enjoy the Season."

"Nonsense," the older woman argued, a delighted expression returning to her round face. "We have accomplished what we set out to do in London, and quite
naturally Lord Carlton will stay at our home until William
returns. In the meantime, my dear, there is no reason at
all that the two of us can not devote our time to planning
your wedding. We have a hundred decisions that must be
made as soon as possible. I daresay we shall have the most
wonderful time . . ."

Thirteen

Seated on the threadbare sofa that had been relegated to the back drawing room, Roma absently stitched at her lopsided sampler. A restless night spent brooding on Lord Carlton's outlandish proposal and her own impulsive agreement had left her unnaturally pale and eager to avoid the ceaseless chatter of her delighted aunt.

No doubt she should never have agreed to his shocking suggestion, she silently acknowledged. Not only was it highly improper, but it had placed her irrevocably in his debt. A realization that was far more disturbing than the fear of a scandal, if the truth should be discovered.

But what choice did she have? As Lord Carlton had so saliently pointed out she possessed few options. She could remain in London until her aunt eventually tired of the glittering whirl, or she could return to Devonshire on her own and perhaps place her brother in even greater danger.

"A fine muddle you've gotten yourself into, Roma Allendyle," she muttered beneath her breath.

Stabbing her needle through the heavy fabric, Roma paid little heed to her uneven stitches. Indeed, she was so intent on her inner turmoil that she even failed to note the sound of approaching footsteps. It was not until the door was abruptly thrust open that she realized her blissful solitude was at an end.

With a small start, she lifted her head to see her cousin

entering the room, an expression of disapproval on his youthful features.

"There you are," he said, his tone almost accusing.

"Good morning, Claude."

"Do not good morning me, Roma Allendyle." Claude immediately launched into an attack, not even bothering with the common civilities. "What the devil are you playing at?"

Against her will, a warm flush spread on Roma's cheeks. The day before Claude had been gadding about the less respectable establishments in town with a handful of cronies, not returning to the house until quite late. Obviously he had just been informed of her supposed engagement to Lord Carlton.

She attempted a bluff. "I fear I do not know what you mean."

"Do not presume to gammon me, my dear." Claude's tone was as forbidding as his countenance. "Not even I am noodle witted enough to believe a gentleman who has dodged every contrivance known to man to lure him into the parson's mousetrap has suddenly succumbed to a country miss with a sharp tongue and disobliging manners."

Despite her flustered unease, Roma could not prevent a wry grimace. "Such flattery, sir. I shall be quite overcome," she chided.

Claude determinedly ignored her reprimand. "Besides which, I know you far too well, Roma. You have never hesitated to share your views on acquiring a husband. I believe you have often likened it to being made a prisoner of war."

She could hardly deny her vehement opposition to marriage. She had voiced her objections far too frequently to pretend otherwise. Instead she busied herself with setting aside the lumpy sampler and conveniently hiding her expressive features.

"Do you not believe that a lady can enjoy a change of heart?"

Claude gave a strangled grunt of disbelief. "So you are telling me that you are now prepared to submit to the dictates of Lord Carlton?"

"Certainly."

"Fah . . ." Claude stomped across the room to halt beside her chair, his polished Hessians glowing in the dim morning light. "Now I am certain you are attempting to bamboozle me. I will see pigs sprout wings and take flight before you allow the leash to be placed about your neck." Reaching down, he firmly grasped her chin and raised her reluctant face for his inspection. "Now, I demand to be told the truth."

For a moment she attempted to meet his challenging gaze with a semblance of bland composure. After all, Claude would not be the only person to react to her engagement with such violent disbelief. But as she forced a stiff smile to her lips, she realized that it was a hopeless task. How could she possibly dissemble to a relative who had known her since the cradle?

"Oh, very well, Claude," she conceded with ill grace, "but you must promise to keep it in the strictest confidence."

"Of course. You know that you can trust me."

With a swift motion, he settled himself on the sofa, his unusually stubborn expression revealing he would accept nothing less than the complete and utter truth. Still Roma wavered. She could not very well confess everything, she acknowledged with a twinge of embarrassment. Despite Claude's indulgence of her peculiar tendencies, he was bound to be mortified by her reprehensible behavior since arriving in London. And, of course, her odd battles with Lord Carlton were somehow far too intimate to share with anyone.

In the end she gave only the sketchiest details.

"The truth is that Lord Carlton was one of the men we met on the beach the night of the ambush. His cousin Jack was the other man there," she reluctantly revealed. "And when Lord Carlton recognized me, he demanded to be told why I was behaving in such an . . . unconventional fashion." She glared at her cousin as he almost choked at her vast understatement. "He then offered to help."

"Help? Help in what manner?"

"He has spoken with some mysterious connection he has within the government and discovered that William was, indeed, acting as a courier, and that six weeks before, he had revealed he suspected one of the other couriers of being a French spy."

Claude gave a startled grunt. "Good God."

"It was obvious that we needed to return to Devonshire. After all, that is where William disappeared and where he presumably found the traitor, but we had to be able to do so without causing any unnecessary suspicion. Lord Carlton suggested that we pretend to be engaged, and he would demand to travel to Greystead Manor so he could speak with William upon his return."

Claude regarded her in silence as she stammered to an uncomfortable halt, the deepening wrinkle in his brow the only indication he found her disjointed explanation beyond the ordinary.

After what seemed to be an eternity, he at last gave a slow shake of his head.

"So it was Lord Carlton who suggested he pretend to seek your hand in marriage?" he demanded.

"Yes."

"How very extraordinary."

Roma felt a strange flare of unease at his pensive tone. "What do you mean?"

Claude abruptly rose to his feet, pacing to the center of the room. Then turning about, he regarded her with a narrowed gaze.

"Do you not find it rather peculiar that Lord Carlton would go to such lengths to help a gentleman he has never before encountered?"

"He feels a sense of duty to William," she rushed to explain. "They were both in the military, you know."

"Along with half of the gentlemen in England, I should presume," he murmured.

Her unease increased. She had expected surprise, perhaps even censure, but not this poorly concealed suspicion.

"What are you implying, Claude?"

A sudden heat stained his cheeks. "Lord Carlton has not . . . I mean . . ."

Roma blinked in puzzlement. "Has not what?"

"He has not behaved in an improper manner, has he?" Claude managed to burst out.

Roma gave a strangled gasp as she lifted a hand to her unruly heart. For a breathless moment the memory of his warm, impassioned kisses blazed through her thoughts. Although it had been two days since she had so shockingly lain in his arms, her body still tingled from the unfamiliar sensation of his masculine frame pressed closely against her own. Then, just as swiftly, she was thrusting the treacherous thoughts aside. She had decided at the time that the unfortunate episode was best forgotten as soon as possible.

"Certainly not," she declared with considerable force. Regardless of their unconventional relationship she would never believe Lord Carlton capable of treating her as anything other than a lady. "I am surprised at you, Claude. Lord Carlton is a gentleman."

Claude tugged at his intricately knotted cravat as if it threatened to choke him.

"Well, dash it all, Roma. What am I supposed to think? It seems deuced strange that a man in Carlton's position would risk his reputation for a family who haven't the faintest claim on his charity."

She conveniently forgot her own initial wariness at his interference. Although she could not claim to know what motivated Lord Carlton, she was quite certain that it had nothing to do with her.

"I assure you, Claude, you have nothing to fear from

Lord Carlton," she said in dry tones. "If he were to offer *carte blanche* to a woman it would certainly not be me."

Claude paused, his gaze unconsciously moving to survey pale features framed by the fiery curls and the diminutive form modestly attired in a slip of pistachio satin overlaid with a delicate gauze. After a detailed inspection he apparently found little to recommend her to a gentleman of discerning taste and the tightness slowly drained from his countenance.

"Perhaps you are right," he grudgingly admitted.

"Of course I am."

"It was just such a damnable shock this morning when Mother announced that you were to wed Lord Carlton."

"Especially when you are no doubt still recovering from a sore head," she managed to tease.

He smiled in a rueful fashion. "Indeed. I thought for a moment I must still be a trifle foxed."

"That is what you get for allowing those scapegrace friends of yours to lure you into behaving like a nodcock."

"They are not so bad, Roma"—his eyes suddenly twinkled with humor—"although I did wonder on their judgment when they all proclaimed a decided desire to seek your favor. They will no doubt be devastated when they learn you have given your heart to another."

Her gaze narrowed in a dangerous manner. "That is not amusing."

A sharp knock on the door brought an abrupt end to their conversation. Waiting a discreet moment, the rigidly somber butler entered the room.

"Your pardon, Miss Allendyle, but Lord Carlton is here to see you."

It took a great deal of effort to control her sudden flutter of nerves. Lord Carlton at such an early hour? What the devil was he up to?

Slowly rising to her feet, she pinned a stiff smile to her face.

"Thank you, Forbes," she retorted.

With a bow, the butler turned on his heel and disappeared through the door. Anxiously smoothing the skirt of her gown, Roma prepared to follow the servant from the room, but as she passed by the silent Claude, he suddenly laid a hand on her shoulder. With a lift of her brows, she turned to meet his concerned frown.

"Roma . . ."

"Yes, Claude?"

"Promise me that . . . that you'll take care."

Not quite certain what he wanted from her, Roma gave a small nod of her head.

"Of course."

Seemingly satisfied, Claude stepped back, and Roma reluctantly left the room to make her way to the formal salon.

She had not expected to see Lord Carlton on this day. When he had left the day before he had made a vague mention of business that he had to attend to before finalizing his plans to leave London. Perhaps being rather cowardly, she had assumed that she would be spared this uncomfortable encounter for several days. Now she found herself battling an unexplainable bout of nerves.

All too swiftly she arrived at the front of the house and, with an effort, forced a smile to her face. Then, smoothing her skirt one last time, she stepped into the salon.

Instinctively her gaze sought the tall male form standing beside the mantel. Almost absently, she noted how the tan coat set off broad shoulders with exquisite perfection and how the skintight breeches emphasized the powerful thrust of his legs. Even in her current state of distraction she had to admit that Lord Carlton was a most handsome gentleman. Uncommonly handsome, she corrected, as a stray shaft of sunlight danced off the gleaming raven hair and warmed the aquiline features.

Lifting her gaze she belatedly realized that Lord Carlton had been well aware of her survey. She shivered as she encountered the glitter in his blue eyes, thankful

that her aunt provided a welcomed distraction as she bustled across the room with an air of suppressed excitement.

"Ah, Roma, there you are. Lord Carlton was just telling
me that you are to be introduced to Lady Chalford this
morning."

Roma's eyes widened in shock. "Pardon me?"

"I fear my grandmother sent a message at the crack of
dawn," Lord Carlton drawled. "I am to present you in
her drawing room at precisely ten o'clock."

"Well, of course she wishes to have Roma introduced,"
the older woman gushed, her cheeks flushed with her
niece's good fortune. "Soon enough she will be a member of the family."

Roma felt a flutter of panic. "But I . . . Surely it would
be best to wait until . . . later?"

With a casual motion, Lord Carlton straightened and
strolled to peer down at her upturned face.

"You do not know my grandmother, my dear, if you
imagine she can be fobbed off once she has taken a notion into her head." He smiled in a lazy fashion. "No
one, including myself, dares to defy such a direct sum-
mons."

Obviously sensing her niece's distress, if not the reason
for it, Clara hastened to provide a measure of reassurance.

"Come, Roma, it is natural to feel somewhat uneasy.
After all, Lady Chalford can be quite intimidating. But I
am certain that she will find you most charming."

Without warning, Lord Carlton reached out to grasp
her hand and raise her fingers to his warm lips.

"Indeed, my grandmother can not help but be en-
chanted. As I am."

That odd shiver tingled down her spine again as her
aunt gave a trill of laughter.

"Ah la, my lord, such a pretty way you have with
words."

The disturbing gaze never left Roma's pale countenance. "Shall we go, my dear?"

Roma wanted to protest. After all, it was one thing to consider the notion of pretending an engagement in the privacy of her own home. She could soothe her conscience with the thought that she was making a noble sacrifice for William. It was quite another to deliberately set out to deceive an elderly woman.

But with her aunt regarding her with open pleasure and Lord Carlton firmly tucking her arm through his own, she had little choice but to allow herself to be led back out of the room and across the foyer to the hall.

In rigid silence she swept through the door hastily opened by Forbes, barely noting the pale warmth of the morning sun or the splendid chestnuts that stood before the glossy black curricle. She even managed to ignore the piercing blue gaze that lingered on her tense profile as she was carefully lifted onto the leather seat and Lord Carlton urged the restless pair into motion.

Her inner brooding was allowed to remain unchallenged as Lord Carlton negotiated the busy London streets, but as they entered the more gracious avenues near the park, he slowed the horses to a sedate pace.

"You are very quiet, Roma," he murmured, his attention shifting to the hands tightly clenched in her lap.

"Must we do this?" she demanded in a low voice.

With her head lowered, she missed his wry smile.

"I fear we must."

"But why would your grandmother wish to meet me?"

"Perhaps because I told her yesterday that I intend to make you my bride."

Her startled gaze flew to his dark countenance. "What?"

"Well, I could hardly abandon London without some explanation," he pointed out with calm composure. "Besides which, she is bound to hear the rumors already circulating through town."

She wanted to argue, to accuse him of putting her in this awkward situation, but in all fairness she realized that he was correct. He could hardly disappear without telling his grandmother where he would be staying and why he would chose such a remote part of the country. That didn't, however, ease her discomfort.

"This is awful. How can I possibly lie to your grandmother?"

"If it makes you feel better, then think of you brother," he commanded.

"But . . . she will never believe that you wish to wed an insignificant country miss." She unconsciously echoed the words of her cousin. "She will think you have taken leave of your senses."

"On the contrary, she will be delightfully astounded by my good fortune," he startled her by insisting as they pulled to a halt in front of an imposing Palladian style town house. Tossing the reins to the groom who leaped to the paved road, Lord Carlton turned to regard her with an encouraging smile. "Come, sweet Roma, I am certain Colonel Allendyle taught you to march into battle with your head raised high."

The mention of her father abruptly stifled her flutters of fear. It was true. Her father had always taught her to face even the most unpleasant experiences with her shoulders squared and her pride intact. It was unlike her to be unnerved by anyone or anything.

"Yes, he did," she admitted with a lift of her chin.

His smile widened. "Then into battle we go."

He gracefully vaulted out of the curricle and was helping Roma to alight when the door was pulled open to reveal a tall, rapidly balding butler of indeterminate years. Leading Roma forward, Lord Carlton smiled with obvious pleasure at the servant.

"Good morning, Grimfeld."

The butler performed a stately bow. "My lord."

Sweeping past the uniformed servant, Lord Carlton steered Roma into a vast foyer. Then, divesting himself of his gloves and beaver hat, he handed them to the waiting Grimfeld.

"And how is my grandmother this morning?"

"She is—"

"She is considerably annoyed that she is the last to be informed that her only grandson is about to acquire a wife," a peevish, decidedly female voice interrupted from across the hall. With a start of surprise, Roma turned to discover a tiny, elegantly attired woman with a puff of white hair and a regal expression viewing them with obvious ill humor.

Lord Carlton performed an elegant bow. "Good morning, Grandmother. You are looking particularly well this morning."

"Fah!" The older woman brushed aside the smooth compliment, stabbing the waiting butler with an unnerving glare. "Grimfeld, we will have tea in the front drawing room."

The butler made another bow. "Very good."

Leaning on an ivory cane that appeared more of an affectation than a necessity, Lady Chalford crossed the hall and went through a set of double doors. Lord Carlton smiled in an indulgent manner before giving Roma's cold fingers an encouraging squeeze and urging her to follow the small figure.

It took every ounce of her courage to keep her expression smooth as she entered the imposing salon with its classic Grecian style. Even though accustomed to luxury, Roma was impressed with the stark elegance of the rosewood furnishings and heavy gilt that decorated the intricate lion's paw feet. She had little doubt that several thousand pounds had been spent to achieve the air of simplicity. Then realizing she was being intimately scrutinized by a pair of shrewd gray eyes, Roma forced herself to calmly perch on the edge of a small sofa. As if sensing her need for reassurance Lord Carlton settled closely beside her, boldly reaching out to grasp her hand in his warm fingers.

With a lift of her brows, Lady Chalford peered down her thin nose at her grandson.

"Now, you shall introduce me to this young lady who

presumes to become a member of my family," she commanded in imperial tones.

"Certainly. Grandmother, may I present Miss Roma Allendyle? Miss Allendyle, my grandmother, Lady Chalford."

"Allendyle?" Lady Chalford frowned, her still handsome features revealing her disapproval. "Where do you come from?"

Roma drew in a deep breath. She would not allow herself to be intimidated, no matter how grand Lady Chalford might be in the eyes of London, and perhaps in all of England.

"Devonshire," she retorted with admirable composure.

Lady Chalford paused, then gave an abrupt thump of her cane on the carpeted floor.

"Ha. I remember your father. Military man."

"Yes, he was."

"Never had two words to say for himself, but managed to snare the Toast of the Season." The gray gaze narrowed as it swept over her pale features. "You don't resemble your mother."

Roma blinked. "No."

"Pity. She was a great beauty."

Oddly Roma took no offense at the blunt pronouncement.

"Yes, she was."

"Hmmm . . . red hair." The older woman continued her detailed list of faults. "I suppose you have a temper?"

"On occasion."

"And more spirit than is proper for a young lady."

Roma ignored the stifled choke of laughter from the man at her side. "So I have been accused."

"That is hardly what is expected for a young lady hoping to enter this family."

"Perhaps not."

Another silence fell as Lady Chalford peered at her in that disturbing manner.

"I wonder, my girl, if you fully comprehend the significance of taking the title of Lady Carlton," she at last accused.

"Are you attempting to frighten off my prospective bride, ma'am?" Lord Carlton inquired, belatedly coming to her rescue.

"I wish to assure myself that she has given the matter serious contemplation. She will be expected to behave in a manner befitting her position."

"I can not conceive of a more tedious fate," Lord Carlton argued. "I prefer her to remain precisely as she is, including her penchant for plunging delightfully from one disaster to another."

Roma blushed as the older woman shifted to regard her with a hint of surprise.

"Indeed?"

"Yes, indeed. I have waited a long while to encounter someone who never fails to surprise me. She is utterly perfect."

Even knowing that Lord Carlton was simply playing a role to distract his grandmother from the truth, Roma couldn't wholly dismiss the renegade tingle of pleasure. It could only be a sense of relief that he wasn't chiding her for her ill-bred behavior or sharp tongue, she told herself firmly.

Lady Chalford banged her cane on the carpet. "And what of your sentiments, child?" she demanded.

Roma gave a tiny shrug. "My sentiments?"

"I presume you wish to sway my opinion by claiming my grandson is similarly without defect."

Something in the sharp tone warned Roma that this was not a lady easily fooled. Indeed, the same shrewd intelligence carved into her grandson's aquiline features could be easily discerned in the softer curves of her own countenance.

Rather on impulse, Roma found herself answering with a blunt honesty. "Actually he is spoiled, proud to a fault and far too fond of having his own way."

She felt Lord Carlton's slender fingers tighten on her

hand, even as a gleam of appreciation entered his grandmother's gray eyes.

"Ha."

"He is also considerate and astonishingly kind when
he chooses," she continued in a low voice.

Lord Carlton gave a sudden chuckle as he lightly
brushed the inner skin of her wrist with his mouth.

"Vixen," he murmured.

"She will never make you a comfortable wife," Lady
Chalford unnecessarily pointed out.

Deliberately leaning forward, Lord Carlton caught
Roma's wary gaze.

"Thank God."

"Clearly your mind is settled," his grandmother complained.

"Unequivocally." With a display of reluctance Lord
Carlton returned his attention to the elderly lady. "Do
you approve?"

"Does it matter?"

"Not in the least."

A thick silence descended at his offhand words and
Roma momentarily feared they had overplayed their
hand. She had no doubt Lady Chalford was as unaccustomed to having her opinion so summarily dismissed as
her grandson. But just as she prepared for an all-out battle of wills a sudden smile softened the autocratic countenance.

"Then I wish you well," she pronounced in noble
tones. "And I hope she leads you a merry dance."

Tilting back his dark head, Lord Carlton laughed with
rich amusement. "I have every confidence that your wish
will be granted, ma'am. Now tell me of the latest scandals
to capture your fancy."

With a tiny smile, the rigid lady settled back into her
seat and, rather to Roma's surprise, began to repeat some
of the more shocking *on-dits* circulating through town.
She also appeared to be well apprised on a variety of
political policies being discussed in Parliament, and she

appeared to delight in debating the issues with her grandson.

After nearly a quarter of an hour, Lord Carlton slowly rose to his feet and gently urged Roma to his side. "I should return Miss Allendyle to her aunt."

Lady Chalford gave a regal nod of her head. "You may bring her back to visit when you return to London."

Loosening his grasp on her hand, Lord Carlton crossed to place a kiss on his grandmother's cheek.

"I will."

Returning to Roma, he escorted her out of the room. In the foyer they encountered the butler carrying a tray with the forgotten tea.

"Ah, Grimfeld . . ." Lowering his voice, Lord Carlton leaned toward the stern-faced butler. "Take care of her until I return," he commanded, collecting his hat and gloves from the side table.

The servant nodded his head. "I shall do my best, my lord."

"And contact me in Devonshire if there is anything you need."

"Of course."

"Excellent."

Roma was once again reduced to silence as Lord Carlton led her to the waiting curricle. This time, however, it was not nerves that held her tongue, but a need to adjust her image of the man climbing onto the seat beside her.

Strangely she had managed to convince herself that Lord Carlton was incapable of such tender sentiments. She had witnessed his courage, his arrogance and on occasion his practiced charm, but she had presumed he preferred the more fashionable habit of dismissing frivolous emotions. Watching him with his grandmother had revealed a genuine attachment that was somehow disturbing.

She swayed slightly as Lord Carlton turned onto the street that would lead to her aunt's home. Lifting her gaze, she realized her companion was surveying her pensive expression with a mysterious smile.

"You managed my grandmother admirably," he congratulated her. "I believe she actually took a fancy to you."

His praise only deepened her sense of disturbance. "I do not like deceiving her."

"Nor do I, but we have decided upon a path to discover the truth surrounding your brother's disappearance." A raven brow arched in a challenging motion. "Have you lost the courage to follow that path?"

Despite her best intentions, she readily responded to his taunt. "Certainly not."

The dark features abruptly softened. "Be at ease, Roma," he coaxed. "Soon you will be at Greystead."

A poignant stab of longing pierced her heart. "Yes," she whispered beneath her breath. "I am going home."

Fourteen

In the end her heartfelt desire to be at Greystead came sooner than expected. Only two days after her visit to Lady Chalford she received a note from Lord Carlton, informing her that he would be prepared to travel to Devonshire by the end of the week.

Not surprisingly the abrupt notice had sent her aunt into a bout of flurried activity as she had set about closing the town house, finishing her last-minute shopping and making a thorough round of calls to preen over her extraordinary success in launching her niece into Society.

Roma found herself included in the general chaos. With a sense of haste, she rushed to complete packing and writing messages to Devonshire to prepare for their arrival. She had little time to brood on Lord Carlton or his sudden absence over the next few days.

Still, she couldn't deny that on occasion she found herself wondering where her supposed fiancé might be and why he hadn't bothered to call on her. And her surprise only deepened when they prepared to leave London and Lord Carlton revealed that he intended to ride the superior black stallion he had arrived on rather than share the well-sprung carriage he had so thoughtfully produced for their comfort.

Not that she wanted to be enclosed with him for one tedious hour after another, she swiftly reassured herself. But after spending the past few days lecturing herself on

the necessity of maintaining a cool composure, she found
it decidedly annoying to have her efforts wasted.

With her nose put out of joint by what she blamed on
the long journey and Clara's inane chatter, Roma determinedly refused her aunt's offer of tea when they arrived
at Rosehill. Instead she waited only long enough for the
weary horses to be changed, and with an indifferent
promise to return for dinner, she headed for Greystead
Manor.

Now she heaved a deep breath as they swept up a tree-
lined drive to the modestly appointed house. As always
she felt a tingle of pride at seeing the weathered gray
stones, the fluted columns and recently paned windows.
Although it was not a lavish establishment, there was a
solid beauty in the main hall and the sweeping wings surrounded by the pristine parkland.

Impatiently waiting for the groom to pull open the
door, Roma clambered out of the carriage and rushed
into the front hall. Almost at once a short, decidedly ro-
tund woman moved forward to sweep her into welcoming
arms.

"Miss Roma!" the housekeeper exclaimed, nearly
smothering the slender woman by her display of affection. Then, slowly pulling back, she subjected Roma to a
detailed survey. "Look at you, so thin and pale. I warned
you that London was no place for a decent young lady."

Roma felt a surge of warmth at looking upon the familiar round face with its twinkling brown eyes and rosy
cheeks framed by a severe widow's cap. Mrs. Stone had
been a fixture at Greystead for as long as Roma could
remember. A kind and loving presence for a motherless
child in desperate need of such tender attention.

"Indeed you were correct, Mrs. Stone," she readily
agreed. "It is delightful to be home."

"What you need is fresh country air and plenty of Mrs.
Emerson's plain cooking."

Roma smiled in a weary fashion. "At the moment a
cup of tea would be most welcome."

"Certainly. I had a tray prepared the moment Peter rode over to say you had arrived at Rosehill."

"Bless you, Mrs. Stone."

Placing herself in the housekeeper's capable care, Roma found herself being steered into a tidy library with a massive window looking over the garden and walls lined with books. The tantalizing aroma of freshly baked scones mixed pleasantly with the scent of leather-bound tomes, reminding Roma of lazy afternoons spent in the company of her father.

"Here we are. You sit down, and I will pour a cup of tea just as you like it."

Placing Roma on a worn couch, Mrs. Stone moved to fuss over the heavily laden tray. In the blink of an eye, she returned with a steaming cup of tea and a platter filled with tempting delicacies.

"Thank you." Roma took a sip of the reviving tea, then heaved a deep sigh of pleasure. "Heavenly."

With the familiarity of a longtime servant, the housekeeper settled her considerable bulk on a Queen Ann chair.

"You look exhausted," she accused with a lowering of her brows. "I suppose you have been gadding about to all hours of the day and night?"

Roma couldn't resist a bit of teasing. "There was some gadding about, I must confess."

The older woman gave a loud snort of displeasure. "Lady Welford should know better."

Roma softly laughed. The housekeeper had always cherished a violent dislike for London and those who abandoned the country in favor of the more sophisticated town.

"Aunt Clara meant well, and I was the one to suggest that I indulge in a London Season." Her momentary amusement abruptly faded. "Now I wish that I had remained at Greystead." She paused, knowing it was ridiculous to ask but unable to prevent the words from spilling past her lips. "Has there been any word from William?"

Kindly refraining from pointing out that Roma had left strict instructions she was to be notified the very moment there was any news concerning her brother, Mrs. Stone gave a regretful shake of her head

"No."

"I had hoped . . ." Her voice trailed away.

The housekeeper gave a sympathetic cluck of her tongue. "Have no fear, Miss Roma. I am certain that Mr. Allendyle will soon be home and right as rain."

With an effort she suppressed the cloud of concern that was her constant companion.

"Of course he will." Roma determinedly reached for a sumptuous piece of sponge cake. It had been hours since her last meal. "Tell me what has occurred since I left."

Easily diverted, Mrs. Stone settled her bulk more comfortably and prepared to vent her justifiable disappointment in the upstairs maid.

"I suppose you know that Maggie left to marry that half-wit farmer?"

Roma hid a sudden smile. Mrs. Stone's opinion of husbands was even lower than her view of London. Whether her bitterness stemmed from her own brief marriage, or the long years she had remained a widow, no one dared to inquire. But she had always been a staunch supporter of Roma's determination to remain a spinster.

She attempted to soften the woman's staunch dislike. "I believe Anthony is a very respectable young man."

"Foreign blood and not a brass farthing to his name," Mrs. Stone stated, in condemning tones; then she gave a wounded sniff. "Still, I did my best to warn the chit. Now she must make the best of her lot."

Roma had little doubt the vivacious maid was vastly more pleased with her lot as the wife of a respectable farmer than she had been as a simple servant, but she kept such thoughts to herself.

"Did you manage to replace her?"

"Yes, I've taken on her younger sister, Liza. A silly girl, but I'll soon have her properly trained."

"I am confident you will, Mrs. Stone," Roma readily agreed. The portly woman could rival Colonel Allendyle when it came to training her small army of staff. "What of my bailiff?"

The housekeeper grimaced with instant annoyance. "That man . . . a born tyrant if I ever seen one. Poor Billy has been in tears every day since you left."

Roma heaved a sigh at the thought of the young stable boy suffering beneath the bullying hands of Fred Barker. As soon as William returned she intended to see the spiteful man thrown off the estate. Until then she would have to keep him far too occupied to bully anyone.

"Never fear, Mrs. Stone," she consoled. "I will see Mr. Barker this afternoon. If anyone is to end the day in tears, I assure you it will not be Billy."

The housekeeper beamed with smug satisfaction. "I knew you would make it right. It is good to have you home, Miss Roma."

"It is good to be home," Roma retorted, although she couldn't deny the dawning realization that she was not as comforted by the familiar surroundings as she had hoped.

And it was all due to that vexing Lord Carlton, she told herself as she set aside the unfinished cake. How could she possibly relax while knowing he might suddenly appear at any moment? Or even worse, realizing that the entire neighborhood would soon be bustling with the rumor she was unofficially betrothed?

As if sensing her hidden unease, Mrs. Stone regarded her with a suspicious frown.

"Is something amiss?"

Roma absently folded the fine linen napkin as she considered the least shocking means of revealing the presence of Lord Carlton at her aunt's home.

"I suppose I should tell you before it has spread all

over the neighborhood that Lord Carlton will be staying with Aunt Clara for the next few days."

"Lord Carlton?"

"Yes, he . . . he is an acquaintance from London. He is here to help in my search for William."

The housekeeper was clearly perplexed. "Oh."

"I only mention him because it became evident while I was in London that I must return to Devonshire without creating undue interest." She made a vague gesture with her slender hand, prolonging the inevitable. "Lord Carlton suggested that he pretend to be my suitor desiring an interview with William."

A profound silence descended as Mrs. Stone gazed at her in startled disbelief. "This Lord Carlton wishes to marry you?"

"No, of course not." Roma hastened to deny it. Why did everyone persist in leaping to such absurd conclusions? "He only proposed so that Aunt Clara would return home."

"So . . . he doesn't wish to marry you?"

Roma heaved a rueful sigh. "I know it is all very complicated, but all you need remember is that Aunt Clara and the neighbors believe Lord Carlton is waiting for William to return from his visit north so that he can ask to marry me. In truth he will be seeking information concerning my brother's disappearance."

"Are you certain you know what you are about, Miss Roma?" the older woman demanded with an expression revealing a growing concern that her mistress was becoming a bit noddy.

"Quite certain," Roma blandly lied.

"And this Lord Carlton is a man of honor?"

"Without a doubt."

Mrs. Stone continued to bristle with disapproval. "I can not think what your dear mother would have to say. Pretending to be engaged, indeed. It's disgraceful."

"For now my only concern is for my brother. I will do whatever necessary to discover the truth." With an effort,

Roma softened her sharp tone. "Besides, it is only a temporary deception, I assure you."

Only partially mollified, Mrs. Stone gave her a speaking glare. "I can not say that I approve, but you have always done precisely as you chose. Stubborn just like your father."

"That particular flaw in my character seems to be pointed out quite frequently of late," Roma retorted.

Seemingly resigned to the younger woman's unyielding nature, the housekeeper heaved herself to her feet.

"Will you be dining in this evening?"

"No, Aunt Clara has requested that I join them for dinner." Roma's expression was decidedly unenthusiastic. "Indeed, I shall be dining there indefinitely."

"Then I shall send word to their cook that you are to be fed a nicely roasted joint and plenty of potatoes to fatten you up," Mrs. Stone announced in decisive tones. "None of those shabby French dishes."

"I am confident Mrs. Davies will provide an ample meal."

The large woman gave a derisive sniff "And I know Lettie Davies well enough to realize that she will be more concerned with impressing a London gentleman with her fancy sauces and pastries than setting a decent table. Now, I have rattled on long enough. You should rest."

Roma could think of nothing she longed for more than a hot bath and a few hours of lying upon her bed. But thrusting aside the tempting notion, she determinedly rose to her feet.

"All in good time. First I would like Mr. Barker to attend me here."

"Should I have one of the gardeners step in as well?"

"That won't be necessary."

"Maybe not, but I will have John in the hallway just the same." The housekeeper named one of the under gardeners who was a burly young man with an abundance of muscles.

Roma shook her head in resignation. She wasn't the only stubborn person in this household.

"As you wish, Mrs. Stone."

Obviously pleased with Roma's swift capitulation, the housekeeper waved a plump had at the neglected tray.

"Now be a good girl and finish your tea. I will send John to fetch Mr. Barker."

Having the last word as always, Mrs. Stone turned and disappeared through the double doors. Once she was alone, Roma absently wandered across the room, her hands stroking the satinwood furniture until she reached the prized library table her father had acquired from Sheraton. Being back in this room reminded her forcibly of just how much she missed the Colonel's steadfast presence and ready sense of humor.

He would know what to do to help William, she thought with a pang of regret. And even if he didn't he never would have made such a bumble bath of the search as she had.

Certainly he would never have found himself pretending to be engaged to an overbearing gentleman with little regard for propriety.

A tiny smile abruptly softened her anxious expression. Perhaps he would not have found himself engaged to Lord Carlton, she acknowledged, but she was uncannily certain that the two gentlemen would have gotten along most famously. Unlike most men, Lord Carlton would not have been intimidated by the Colonel's gruff manner and habit of barking out orders, while her father would have respected the nobleman's shrewd intelligence.

Her hand drifted from the desk as she straightened her shoulders. The Colonel was not here, and it was up to her to somehow solve the seemingly endless list of troubles.

Beginning with her ill-mannered bailiff who clearly forgotten her stern warnings. A mistake he would not soon make again.

* * *

Across the wide meadow, Lord Carlton sat astride his stallion regarding the well-tended farms and livestock with a judicial gaze.

"Prime bit of lad you have, Welford," he congratulated with sincere appreciation.

Well aware that Carlton's vast estates must cast his own in the shade, Claude was nonetheless grateful for the compliment. He was feeling decidedly overwhelmed at the task of entertaining such a grand guest and feared the aristocrat might find the simple surroundings beneath his contempt.

"Thank you, my lord."

"Please . . . can we dispense with such formality?" Giles pleaded. "I far prefer Giles."

A pleased flush touched the younger man's cheeks at the honor. "Very well . . . Giles."

"Good." Turning in his saddle, Lord Carlton pointed his riding crop at the distant house. "Is that Greystead?"

"Yes. Not as ancient or as large as Rosehill, but a fine house," Claude answered.

"Yes, indeed."

Claude gave a sideways glace at his companion, who was peering at the house with inordinate interest. "It is entailed to William," he added unnecessarily.

"So I assumed. Although Roma did mention she had inherited a legacy in her own right."

"A modest legacy, I fear," Claude corrected.

Giles swallowed a smile, wondering if Welford feared he considered Roma an heiress. After all, it was not unusual for a gentleman, even in his comfortable position, to seek a wealthy wife. Absurd of course. There wasn't enough money in all of England to have induced him to marry the exasperating Roma Allendyle. Only love could have accomplished that amazing feat.

"Too large for my peace of mind," he answered with blunt honestly.

Claude blinked in surprise. "What's that?"

"She has become far too fond of her independence."

Giles unconsciously frowned. "She seems to have no interest in sharing her life with anyone."

The hint of wariness disappeared from Claude's youthful features, to be replaced with a sly smile.

"True enough. Although I suspect if the right gentleman were to come along he could convince her to change her mind."

Giles was well aware he was being discreetly led into a declaration. He smiled with wry amusement.

"Perhaps."

"Of course, my cousin is not the most biddable of creatures," Claude was forced to acknowledge.

"She is trying beyond all measure."

"It would take a gentleman of considerable patience."

"It would take a gentleman who has lost all sense." Giles snorted; then, with a rueful shrug, he turned to meet Welford's narrowed gaze. "Fortunately I have never been overly blessed with good sense. Now, I believe you were going to show me the path to the cove?"

Claude paused, as if wanting to pursue the subject further, but with a shrug, he gestured toward the narrow lane.

"This way. But take care. The path becomes very steep just over the ridge."

Giles gave a decisive nod, vaguely recalling the dangerous road from his previous visit to Devonshire, and with a gesture of his slender hand, he indicated that Claude should lead the way.

In silence they traveled along the dirt road, winding through the rolling fields and thicket of trees that lined the ridge. Giles felt an odd prickling as they carefully made their way down the cliff to the crescent-shaped beach below. He recalled all too vividly the stormy night and terrifying sounds of gunshots.

With a shake of his head, Giles swung himself out of the saddle and loped the reins around a protruding rock. He had enough to occupy his thoughts without the distractions of that terrifying evening. Paying little heed to the sand marring the gloss of his boots, he made his way to where Claude had bent to inspect the ground.

"It looks as if someone has been here," Claude pointed at the unmistakable prints sunk in the soft sand.

Giles glanced about the remote beach. "Strange."

"Perhaps a local farmer in search of a hidden love nest?" the younger man suggested without much conviction.

"I doubt many maidens would be willing to traverse such a dangerous path, even for the sake of love." Giles nodded his head toward the steep path. Then, as he turned back to more closely inspect the footprints, a glitter of gold captured his attention. Reaching out, he plucked the object from the sand. "What is this?"

"A pocket watch." Claude leaned forward, his breath suddenly catching in a loud gasp. "This belongs to William. He was here."

Giles's heart leaped at the exclamation, but he swiftly tempered his excitement. What was needed now was calm reason, not foolish emotion.

"We must not jump to conclusions. We have no means to determine on how many occasions William came to this cove. He might have dropped this watch months ago."

Claude gave a violent shake of his head. "No. I recall William pulling it out to check the time on the day he disappeared. I remember it distinctly. He had stopped by to view my new mare."

"Did he appear concerned?"

"More . . . distracted," Claude explained, his brow furrowed as he attempted to recall the events of the day. "I assumed he was thinking of the unnaturally dry weather. He took his duties as a landowner quite seriously."

"And he did not mention any appointments?"

Claude struggled to remember a name or place that William might have brought up, only to sigh in a regretful manner.

"Nothing. He glanced over to the horse; then, pulling

out his watch, he muttered something about attending to unfinished business."

Giles settled back on his heels as he contemplated the watch he held in his slender fingers.

"He must have been meeting someone. But who?"

With a sudden movement, Claude rose to his feet. "I will search the rest of the beach."

Giles also rose to make a thorough tour of the cove, kicking aside rocks and pieces of driftwood in an effort to discover further clues. After a futile circle from one end of the beach to the other, he called a halt.

"I fear that we have accomplished all we can here to-day."

Claude came to a reluctant halt, his expression troubled. "What of the watch? Shall we return it to Roma?"

Giles gave a swift shake of his head. Although the watch confirmed that William had been to the beach on the day of his disappearance, it did not prove where he was now or indeed if he were alive or dead.

"Not at the moment. Roma might very well view the finding of the watch in so remote a location as an ill omen. I have no wish to increase her anxiety. For now, I think we should keep this between the two of us."

Claude regarded the older man in a distinctly skeptical manner. "She will not thank you for attempting to protect her."

"You are no doubt correct," Giles agreed with a grimace, all too familiar with his beloved's fiery temper. "Unfortunately I find it difficult to alter the habits of a lifetime."

A swirling gust of wind sent the sand sweeping through the damp air. Overhead a lone bird cried a shrill protest at their presence.

"Gad the wind is chill." Claude abruptly shivered. "Let us seek the warmth of Rosehill."

"Excellent notion."

Together, they collected their mounts and retraced the treacherous path up the cliff and over the ridge. Once away from the cove, Giles breathed a sigh of relief. There was something rather ominous about the deserted beach. As if unseen eyes were watching his every movement. Perhaps an absurd notion, but one he could not shake.

Lost in his troubled thoughts, Giles barely noted his surroundings until a familiar clump of trees suddenly captured his attention. Bringing his horse to a halt, he regarded the copse with an unconscious smile. Ahead of him, Claude slowly pulled his own horse to a stop and turned to frown at him in puzzlement.

"Is something the matter?"

"I was just noticing that building over there." Giles pointed at the barn barely visible in the distance.

"It is nothing but an abandoned barn," Claude retorted.

Giles's smile widened, a tingle warming his blood as he recalled the slender young woman who lay upon the straw. It was an experience he would dearly love to repeat in the near future.

"Much more than that, I think," he murmured in soft tones.

"Would you like to ride over and see it?"

"Not today." Giles urged his horse forward. His quick mind was already making plans on how to coax his reluctant fiancée to the secluded barn. "At the moment I far prefer the thought of a toasty fire and something from your cellar to ease the chill from my bones."

Claude smiled in instant agreement. "As easily said as done."

Fifteen

Several hours later, Roma was reluctantly entering the carriage her aunt had sent to fetch her. After sternly lecturing her unctuous bailiff, she had devoted a good part of the afternoon to updating the household accounts and inspecting the gardens. Activities she had performed on dozens of occasions without undue thought, but which today had taken an inordinate amount of effort. Her unruly mind simply refused to concentrate on the tasks at hand. And even when Mrs. Stone had bullied her into taking to her bed for a few hours of rest, she had found herself tossing with a restless dissatisfaction.

It was concern for William, of course, she had told herself severely. Being back at Greystead only more forcibly reminded her of her dearest brother and the strange manner of his disappearance. It also reminded her of her dismal failure to locate the smallest trace of a clue.

At last she had been driven into rising and dressing for the evening ahead. In an effort to distract her thoughts, she had allowed her maid to arrange her fiery curls in an elegant knot atop her head and to dress her in a gown of ivory satin with velvet trimmings in a becoming emerald shade.

Now she felt decidedly self-conscious as they rolled across the short path from Greystead to Rosehill. She had no desire for Lord Carlton to presume she had attired herself in so fashionable a mode for his benefit. After all, she had no doubt any number of foolish maidens would attempt such blatant methods of attracting his attention. And he was certainly odious enough to make such an assumption.

She would simply have to treat him with the cool composure that she had practiced, she reassured herself. It should prove her indifference. Tilting her chin to a determined angle, she watched as Rosehill came into view.

An older home than Greystead, the manor followed the picturesque Gothic style. Much to the pride of her aunt, the house had recently received the attentions of the extraordinarily talented James Wyatt. His work had renovated the sadly disrepaired building into a showpiece. He had even consented to extend his efforts to the large chapel and conservatory.

The carriage drew to a halt, and Roma allowed the uniformed footman to help her to alight. Then, crossing to the open door, she gave a sudden smile as she caught sight of the tall, wiry man waiting in the wide entrance hall.

"Good evening, Miss Allendyle," the butler intoned with all the dignity of his London counterpart.

"Good evening, Polsun." Roma ignored the polished dignity of the servant. She had known Bob Polsun since she was old enough to walk. "How is your son?"

An answering smile abruptly softened his rigid expression. "Much improved. Why, only this morning the doctor was saying he was astonished with the boy's progress." His voice grew husky with affection. "I do not know how we can possibly express our gratitude."

Roma waved aside the words with a hint of embarrassment. When Mrs. Stone had written to inform her that the poor boy was suffering from an inflammation of the lungs, it had seemed only natural to seek the advice of a London specialist and to send back the powders he recommended.

"Let us only be happy with the knowledge that Richard

is on the mend." She brought a firm close to his words of thanks. "Has my aunt come down yet?"

"No"—his regard became watchful—"but I believe that Lord Carlton is in the formal drawing room."

"Oh . . . thank you." She conjured a stiff smile. "I will show myself in."

Moving though the hall, Roma halted to feign an interest in the elaborate ebony side table. It wasn't until she heard the butler retreat toward a side chamber that she glanced about to ensure she was alone. Then, picking up her skirts, she quickly hurried down the vaulted gallery toward the narrow door that would open into the gardens. It might be the act of a coward, but she had no wish to see Lord Carlton without the distracting presence of her aunt and cousin.

She hurried past the tall windows with the thick scarlet curtains and bookcases that contained her uncle's rare collection of antique books and maps. She didn't even glance toward the doorway that would open into the drawing room. She hoped to be safely in the garden before anyone even realized that she had arrived.

Unfortunately, Lord Carlton seemed to possess an uncanny knack of thwarting her plans, and she was less than halfway down the hall when the familiar sound of his voice brought her to a sharp stop.

"Searching for someplace to hide, Roma?" he drawled with lazy amusement.

The knowledge that his accusation was far too close for comfort instantly put her on the defense. She might reluctantly admit to herself she was a coward where this man was concerned. It was quite another thing to allow him to suspect the humiliating truth.

Slowly turning about, she forced herself to squarely meet his glittering blue gaze. "Certainly not. I . . . I simply wished to stroll through the garden before dinner."

Leaning negligently in the doorway, Lord Carlton slowly straightened, his muscular form exquisitely outlined by the black coat and white satin pantaloons.

"Indeed? A rather chill evening, but I am always eager to fulfill the wishes of a beautiful lady."

Her eyes widened as he gracefully strolled to join her in the hallway.

"There is no need for you to join me."

"Of course there is," he argued. "Why do you think your aunt is so conveniently absent?"

"I haven't the least notion."

"She is discreetly allowing us a few moments alone." He smiled with wicked pleasure at the ready heat that brushed her cheeks. "Do you not think she would find it odd to come down and discover you wandering in a dark garden while I remain by myself in the drawing room?"

Roma clenched her teeth in frustration. Did he always have an answer for everything?

"Oh . . . very well," she conceded with ill grace.

Thoroughly indifferent to her pointed lack of enthusiasm, Lord Carlton drew her arm through his own and politely escorted her down the hall and out of the door. Roma held herself stiffly as they entered the shadows of the formal garden, but with her usual bad luck she couldn't prevent a shiver as the night breeze cut through her thin shawl. Taking full advantage of her weakness, Lord Carlton pulled her shockingly close, using his large form to block the wind.

In silence they passed around the sparkling fountain, turning down a wide path lined with a delicate framework of trelliswork and archways.

"I presume you are delighted to be back at Greystead?" He at last broke the silence.

"Of course." She couldn't resist a sideways glance at the noble profile. "Although I fear that you must be insufferably bored?"

"Not at all. Your aunt and cousin have taken great care to see to my comfort. Besides, as I once told you I far prefer to stay in the country."

She gave a disbelieving shake of her head. "I find that difficult to believe."

"Why?"

"I do not know." Roma unconsciously frowned. "You simply seem very much at ease in London."

"Ah . . . a deadly insult coming from you, eh, Roma?" he taunted in soft tones.

Her heart fluttered in an odd fashion. In truth, she had not intended to insult him. She had merely been thinking of his elegant sophistication and his ease of moving through society. Far different from the makeup of most country gentlemen.

Feeling his gaze closely inspecting her uncertain expression, she hurried to divert his attention.

"Have you seen my uncle's collection of rare maps?"

For a long moment he continued to regard her in amusement; then, with a shrug, he followed her lead.

"Yes, Claude was kind enough to give me a viewing. He possesses some fine pieces."

"One day they will be given to a museum, but for now Aunt Clara refuses to part with them. She claims that each one holds a special memory."

"I admire her decision," Lord Carlton retorted in a surprisingly sincere tone. "She must have cared a great deal for your uncle."

"Yes. Like my mother, she was allowed to marry for love."

"A family tradition?"

"I . . . I suppose."

Lord Carlton smiled again as they rounded a corner.

"What did you think of my grandmother?"

Roma glanced at him in puzzlement, wondering why he would be interested in her opinion.

"I found her to very elegant and refined," she replied in all honesty.

"And?" he persisted.

"And rather outspoken."

"Did she offend you?"

"Not at all," Roma admitted. "I prefer outspoken women."

Lord Carlton laughed softly. "Why does that not surprise me?"

A small silence descended as they turned a corner that would eventually lead back to the main house. At last, Roma spoke the words that had been at the back of her mind since her visit to the elderly lady's home.

"You seem to be very fond of Lady Chalford."

"Yes." His tone was indulgent. "Like you, my own mother died when I was very young. When my father chose to marry again, I was sent to live with my grandmother."

"Did that bother you?"

He glanced down at her. "My father choosing to remarry or going to live with my grandmother?"

"Your father deciding to marry," she clarified, wondering how she would react if her own father had taken the same path.

"Actually it bothered me a great deal," he startled her by admitting. "I thought my father to be a heartless cad. In my mind, he was betraying the memory of my mother. It wasn't until I grew older that I realized he was simply attempting to relieve the loneliness of her death." He gave her a faint smile. "Thankfully we made our peace before he died."

"So now it is just you and your grandmother?" she asked softly.

He grimaced in a rueful fashion. "And a handful of distant cousins who go to bed each evening with the prayer I remain unwed."

She felt a strange pang in the center of her heart.

"And will you?" she inquired before she could halt the words.

"Remain unmarried?" A disturbing glint entered those blue eyes. "No. I intend to marry. In the not too distant future as a matter of fact."

"Indeed?"

The annoying pang once again made itself felt. Ridiculous, of course. Whether this man decided to marry or not was none of her concern. Indeed, it should be of the utmost indifference if he were to wed a half-a-dozen witless debutantes.

But while she firmly reassured herself that she hoped he landed with a harpy that plagued him night and day, the image of him standing at the altar with a porcelain beauty at his side sent her stumbling forward in an awkward motion.

"Take care," Lord Carlton warned, but even as he grasped her waist in a steadying gesture, Roma felt a painful tug on her hair.

"Oh . . . blast," she gritted as she realized her elegantly arranged curls had managed to become entangled in the wooden archway.

This was what came of wool-headed girls with more vanity than sense, she chided herself sternly, illogically blaming her predicament on her elegantly styled curls rather than her ludicrous reaction to his bland announcement of his intent to wed.

"Hold still," Lord Carlton commanded, loosening his grip on her waist to inspect her tangled curls. "I fear you have made a devilish mess of this, my dear."

She sucked in a sharp breath, far too conscious of his nearness.

"Could you please just untangle me?" she demanded.

"Patience, Roma," he murmured gently pulling at her uncooperative locks.

"Surely it can not be that difficult?"

Glancing down, he met her rigid embarrassment with a slow smile. "Actually it is quite difficult. How am I to concentrate when I am being so thoroughly distracted by that enticing scent of honeysuckle?"

"My lord . . ."

"Giles," he corrected in low tones.

Her breath was disturbingly elusive as she sought to retrieve her shattered composure.

"Are you going to assist me or not?"

"Well, I have no intention of leaving you to pass the evening in this garden," he teased in light tones. "You needn't work yourself into a panic."

"I am not in a panic," she denied, wincing at her breathless tone.

"No, of course not," he drawled.

"I am not—ouch."

"I told you to hold still." His breath sweetly brushed her cheek as he gave a last tug. "There. You are free."

Thoroughly unnerved, she waited for him to step back so that they could resume their circuit to the house. Annoyingly he remained towering over her with that devilish amusement softening the angles of his magnificent countenance.

"We should return to the house," she at last charged, hoping she did not appear as flustered as she felt.

"There is no hurry."

"Aunt Clara will be wondering what we are doing out here for such a length of time."

"I am confident Lady Welford's romantic disposition will provide any number of reasons why we chose to linger." A slender finger lightly brushed her heated cheek. "The moonlight, the scent of the night air, the pleasure of a few stolen kisses."

"This is absurd," she breathed out.

"We really should not disappoint the excellent lady." His voice dropped to a husky pitch as his dark head angled downward.

A flare of sharp excitement unsettled her stomach. How often had she recalled the feel of his lips against her own? Or the warmth of his hard body? Far too often for her peace of mind.

"No . . . you must not."

"Indeed, I must," he corrected in a breathy whisper. "I most assuredly can not help myself."

She might have screamed or dodged aside as the dark

head neared. She might even have stomped on his toes as she had done to other overly forward suitors. But in the end she did nothing to halt the searching mouth from claiming her own in a bold kiss.

A searing pleasure raced through her body as he gently pulled her close, one hand cradling the back of her head as his lips became more insistent. This time her shiver had nothing to do with the chill-edged breeze. The delicious sensations overrode common sense and even fear as she leaned helplessly against his wide chest.

Oblivious to all but the man holding her with tender strength, Roma was unprepared for the shocked gasp that echoed through the still garden.

"Oh . . ."

Raising his head with obvious reluctance, Giles regarded the wide-eyed young man with resigned amusement.

"Hello, Welford. Haven't you someplace better to be?"

Tugging at his collar, Claude shifted his feet in acute embarrassment. "Yes . . . well . . . Mother sent me to tell you that dinner is being served."

Ignoring Roma's frantic attempts to free herself from his steely embrace, Giles gave an imperious nod of his head.

"We will be along in a moment."

"What? Oh, of course. Yes. Very good."

With an awkward bow, Claude backed his way around the corner, nearly falling over a marble bench.

Watching the rather ridiculous display, Roma determinedly conjured up a brittle shell of composure. Nothing would induce her to reveal the depth of her disturbance. Not even if it choked her. Stilling her struggles, she forced herself to meet his laughing gaze.

"I believe we embarrassed your poor cousin," he murmured.

"Can you be surprised? Your shocking conduct would embarrass anyone with the least amount of propriety."

"It was only a kiss, Roma," he said, his tone so reasonable that she longed to plant him a facer. Just a kiss? Then why did her blood still tingle and her heart race with excitement? "Besides, when I heard the footsteps approaching I assumed that it was your aunt. As I told you, I did not want to disappoint such an obvious romantic."

"Well, it was not my aunt, and I can not conceive what Claude must be thinking," she accused.

"He is thinking that I was bewitched by your beauty in the moonlight. That I was unable to resist temptation. And"—his fingers carefully smoothed a curl lying against her temple—"he would be correct."

"Giles . . ."

His finger moved to press against her lips, effectively halting her strangled denial. "Shall we return to the house?"

She snapped her lips together as he stepped back and waited for her to join him. She had risen to his bait enough for one evening.

With a belated attempt at dignity, Roma swept past his tall form and up the shadowed path. She maintained her rigid silence as they once again skirted the fountain and entered the narrow door. Once they were in the corridor, Lady Welford hurried forward with an arch expression on her round face.

"There you are, you naughty children. I see that I will have to keep a close guard on you two." She wagged her finger at the darkly handsome gentleman. "The sooner William returns the better."

Claude entered the hallway at the same moment the butler threw open the doorway to the dining room.

"Dinner, my lady."

"Thank you, Polsun."

Taking the proffered arm of Lord Carlton, Clara moved toward the open doorway, leaving behind a blushing Roma.

"You appear to be taking your engagement quite to

heart, Roma." Claude stepped to her side, offering his arm.

"I am not engaged," Roma snapped.

Tempting fate, Claude arched a chiding brow. "Then I really must scold you on your improper behavior. It is one thing to kiss a fiancé in a dark garden—it is quite another—"

Roma's eyes flashed a clear warning. "That is enough, Claude."

"You needn't be so prickly." He laughed softly. "No doubt many females have succumbed to Lord Carlton's charms."

"No doubt," she gritted out.

Claude regarded her stiff features with a speculative expression. "Do not tell me that you are jealous?"

"That is absurd. I am not jealous, and I did not succumb to any supposed charms. Lord Carlton simply caught me off guard."

"You mean to say he forced himself upon you?"

The treacherous memory of her body swaying into his arms made it impossible to lie.

"I would prefer not to discuss it further."

As if sensing her inner turmoil, Claude smiled with aggravating humor.

"Very well." Reaching out, he placed her hand on his arm and steered her toward the wide door. "You know, I must admit that your Lord Carlton has proven to be something of a surprise."

Wishing the entire night to be over, Roma reluctantly followed his lead.

"What do you mean?"

"I thought he might find his days at Rosehill sadly flat, but not only has he proven to be an amiable guest, but he is remarkably well informed on the latest techniques in farming. He made a number of suggestions that I intend to have implemented as soon as possible."

"Really?" Her voice expressed her disbelief.

"Yes, really," Claude insisted. "He also spoke of his own estates."

She attempted to pretend a supreme indifference. "Oh?"

"They sound splendidly situated, and of course, everyone is aware that Markstone is one of the most magnificent homes in all of England." Claude paused, casting a covert glace at her profile. "Naturally it must be a great burden for one person to oversee not only his land and tenants but his household as well. What he needs is a wife."

An instinctive grimace tightened her features. "Do not concern yourself on that matter, Claude. Lord Carlton has already stated his intentions of acquiring a wife. Although I can not imagine any woman foolish enough to pledge herself to such an arrogant, overbearing creature."

Claude's smile only widened. "Can you not?"

"Claude . . . Roma . . ." Standing in the doorway, Clara regarded them with impatience. "Come along, children."

Relieved to bring an end to the conversation, Roma hurried forward, entering the large dining room. Soft candlelight glowed off the chandelier hanging from the timbered ceiling, adding a sheen to the polished table. Figured damask covered the seats and windows, while the paneling was patterned with inset mirrors. Over the door a painting of knights in pageantry complemented the ceramic armor hanging in the corners.

A lovely room, but Roma barely noted her surroundings as she took her seat and absently tasted the various dishes placed before her by the uniformed servants. It was simply impossible to appreciate turtle soup or the delicate trout in cream sauce while her aunt coyly maneuvered the conversation to every wedding she had ever attended in the past fifty years.

At long last dinner came to a close and her aunt suggested they retire to the drawing room for Roma to display her talents on the harp. Unable to think of anything more torturous for all concerned, Roma dug in her heels with the excuse of excessive weariness.

As she was on the point of leaving the room, Clara glanced at her niece in surprise. "Surely you can not wish to leave at such an early hour?"

Glancing at the gilded clock, Roma resisted an urge to point out that it was well past eleven. Even in the country Lady Welford preferred to keep town hours.

"I fear I must. With William away I have a great deal of work to oversee."

"Nonsense," Clara chastised with a horrified glace at Lord Carlton. "Your bailiff can oversee any work until William returns. Why else do you pay him a salary, for goodness' sake?"

"I have often wondered that myself, Aunt Clara. Unfortunately for the moment I am unable to rid myself of his presence. Which means I must keep a close guard on his every movement."

Clara frowned and made a dampening motion with her hand. "Really, Roma, what will Lord Carlton think of you?"

"I believe I shall make an early night of it myself." Giles smoothly stepped into the argument, holding out his arm. "May I escort you to your carriage, my dear?"

She had little option but to accept his offer, and together they entered the long gallery that led to the entrance. With a discreet movement, Polsun opened the door, and they walked onto the shadowed porch. As they went down the steps to her waiting carriage, however, Giles pulled her to a gentle halt.

"Hold a moment, Roma."

Raising her head, she met his probing gaze with commendable calm. "Yes?"

"Have you considered what actions you intend to undertake to search for your brother?"

Her expression grew guarded. She had no intention of revealing the various plots and schemes she had dwelt on during the long afternoon. She was quite certain he would disapprove of each and every one.

"I have given it some thought," she replied in a vague manner.

His gaze narrowed. "And what fearsome scheme have you concocted this time?"

"None."

With a click of his tongue, he reached out his hand and firmly grasped her chin. "Do not take me for a simpleton, my dear. Such a meek expression does nothing but assure me that you are hiding something from me."

"There is nothing to hide," she denied, even as the ready heat crawled beneath her skin.

"Roma—"

"It is late, Giles," she swiftly interrupted. "I must go."

For a long moment he regarded her delicate features with smoldering suspicion; then, removing his fingers from her chin, he instead grasped her hand.

"I shall be keeping a close guard on you, Roma," he warned in stern tones. "You can not hide from me."

Her independent spirit was instantly riled by his possessive manner. "Please remember you are here to search for my brother."

"That is only one of many reasons I am here." With a firm movement he was handing her into the dark recesses of the carriage, maintaining his grip on her hand despite her attempts to pull free. "Remember, my dear, there is nothing you can do that will escape my notice." Bending his head, he pressed warm lips to the sensitive skin of her inner wrist. "Sleep well."

He had stepped away and firmly shut the door before she could chide him on his reprehensible behavior. But what did it matter? she asked herself, absently rubbing at her tingling skin. She seemed incapable of resisting his practiced charm. Even when she told herself she was behaving like a nitwitted fool.

But while she might be vulnerable to his touch, she refused to cowed by his heavy-handed warnings. She would search for William using whatever means necessary. And if it didn't suit the imperious Lord Carlton, then so much the better.

The cumbersome carriage swayed down the narrow lane while inside Roma brooded on a means of searching for her brother. Even if it meant going through every home in Devonshire.

Or England.

Sixteen

From his position at the edge of the woods, Giles watched as Roma jumped the nearby hedge, the massive stallion in complete control as she plunged on at a full gallop, her auburn curls flying with abandoned freedom.

A rueful smile touched his dark countenance as he noted her masculine breeches and shirt. Since her return to Greystead Manor the week before, Roma had gratefully reverted to her more normal habit of forgetting that she was a young woman, and more often than not could be found striding about the estate giving commands in a military manner that would have rivaled her father's. Except, of course, during the evenings when she was expected to make an appearance at her aunt's home where they would spend a few hours discussing the upcoming wedding.

Only Giles knew how she dreaded the nightly sessions, and he accepted the irony of the situation with grim humor. After years of avoiding the parson's mousetrap he was now reduced to employing the same desperate measures he had scorned to achieve his own ends. He knew that he was shamelessly abusing Roma's anxiety for her brother to force his way into her life, but even as she grew more wary of the wedding plans that were proceeding at a rapid pace, the more determined he became to turn the pretend engagement into a very real commitment.

But while he might be toasted as England's most eligible bachelor, with a string of mistresses and a past paved with broken hearts, he hadn't the least notion of how to woo this impossible woman. With a shake of his raven head, he watched as she once more turned the stallion and made a leap that would terrify most men.

She was quite simply like no other woman he had ever met. She had no interest in his wealth or title. Not even his enviable position in the *ton* seemed to have made any impression on her distant heart. And if he had ever vainly considered himself irresistible to the opposite sex, she had swiftly managed to correct this error.

More often than not she managed to make him feel like an unwanted intrusion into her life, endured only for the sake of her brother. And not even the potent memory of her passionate response to his kisses could change the stark knowledge that she was barely conscious of him as a potentially attractive male.

Perhaps it was retribution for the years he had seen women as mere objects for his own pleasure, he acknowledged with a small sigh. What better punishment than falling in love with a young woman who not only considered him a foolish coxcomb, but who would be a constant trial on his nerves even if he did succeed in winning her heart?

With a small laugh at his ridiculous position, Giles abruptly urged his own horse forward. There was little use in regretting his unorthodox wooing of Roma Allendyle. Their relationship had begun in a bizarre manner, and he had no doubt that it would continue in the same fashion. At least he was assured that he would never be bored.

He crossed the field at a leisurely pace, waiting for Roma to reluctantly rein her mount to a halt before joining her beside the road that led to Greystead Manor. As always she eyed him with a wary mistrust that made him long to shake some sense into her.

"Good morning, Roma."

Her gaze narrowed at his mild tone, and he suddenly realized that she had expected to be reprimanded for her hoydenish behavior.

"Good morning, my lord," she said; then, as he flashed her an annoyed frown, she gave him a small smile. "Giles. Did you need something?"

"Simply a desire to speak with you in private. Something that is impossible with Aunt Clara fluttering about."

Her glace was dry. "This was your brilliant plan."

"Yes, I know. Unfortunately I was not acquainted with your relative at the time."

Surprisingly, an expression of sympathy crossed her flushed face. "Has it been very bad?"

An urge to play upon her unexpected compassion was swiftly thrust aside as they casually turned the horses toward the graceful country house that slumbered peacefully beneath the lazy spring sunlight.

"Nothing unbearable. Certainly your aunt means well."

"Yes, but that does not make her any less irritating." Her smile faded as she shot him a sideways glace. "And I fear she will only become worse as this mythical wedding draws closer. I do not suppose you have given any thought as to how we are supposed to end this farce without breaking her heart?"

He shrugged. "I assume that if worse comes to worst we could go through with the ceremony."

She gave an audible gasp, the spirited stallion tossing his magnificent head as if sensing Roma's sudden tension.

"That is not amusing," she gritted out, regaining control of the skittish horse.

"It was not meant to be," he confessed, his tone self-derisive. "After all, there is no legitimate reason we should not wed. We are both at an age where neither one of us has unreasonable expectations or foolish romantic notions when it comes to marriage, and we are both old enough to consider setting up a proper household. Besides, we tend to rub along well enough and—"

"Don't be absurd. We do nothing but snap at one another," she interrupted, her hazel eyes flashing with something that looked remarkably like panic. "And if you are suddenly in the market for a bride of convenience, then I suggest you search for a biddable woman who can grace the position of Lady Carlton. I assure you I would prove to be nothing more than an embarrassment."

"And I assure you that you could not possibly be more mistaken," he said quietly. "It takes more than expensive clothes and a flirtatious manner to be a lady. My own mother was a woman of uncommon spirit and courage. I know she would have taken a great liking to you."

She blinked, obviously caught off guard by the sincerity in his words.

"I . . . no, this is a ridiculous conversation. I have no intention of marrying anyone, whether it is for convenience or not."

Sensitive to the sharp edge that entered her voice, Giles strategically backed away. If nothing else he had planted a seed in her mind.

"There is no need to fly into a pet, my dear," he soothed, his expression bland. "I was simply pointing out that we have a considerable number of options when it comes time to end our engagement."

"That is easy for you to say," she grumbled, clearly relieved at his determinedly light tone. "You are not forced to endure Aunt Clara's tedious insistence that we discuss every detail of the wedding, or the next evening to hear her change every decision we made the night before."

"Yes, it must be quite wearing," he agreed. "But do not imagine I have not suffered. I have heard a dozen different lectures on training you to be a suitable bride, from burning your breeches to selling that monstrous beast you insist on riding rather than a proper lady's mount."

Her mouth dropped open with her sheer indignation at his teasing words.

"Sell Diablo? Over my dead body."

He swallowed the urge to inform her that the first time he had witnessed her thundering across the field on the great brute of a horse he had been seriously tempted to pull her across his knee and beat some sense into her thick head. But after choking back his terror and forcing himself to watch the two with his mind rather than his heart, he had grudgingly conceded that Roma not only maintained full control over the large animal, but that they moved together with a silent understanding that was beautiful to see. It was clear the two possessed a rare trust, and Giles easily sensed that the stubborn woman would firmly dig in her heels at the mere suggestion of finding a more suitable mount. That did not, however, make him wish she did not possess quite so much spirit. It was distinctly uncomfortable to live in constant fear that she was putting herself in some type of mortal danger.

"I doubt if that shall be necessary, my dear." He flashed her a mocking smile. "No one possesses the required nerve to challenge you in an open confrontation. In fact, as far as I can tell, you terrifying everyone in the neighborhood with your sharp tongue and ever-ready riding whip."

A crimson blush stained her cheeks, but she couldn't fully hide the renegade smile that tugged at her lips.

"I am quite sure you are greatly exaggerating," she retorted. "I certainly do not frighten you."

"No," he agreed readily, although that wasn't quite true. There were times when his unfamiliar emotions for this tiny woman terrified the life out of him. "You won't be allowed to frighten me away. It takes more than an unruly tongue and a riding whip to intimidate a Carlton."

She rolled her eyes at his deliberately arrogant tone. "I am sure that is very noble; however, I do not have the time to discuss the questionable merits of the Carlton clan. I have a meeting with my bailiff in half an hour."

"Please give me a moment, Roma."

With a small frown of surprise she brought Diablo to a halt and gazed at him with vague impatience.

"Yes?"

He hesitated, suddenly aware that he disliked the notion of creating even more antagonism between them. Still, he wasn't about to allow her to continue with her dangerous games of cat and mouse.

"Roma, you can not keep up this house-by-house search for your brother."

"I do not know what you mean," she retorted, her guilty expression giving her away. It was obvious she had hoped he had remained in ignorance of her covert activities.

"Your ploy of playing Lady Bountiful and calling on every house and cottage in the neighborhood has not gone unnoted," he informed her in a severe tone. "Not only are people speaking of your uncharacteristic burst of social activity, but the vicar and his wife are offended by the endless stream of soup and blankets you are taking to the poor. They assume you are dissatisfied with their own charitable endeavors."

She gave a proud toss of her fiery curls. "There is nothing unusual in my behavior. Most ladies devote a great deal of their time to visiting their neighbors and caring for the poor."

He gave an inelegant snort. "Most ladies perhaps, but not you, Roma. I have no doubt that you care as much as the next person, perhaps even more, for the plight of the less fortunate. I have, in fact, heard your aunt speak of your attempts to establish a school for both boys and girls in the area. But you are not in the habit of personally trailing from one house to another, and quite frankly, it is beginning to stir exactly the type of gossip that we were trying to avoid."

"What does it matter?" she demanded, the frustration that smoldered just below the surface suddenly overflowing. "We came here to search for my brother and so far you have done nothing. I can't simply wait around and hope he somehow manages to save himself."

Giles smiled wryly at her less than subtle insults. He

knew it was impatience and fear that made her strike out, but it didn't make the blow any easier to take.

"And so you would rather endanger your brother by openly searching for him house to house, and even worse, placing yourself in danger? Just what do you think would happen if you did stumble across a house where your brother was being held captive?" he demanded, his eyes narrowed. "Do you think the kidnappers would kindly thank you for your soup and then hand William over to you? Surely you have more sense than that?"

Hazel eyes snapped with instant fury at his attack, but he also noted the uncertainty that fluttered across her delicate features. Perhaps he had managed to make her at least consider how futile her risky plan was.

There was silence as she struggled to hide her sudden indecision; then her gaze abruptly narrowed.

"How did you know about my visits in the first place?"

Giles shrugged, refusing to admit that Jameson was currently staying at the local inn, picking up the latest gossip and asking discreet questions. Nor would he admit that he had bribed one of her own servants to follow her wherever she went.

"As I said, people are already talking about your unusual behavior," he lied with casual ease. "Which is why you must stop at once."

"And do what?" she demanded angrily. "Waste my time discussing a mythical wedding with my aunt?"

He heaved a small sigh. "Could you not simply trust that I am doing everything possible for William?"

"You?" She didn't bother to hide her amazement. "What do you mean?"

He hesitated, wondering exactly how much he should tell her. It wasn't that he didn't trust her to keep his covert activities a secret. He was just well enough acquainted with her stubborn nature to realize she would insist on being thoroughly involved in his every movement, no matter how risky.

"I am not sure that—"

His reluctant words were abruptly broken off as the sound of an approaching rider echoed through the still air. On instant alert, he shifted in his saddle to peer down the dusty road. Within moments he could make out the shape of a man trotting toward them at a leisurely pace. The two watched in silence as the unknown rider approached, but as he drew near Giles felt himself stiffen in surprise.

There was no mistaking the small but elegantly attired form or the arrogant tilt to the dark head of Lord Scowfield. Giles bristled with instinctive antagonism, unconsciously assuming his most aristocratic demeanor. Not only did he dislike the overly suave man; he didn't trust him any farther than he could toss him. It seemed highly suspect for him to return to the country at the same time as Roma.

His companion, however, had no such suspicion, and with an openly pleased smile, she urged Diablo forward to greet the approaching guest.

"Freddie, what a wonderful surprise. I thought you were cutting a dash through town?"

Sweeping an elegant bow from the back of his flashy black stallion, Freddie ran an indulgent glance over her tousled appearance, completely ignoring the menacing man in the background.

"London was sadly flat without you, Roma. I remained long enough to visit my tailor, and attend my aunt at her tedious soirees, before I made my excuses and fled home with all possible haste. Naturally I came over as soon as I was settled." He flashed her a teasing smile. "I had hoped to convince you to take a short ride with me, but I see that I am too late."

"Yes, well . . ." Roma suddenly seemed to recall her less than immaculate appearance. "I did not expect any visitors this morning."

Freddie chuckled as she lifted a self-conscious hand to her tumbled curls in a thoroughly feminine motion.

"Do not worry. I think you look quite charming."

Already gnashing his teeth at Roma's obvious pleasure in the man's sudden appearance, Giles had nearly exploded at the smooth compliment and the overly familiar manner in which Scowfield's gaze swept over her too tight clothing. With a strangled hiss, he jerked his horse next to Roma's and sent the unwanted intruder a warning glare.

"My fiancée always manages to look lovely," he informed Lord Scowfield in a haughty tone. "But, like most women, she prefers to have advance warning of visitors so that she can entertain them in a conventional manner."

"Giles . . ." Clearly startled by his unexpected attack, Roma turned to toss him an angry glace, but Freddie Scowfield remained unperturbed.

"You are quite correct, Lord Carlton, and I extend my full apologies. You can put my lack of manners down to my long-standing friendship with Roma and my eagerness to announce my return home." His smile did not reach the piercing dark eyes. "And, too, there was a bit of curiosity about the rumors flying about London. I see it is true that the two of you have become engaged."

There was no way to decipher what the man felt about Giles presence, and he could only assume Scowfield was a master at hiding his inner emotions.

"Yes, it is true, although we must wait for Mr. Allendyle to return from the north before we can make an official announcement."

This time it was clearly more difficult for the visitor to hide his surprise.

"The north?" He gave a slight cough. "I see . . . Well, of course, William will be delighted to learn the happy news. He is quite devoted to Roma."

Giles felt a tingle of warning inch down his spine. He was absolutely certain this man knew more than he was admitting, and he was suddenly determined to discover much more about Lord Scowfield. It could very well be this man held a clue to William Allendyle's disappearance.

Conjuring up a stiff smile, Giles forced himself to momentarily forget the white-hot jealousy that threatened to cloud his reason and to think of what was best for Roma.

"There are quite a number of us devoted to Roma," he said in an indulgent tone. "Unfortunately her bailiff is not one of her loyal followers and seems to be in constant need of her firm guidance. I was about to leave her to her daily bout with the troublesome man and take a cup at the inn. Perhaps you like to join me?"

Caught off guard, Freddie hesitated, his gaze flickering toward the puzzled Roma.

"Actually, I—"

"Come, I insist." Giles deliberately moved his horse between the two, his expression pleasant but determined. "As an old friend of my fiancée I think it is important that we get to know one another. You can regale me with amusing stories of Roma as a young girl." With a casual movement, be glanced over his shoulder at Roma. "Do not be too harsh on the poor bailiff. Oh . . . and leave your riding whip in the hall; I have no doubt he is already shaking in his boots at the mere thought of being hauled upon the carpet by your sharp tongue without adding another weapon. Until later, my dear."

Seventeen

"There, Miss Roma." The maid tucked the last curl into the topknot, then stepped back to admire her handiwork. "Don't you look pretty?"

With a far more critical eye, Roma studied the reflection gazing back at her in the oval mirror. Attired in a pale lemon gown with a trim of silk roses, she appeared far different from the hoydenish miss who had been visible about the estate the past few days. A change that she would bite off her tongue rather than admit she secretly enjoyed. What was the use of fripperies when she had an estate to manage?

"Thank you, Anna."

"And such a lovely day for a picnic," the maid continued, her round face turning toward the window where a stray slat of sunlight spilled through the chintz curtain.

Roma followed the servant's glace, although a small frown tugged at her auburn brows.

"Yes, I suppose it is, although I can not conceive what induced my aunt to plan such an outing. She has always abhorred such rustic entertainments."

Roma had indeed been startled when she had received a note that morning begging her presence at an informal picnic to be held on the grounds of Rosehill. She could only suppose that her aunt, grown exasperated by her polite evasions and insistence that she was far too occupied to come to dinner over the past few days, had devised a means of ensuring her presence.

A twinge of unease plucked at her conscience. It was nothing short of cowardice to have avoided Rosehill with such diligence. But Lord Carlton's offhand proposal had bothered her far more than she cared to admit. Even knowing that he was simply attempting to put her to the blush did not dismiss the disturbing quivers in the pit of her stomach.

"Perhaps she thought to please Lord Carlton," the maid suggested.

With a slight shake of her head, Roma attempted to dismiss her troublesome thoughts. She was a fool to dwell on his teasing words. She had no doubt that he had forgotten them the moment he had ridden away with Freddie Scowfield. Certainly he had not bothered to press her on the subject. Or any other subject since he had been decidedly absent over the past few days.

"Perhaps," she agreed with a tiny shrug.

Setting aside the silver-handled brush, the plump young woman sent her a shy smile.

"Such a handsome man," she said in soft tones.

There was little Roma could say to that. "Yes."

"And quite without airs," the maid continued. "My Peter says he comes right into the common room at the inn, not demanding a private parlor like that other gentleman who used to go there."

The surprise that Giles had condescended to enter the disreputable inn at all was swiftly overset by a sudden suspicion.

"Gentleman? What other gentleman?"

Anna blinked in surprise at her sharp tone. "Peter has only seen him on a couple of occasions. He comes in dressed like one of them fancy gents from London and hides himself in the front parlor."

"Really? How peculiar."

Once started, the maid needed little coaxing to continue. The mystery gentleman was clearly a source of speculation among those of the neighborhood.

"Yes, and he don't want to be disturbed. Peter once heard the man threaten to blow the innkeeper's head clean off if he dared to open the door."

Roma abruptly turned about, her hazel eyes narrowed. "And he stays in there alone?" she demanded. "I mean, no one comes to visit him?"

Anna gave a decisive shake of her head. "Not that anyone knows of. Just stays in there by himself for half the night and then leaves without so much as a by your leave."

"I wonder who he could be?"

"I am sure I couldn't say, Miss Roma."

Not certain what she suspected, Roma nevertheless felt that the strange gentleman was worth inspecting further. Since Lord Carlton's aggravating pronouncement that her visits throughout the neighborhood had become the source of speculative gossip, she had been reduced to once more simply waiting for some sign of William's presence.

"Perhaps you could ask Peter to inform me when next this mysterious guest arrives at the inn?"

"You think he might be an acquaintance of yours?"

Roma gave a noncommittal shrug. "That is what I would like to discover."

There was a brief knock on the door before it was pushed open to reveal the downstairs maid.

"Mrs. Stone asked me to tell you that the carriage is waiting, Miss Allendyle," she announced with an awkward bow.

"Thank you, Liza."

The girl retreated with another clumsy bow, and Roma turned for one last glance in the mirror. She regarded the reflection of a slender young woman with little concern for the beauty of her delicate features or the grace of her unstudied movements. She only wished to assure herself that her unruly curls remained pinned in place and her gown unsoiled.

Satisfied that all was in order, she picked up the lacy parasol and glanced at the maid.

"You will remember to speak with Peter, won't you?"

"Of course."

"Thank you, Anna."

With a smile, Roma turned and made her way out of the room and down the long staircase. She paused, however, as she stepped out of the house and raised her face to the sun.

It was a glorious spring day. Overhead the sky shimmered, a vivid blue without a cloud to mar the perfection. The faint breeze carried the spicy scent of wildflowers. And the dazzling sunshine added a pleasant warmth. It was indeed a glorious day for a picnic.

About to enter the carriage her aunt had once more sent to fetch her, Roma was halted by a glimpse of a young woman crossing the grounds toward the back entrance. With a motion to the groom to hold the horses, Roma moved across the paved drive to intercept the tall, dark-haired woman carrying a basket of freshly cut flowers.

"Hello, Maggie." She greeted her former maid with her usual lack of pretension.

A genuine gleam of pleasure lit Maggie's dark eyes at the sight of her former employer. Not precisely a pretty woman, she did possess a pleasing countenance and unaffected manners.

"Miss Allendyle." She held up her basket of flowers. "I came to visit Mrs. Stone."

Roma gave a low chuckle. "I am not certain that she has forgiven you for your unconscionable treason."

Maggie joined in her amusement even as a becoming blush touched her cheeks. "No, I believe that she has taken it quite to heart."

"I, however, am delighted with your good fortune."

"Are you?" There was a touching eagerness in the

young woman's expression. "And you think Anthony a good match?"

"I think him the finest match," Roma assured her.

Clearly delighted that the woman she had always held in the highest esteem regarded the marriage in so providential a manner, Maggie positively glowed with happiness.

"Thank you, Miss Allendyle."

Roma allowed her gaze to travel over the simple but well-cut gown and bonnet.

"I must say, marriage appears to agree with you."

"I have never been so happy," Maggie admitted. Then with a shy glance from beneath lowered lashes, she added, "But then, you will soon know for yourself."

Disconcerted by the unexpected words, Roma gave a small cough.

"Oh . . . yes."

"I have caught a glimpse of Lord Carlton. He is quite dashing," Maggie assured her, clearly unaware of Roma's discomfort. "And Anthony tells me he is a most charming gentleman. Not at all too grand to spare a word for a mere farmer."

Roma's unease dissolved with a flare of wry humor. Lord Carlton appeared to have won the approval of the entire neighborhood. She could only hope she was not sent to the gallows when it was discovered she was not to wed the irresistible lord.

"Lord Carlton appears to have made quite an impression since his arrival in Devonshire," she murmured.

Erroneously fearing that she had managed to imply Lord Carlton was more beloved than Roma, Maggie rushed to correct the error.

"Only because most wish to see you happy, Miss Allendyle," she said in anxious tones.

"Oh, I am delighted he has made himself so pleasing," Roma corrected with a dry smile. "He does not always make such an effort." Then, as one of the horses could be heard protesting the groom's admonishment to hold still, she gave a glance toward the carriage. "I should be on my way, or I shall be shockingly late."

"Forgive me for chattering on."

"Nonsense, it was lovely to see you. Give Anthony my best."

"Yes, yes, I will."

Retracing her steps, Roma allowed the groom to hand her into the carriage. Then, settling against the squabs, she pondered the vast changes in her maid.

There was no doubt of Maggie's happiness. It had shimmered in her eyes for the world to see. But there was also a new confidence in her step and an added hint of dignity in her manner.

Odd really. Roma had always presumed the bonds of matrimony to be heavy indeed. After all, a lady was expected to submit her will to that of her husband. How could she feel anything but oppressed?

But far from appearing trod upon, Maggie had acquired an assurance in her bearing that had never been present before.

Roma continued to brood on the unexpected dilemma as the coach rattled over the uneven ground. She paid scant attention to the passing scenery or even the direction in which they headed. Not until the carriage halted and she was climbing onto the overgrown field did she note the isolated surroundings. With a flicker of suspicion, she watched as the tall, dark form of Lord Carlton stepped from the shadows of the derelict barn. Her aunt would never condescend to be seen next to the ramshackle outbuilding, let alone plan to serve an elegant meal in such a place. In fact, Roma was confident no one had trespassed in the area for the past twenty years. Except of course for her and Lord Carlton on the fateful night they had hidden from the gang of ruffians.

Clearly the gentleman was once again plotting some mischief, she acknowledged.

"Good afternoon, my dear." Giles claimed her hand

in a firm grip, as if he feared she might bolt like a frightened rabbit.

The thought had her chin instantly tilting to a militant angle. "Where is Aunt Clara?"

"No doubt enjoying a delicious luncheon at Rosehill."

She met his lazy grin with a narrowed gaze. "Then what are we doing here?"

"Hold a moment." Suddenly moving to the front of the carriage, he gave a low command to the waiting groom. Then, before she could recover her senses, he had returned to reclaim her hand. "Come along."

She dug in her heels with a frown. "I asked you what we are doing here."

A raven brow flicked upward. "We are about to enjoy a picnic, of course."

Her gaze darted toward the large cover spread beside the barn. At the same moment the carriage abruptly lurched into motion. Her heart gave a decided flip-flop.

"You must be jesting?"

"Not at all," he denied.

"But . . . you tricked me," she accused, remembering the note she had received early that morning.

"Yes." He was thoroughly unrepentant. In fact, he appeared disgustingly self-satisfied. "I have also taken the liberty to order the servants to make themselves scarce for the next hour. You might as well sit down and enjoy this delectable food."

For a moment she could only glare at him in affronted disbelief. Over the past few days she had convinced herself that this encounter with Giles would be fraught with awkward embarrassment. At least for her. But the unexpectedness of the situation had banished all thoughts of their previous meeting.

"You really are the most odious cad, sir."

"Irrefutably," he agreed with a smile. "It is a part of my charm."

She heaved an exasperated sigh. The devil of it was that his sweeping determination was indeed a part of his charm. A charm that was far more potent than she wished to admit.

"I should walk home rather than give in to such blatant manipulations."

"Ah, no, my dear." He firmly placed her arm through his own. "On the last occasion I was foolish enough to turn my back on you, you slipped away. I shall not be so easily gulled again."

She glared at him in annoyance even as he gently tugged her up the grassy slope.

"I have requested you not to remind me of that evening."

Dark head tilted back, he laughed at her prim reprimand. "There seems to be an ever-lengthening list of evenings you wish not to be reminded of, my dear."

She captured her lower lip between her teeth. It was all too true. She did wish she could put out of her mind more than one of their stormy encounters. Still, it was decidedly ill favored of him to point out that he was conscious of such sentiments.

"I am glad you find my discomfort a source of amusement," she said in stiff tones.

"Of course I do not, you goose," he chided. Then, coming to a halt, he placed a finger beneath her chin and forced her to meet his piercing blue eyes. "Come, Roma, all I wish is for a restful meal that does not include a discussion of the wedding guest list, the floral arrangement, or the merits of a custard rather than a pudding."

She hesitated, far from immune to his cajoling manner. "You will not . . . I mean . . ."

He slowly smiled at her stammered words, clearly aware of her concern.

"You are perfectly safe with me, Roma," he assured her in even tones. "Shall we declare a truce and enjoy this beautiful day?"

She knew that she should decline. That she should demand he return her to Greystead Manor without delay. But absurdly she found herself nodding in agreement.

"Very well."

The blue eyes flashed with an indefinable emotion. "Good." Moving his hand back to her arm, he steered her the short distance to the cover. "Here we are. A veritable feast."

Her eyes widened at seeing the lavish bounty that was spread across the ground. Platters of salmon, thinly sliced ham, delicately braised new potatoes and stuffed mushrooms. There was even imported caviar spread onto triangles of toast and a large platter covered by a linen napkin. She settled herself on the edge of the cover, absently accepting the glass of champagne that he pressed into her hand.

"Thank you," she murmured as he sat down beside her, resisting the urge to scoot away from his large form. To do so would be admitting he had the power to disturb her with a mere touch. Then she gave a small gasp as he reached forward to pluck the linen off the platter and reveal the delicate pastries beneath. "Apricot tarts," she exclaimed in delight.

"I happened to meet your old nanny the other day, and she mentioned that they were a particular favorite of yours."

The small warmth at his thoughtful gesture was offset by the wry acknowledgment that there appeared to be no one in the neighborhood he had not yet encountered.

"Really?"

"Yes, a most charming woman."

"What else did she happen to mention?"

"Let me think . . ." He pretended to consider his reply. "Ah, yes, she did happen to share a few childhood incidents. I believe my favorite was the evening you decided to help yourself to a bottle of your father's finest brandy."

Roma gasped in horror. How could her nanny possibly have revealed such a humiliating event? It was bad enough that she had downed an entire bottle of brandy to prove she could hold her drink as well as a man. It was perfectly mortifying to realize that this man was aware of her childish attempt to mold herself into the beloved image of her father and older brother. How could he understand the uncertainty of a young girl being raised in a household of men?

"I had seen Father and William drinking from the decanter," she muttered in defensive tones. "It seemed utterly unfair that I should be denied my share."

Surprisingly his expression was one of rueful admiration rather than admonishment. "I can well imagine. Let no challenge go untried, eh, Roma?"

A reluctant smile melted her stiff expression. "Unfortunately I had no notion the wretched stuff would make me so ill."

He laughed in sympathy as he filled her plate with the tempting delicacies.

"A thick head is no pleasure."

She grimaced in memory of the dreadful morning after. "I find it beyond comprehension that anyone would knowingly seek such an unpleasant condition."

"I do not believe it is so much a conscious decision to become top-heavy, as a lack of concern on what the morrow will bring."

"Perhaps," she agreed, accepting the plate he pressed into her hands. "What else did my nanny tell you?"

"A great many things." He gave a shrug, a wicked glint in his blue eyes. "She told me you were an insatiable student and that you had read your way through your father's library by the age of sixteen and that you could outride and outshoot any gentleman in the county." He ignored her growing discomfort. "She also said that you possessed a fiery temper which is fortunately offset by your generous heart and incurable habit of protecting the weak and defenseless."

"Infamous," Roma breathed out, inwardly deciding she needed to have a firm talk with her former nanny. "I can not imagine what possessed her to rattle on in such a manner."

Giles popped a mushroom into his mouth. "Because she obviously adores you."

"If she adored me then she would refuse to discuss my disreputable childhood," Roma corrected in dry tones.

"Would it ease your embarrassment if I were to share a few of my own childhood mishaps?"

"You?" She arched a disbelieving brow. "I find it difficult to believe you have ever had any mishaps. You are always so annoyingly perfect."

"I assure you, I was a gangling, awkward youth who was constantly tripping over my own feet," he insisted, watching her absently devouring the delectable meal with obvious satisfaction. "My grandmother swore that I could never walk through a room without breaking at least one vase, or return from a walk without having tumbled into a lake."

The image of the exquisitely sophisticated man as a grubby schoolboy was impossible to conjure.

"Ridiculous."

"Not at all." He leaned forward to press a bit of toast with caviar between her lips. "And, like you, I also pinched my father's brandy on one never-to-be-forgotten occasion. I shared it among several of my cousins, and we spent a delightful evening entertaining the entire family. I believe I may even have played the harp until the servants were called in to haul us up to our chambers." His smile widened at her startled expression. "In any event I still have more than one aunt who refuses to speak with me to this day." He shrugged his unconcern. "Hardly a tragic loss."

She gave a rueful shake of her head at his absurd tale. Somehow the thought of him making a cake of himself in such a fashion made him less unapproachable.

"Did you miss not having any brothers or sisters?" she asked before she could halt the question.

"Every day." Leaning back, Giles regarded her with a rather regretful expression. "Although there were children in the neighborhood and even children on our estate, they were always kept at a distance. My position made them uncomfortable to be around me." His smile twisted. "Possessing a title and fortune can be a lonely business."

Her heart gave an unexpected wrench of pain at his simple honesty. She could easily imagine him as a young child surrounded by opulent furnishings and lavished with every luxury, but isolated by his rank. How difficult it must have been to see the other children playing without him. It was little wonder that he had grown into an aloof, rather forbidding man. At least until one managed to slip past his stern facade.

"I am sorry." Without thinking she leaned forward to gently touch his arm.

Glancing down, Giles studied the pale fingers lying against the blue fabric of his jacket; then, with a strange smile, he covered her hand with his own.

"There is no need to pity me, my dear." His gaze lifted to meet her softened hazel eyes. "It taught me to be self-sufficient and able to appreciate those friends I do possess."

Lost in the probing gaze, Roma found it a struggle to catch her breath. He was so handsome, so utterly irresistible. Quite beyond anyone she had ever encountered before.

With a nervous motion, she jerked her hand free and gazed desperately at her empty plate.

"More champagne," he inquired, his voice annoyingly composed. But then, why shouldn't it be? He was not the one assaulted with these ridiculous bouts of awareness.

"Thank you, no."

"At least have another apricot tart?"

Gathering control of her nerves, she forced herself to lift her head. She was behaving like a skittish schoolgirl, for goodness' sake.

"I have eaten three already. One more and I shall be beyond all shame."

"Fustian. There is no need to act the dainty female with me, my dear."

"No." She smiled with wry amusement. "I suppose you already think my behavior to be shocking?"

"Quite shocking," he mocked.

"Well, you needn't think that your opinion matters a wit to me."

"I am painfully aware that it does not," he replied, his darkly lean features surprisingly set in lines of self-derision.

"Giles . . ."

"Yes?"

Once again overwhelmingly conscious of his potent appeal, Roma hastily rose to her feet. Being seated so close together in this isolated place was far too intimate for her peace of mind. It made her remember all sorts of feelings she was determined to forget.

"Shall we take a stroll?"

He paused and then heaved an audible sigh, as if regretting her sudden retreat, but after the barest hesitation he was rising to his feet and graciously offering her an arm.

"By all means," he said in smooth tones. "You can pick wildflowers while I describe the delectable soiree your aunt has devised to introduce me to the neighborhood."

Roma glanced at him in horror.

"Oh, no . . ."

Eighteen

Two days later Lord Carlton turned his stallion off the main path and into the increasingly familiar copse of trees. He could never have supposed on that stormy night weeks ago that he would willingly return to the overgrown thicket. But then again, he never would have supposed he would be besotted over an ill-tempered, unruly chit, or that he would be using every nefarious trick he could contrive to lure her into marriage.

Moving through the lengthening shadows, Giles ruefully recalled his carefully calculated attempts to repair the damage done by his impetuous proposal. He had never meant to allow the words to spill past his lips. After all, he had been grimly aware of the response he would receive. The merest suggestion of marriage was enough to make Roma bolt like a terrified rabbit. And indeed, she had all but disappeared from Rosehill after his reckless words. But for far too long he had waited for some sign, some hint that she considered him more than a necessary encumbrance. Was it any wonder his sorely tried patience had momentarily faltered? He could only hope the more lighthearted picnic had managed to soothe her ruffled emotions.

With an exasperated sigh at his wandering thoughts, Giles forced himself to concentrate on the thickening trees. He would find himself knocked off his mount by a low branch if he did not have a care, he warned himself sternly. Hardly the thing for a noted Corinthian.

Entering the small clearing, he glanced about and then frowned with mild impatience. He had requested Jameson meet him in the copse at precisely eight o'clock. It was unlike the staunchly competent groom to be anything but punctual.

"Jameson?" he called in a low voice.

There was a rustle from above and without warning, a solid form dropped from a branch to land on the spongy ground. Giles stiffened as he regarded the tattered breeches and smock, briefly wondering if he had stumbled upon a local thug hoping for an easy picking. Then the familiar countenance put the absurd thought from his mind. Only the most mutton-headed thief would wait in such a remote location for a potential victim.

Straightening, the groom gave an instinctive tug on the rough smock, as if he forgot he was not in his usually pristine uniform.

"Good evening, my lord."

Giles arched an amused brow. "Practicing to be an owl, Jameson?"

"Simply ensuring you were not being followed, my lord," he explained with his usual unflappable dignity.

With a fluid motion, Giles dismounted and regarded his servant with open admiration.

"You are worth your weight in gold, Jameson."

"I do my best, sir."

"What do you have for me?"

The groom grimaced as he gave a reluctant shrug. "Unfortunately I have discovered very little," he admitted in regretful tones. "No one appears to find anything suspicious in Mr. Allendyle's absence."

Giles was torn between a mixture of relief and frustration. He wanted the damnable mess to be over and done with, but at the same moment, he was realistic enough to sense that the fact William's disappearance remained a mystery was all that kept Roma out of danger.

"I suppose we should be thankful his disappearance has gone unnoted," he grudgingly conceded. "For the moment Roma should be safe enough."

Jameson gave a slow nod of his head. "Yes."

"Is there anything else out of the ordinary?"

There was a pause as Jameson gave the question serious thought.

"I am attempting to discover more on an unknown gentleman who occasionally appears at the local inn and demands a private parlor."

Giles brows lowered. "Yes, I have heard of the elusive guest."

"The innkeeper refuses to admit that he knows anything beyond the fact that the man arrives without warning and never remains more than a few hours." Jameson allowed his distaste for the fat, insatiably greedy proprietor to mar his impassive countenance. "He claims that the man pays in advance and never creates a mess. Precisely the type of guest he has no wish to offend with impertinent questions."

Giles own features reflected the groom's disapproval. He had visited the inn on more than one occasion and had been offended by the man's oily smile and groveling manner.

"I can well imagine. The innkeeper struck me as a man singularly devoted to acquiring his blunt with as little effort to himself as possible." He crossed his arms over the width of his broad chest. "Do any of the regulars have an opinion on this gentleman?"

Jameson shrugged. "A few presume that the man comes to indulge in a secret tryst with a maiden who is smuggled through a back door. Others have claimed that he is a highway robber who is lying low from the constables." Jameson gave a derisive snort. "I even had one bloke tell me that he was convinced the stranger was the illegitimate son of a local lord who comes to demand his quarterly allowance."

Giles couldn't help but chuckle at his groom's condemning tone.

"If you were a betting man on which supposition would
you lay your money?"

"None, my lord," he replied promptly.

"Why?"

"In the first place you could not hide a young maiden
traveling across the countryside to a remote inn." He explained without hesitation. "And in the second a highway
robber would not chose a public inn to hide from the
law."

As always Giles was impressed with his groom's swift
grasp of the pertinent facts. He had always felt it was a
shame the man had not been born into a position that
would allow him a role in the government. He would
have been a shrewd asset. But then again, he had to admit
he wouldn't know what to do without his most trusted
servant.

"What of the illegitimate son?"

Jameson cleared his throat in a disapproving manner.
"It has always been my experience that any gentleman of
means would have his lawyer deal with such a delicate
task."

"Precisely," Giles agreed, his gaze narrowing in a
thoughtful manner. "So why would a gentleman ride to
an isolated inn and hide himself in a room?"

"A mystery, my lord," the groom was forced to admit.

"Such behavior attracts far too much attention to be
of use to any man indulging in illegal activities."

Jameson nodded "Quite right."

"Unless . . ." Giles came to an abrupt halt as he was
struck with a brilliant flash of insight. "Damn, of course."

"What is it, my lord?"

Giles paced across the small clearing, attempting to arrange his tumbled thoughts into a semblance of order.
Beneath his restless feet, a tiny animal burrowed through
the tall grass and into a fallen log.

"Unless he wishes to attract attention to the fact that

he is at the inn to distract people from realizing he is not there at all."

Not surprisingly, Jameson frowned in puzzlement. "Not there?"

"It is a conjurer's trick." Giles attempted to be more concise. "Just consider, Jameson, if you wished to perform some covert activity in this remote area. It would be impossible to avoid being noticed by the locals. Strangers are too rare not to attract some notice."

"True enough, sir."

"So, if you can not avoid detection, the only choices are to discover a legitimate means of staying in the area, or . . ."—he paused for dramatic effect—"diverting attention from your real purpose."

A dawning comprehension slowly glinted in Jameson's eyes. "Yes."

Giles restlessly paced back across the clearing.

"This gentleman has ensured that all speculation is centered on the mystery of what he could be doing in the locked parlor. They never consider the notion he is using their distraction to slip out the window and complete his activities with no one the wiser."

Jameson gave a low whistle as he considered the devious scheme. "I think perhaps I should have a closer look at that parlor."

"You might want to check and see if the window has been recently greased."

"Very good."

Knowing the groom could adequately investigate the inn, Giles turned his thoughts to other matters.

"Is there anything else I should be aware of?"

A distinct gleam entered Jameson's eyes, even though his features remained stoically impassive.

"To own the truth, most of the customers are devilish reluctant to discuss anything beyond the shocking engagement of Miss Allendyle."

"Indeed?" Giles drawled. "And how does the wind blow, Jameson? Am I judged to be a suitable fiancé?"

"I fear that it is as yet undecided. Miss Allendyle is a favorite among the neighbors, and many are of the opinion she is deserving of a husband who is of the first consequence."

Giles felt a twinge of bittersweet longing. "I could not agree more, Jameson."

"Neither can I, my lord," the groom surprised them both by admitting.

With a faint shake of his head, Giles returned his attention to the matters at hand.

"Did you make any inquires about Lord Scowfield?"

"Yes, and for all that he has a title, I can tell you he is not as well thought of in the neighborhood as the Allendyles," Jameson swiftly responded. "Doesn't like to rub elbows with the common folk, unless it happens to be a pretty barmaid, if you know my meaning."

Unfortunately Giles knew his meaning all too well. Not that Scowfield was the only gentleman to seek his entertainment among the local servants. Still, he had always considered the notion of playing the grand signor decidedly contemptible.

"But no suspicion of illegal activities?" he demanded.

Jameson shrugged. "Seems to keep to himself. Not many who know much of his movements."

"It is to be hoped that I shall know more after tonight," Giles said. "I managed to force a dinner invitation from dear Freddie. Quite a reluctant one, I might add. He doesn't appear to care for guests."

"Shall I follow you?"

Giles gave the offer a moment of thought. "Yes," he at last decided, realizing that it would be foolhardy to take any unnecessary risks. "Although I would prefer that no one suspect we are acquainted."

"I have met Lord Scowfield's head groomsman. Perhaps I will call on him tonight with his favorite bottle of gin," Jameson suggested with a hint of a grin.

Giles reached out to give him a grateful pat on the

shoulder. "Wait for me just beyond the gatehouse at midnight."

"I shall be there, sir."

Giles allowed his hand to linger on his groom's shoulder, his expression becoming somber. "Take care, Jameson. I shouldn't know how to go on without you."

A surprising blush stained the pleased man's lean cheeks.

"Oh . . . yes. Thank you, sir."

Grasping the reins of his horse, Giles vaulted into the saddle; then with a wave at his groom, he turned to retrace his steps to the pathway.

Once more headed in the proper direction he attempted to review the brief conversation with Jameson. He was determined to ensure that he had missed nothing. With careful precision, he pieced together the various facts and suppositions as if the mystery surrounding William Allendyle were a gigantic puzzle.

If only there were not so many pieces missing, he thought with a flare of frustration.

Turning onto the tree-lined road, Giles allowed himself to be diverted by the vast parkland surrounding him. Between the trees he could glimpse the closely scythed lawn, classical temples and marble statues scattered about. In the distance a large lake glittered with the soft crimson light of the setting sun. And centered in the framework of nature loomed a classically austere hall with a portico of towering Ionic columns that formed a shallow bow.

A most impressive home, he had to admit, and one that must cost a small fortune to keep in such prime condition.

Halting in front of the waiting groom, Giles dismounted and allowed the servant to take the reins. Then, plucking a tiny twig from the sleeve of his claret kerseymere coat, he crossed to the large door being opened by a stern-faced butler.

"Lord Carlton." The silver haired man gave a stiff bow.

Then, taking Giles's hat and gloves, he motioned across the vast entry hall. "If you would follow me, my lord."

Giles followed the stiffly upright form down the long gallery with its bronzed candelabra-form pillars and marble busts placed in niches overhead. The Pompeian style was continued in the blue and buff drawing room, with one wall devoted to a display of Grecian urns and pottery. Across the room antique draperies were arranged to allow a glimpse of the mirrors beneath, and on another wall the fireplace boasted a gratework of gilt bronze.

"Fine establishment," he congratulated as he turned to regard the butler standing in the doorway.

"Yes, sir. It was built in the early seventeen hundred's by the fourth earl," he explained. "I will inform Lord Scowfield you are here."

"Thank you."

Waiting until he heard the butler's footsteps recede down the gallery, Giles moved across the room to more closely inspect his surroundings. With blatant disregard for propriety he pulled open drawers and leafed through papers in the hope of discovering some clue to William Allendyle's whereabouts. Unfortunately he had to at last concede that there was little to discover in the room beyond the knowledge that Scowfield possessed as fine a taste in his furnishings and art collections as in his architecture. A fact that Giles found oddly annoying.

Standing next to the shelves that held the urns, he was on the point of risking a quick glimpse through the adjoining room when he suddenly noted the chess table situated beside a klismos-style chair. Leaning forward he studied the black and white carved pieces situated on the board. Clearly a well-matched game was in progress, he acknowledged with a flare of excitement.

At that moment the door opened and Giles turned to watch the thin, rat-faced man enter the room. As always Lord Scowfield's appearance was impeccable. Tonight he had chosen an exquisitely molded coat of pale green and breeches in a soft dove hue. Giles was forced to admit the man could as easily fit into the salon of the finest hostess in London as this remote country seat.

Discovering his guest standing across the room, Lord Scowfield arched an inquisitive brow.

"Interested in Grecian urns, Carlton?"

"I am interested in a great many things." Giles forced himself to smile in a bland manner, even as he covertly allowed a gold pocket watch to drop behind his back. Then, with a negligent motion, he waved toward the small table at his side. "Exquisite chessboard. Do you play often?"

Only the barest flicker of discomfort was allowed to mar the Scowfield's cool composure before he was calmly pulling out a snuffbox and busying himself with the task of securing a small pinch.

"No. Unfortunately I rarely entertain."

The brief betrayal was enough to convince Giles he was on the right trail.

"How unfortunate. Quite a large home for a man to rattle around in on his own," he drawled. "I would imagine it would be deuced lonely."

Scowfield shrugged with seeming indifference. "Not at all. I prefer to be on my own."

"Do you? I suppose it has it's benefits," Giles deliberately allowed himself to admit, his gaze narrowing to intimidating slits. "One is not obliged to be constantly tripping over another's toes, or to be having one's movements under constant surveillance." His smile was without humor. "You are quite at liberty to do whatever you might choose with no one being the wiser."

Much to his credit, Lord Scowfield met the subtle thrust with a cold smile. "Quite right. Although I would hasten to add that I rarely indulge in any behavior that I would fear to be put under surveillance."

"No?"

Abruptly moving to the heavy mahogany sideboard, Scowfield held up a crystal decanter.

"Brandy?"

"Yes, thank you."

Pouring two generous portions, Scowfield crossed the room to hand Giles a glass; then, raising his own, he regarded his guest in a mocking fashion.

"A toast," he offered in a challenging tone. "To you and my dearest friend, Roma."

Giles swallowed the urge to knock the superior smile off the rodent face and instead lifted his glass with a laconic gesture.

"I will certainly drink to that."

Leaning against the shelf, Lord Scowfield didn't bother to hide his obvious suspicion.

"I must admit that I am quite surprised by this engagement, Carlton. Roma has always been adamantly opposed to the mere mention of marriage. How did you ever manage to sway her opinion?"

Giles shrugged in a rather self-derisive manner. "I would like to claim that she was felled by my fatal attractions, but in all honesty I must admit it was more persistence than charm that won the fair damsel."

Seemingly surprised by such a blunt confession, Scowfield raised his dark brows. "Indeed?"

"Yes, I simply refused to be dismissed." His expression abruptly hardened, suggesting a hint of danger. "I can be quite tenacious when I choose."

"So I have noted," Scowfield admitted in dry tones. "Still, I can not help but be curious at her abrupt change of heart. I believe you have only known each other a short while?"

"Long enough to be certain that we shall suit quite well," Giles stated in a voice that dared opposition.

"I do hope you are right, Carlton. I should hate Roma to regret her rather . . . hasty decision later."

"I shall ensure that she never has cause to regret our marriage," Giles retorted. Then, realizing he had managed to lose control of the confrontation, he set about remedying his error. "Of course, any wedding will have to wait until I have formally obtained permission from Mr. Allendyle."

A guarded expression descended on the thin countenance. "Yes, indeed. I believe you mentioned William is in the north visiting friends?" His tone was determinedly casual. "Is he expected to return soon?"

"I had hoped you could tell me, Scowfield."

The small man visibly stiffened. "I? What a perfectly ludicrous notion! How could I know when William is to return?"

Giles pretended an interest in the golden brandy he was currently swirling in the bottom of his glass.

"Did he not speak with you about his visit?"

"Not at all," Scowfield swiftly denied. "I haven't spoken with William for . . . oh, several weeks, I daresay. Indeed, I had no notion he was even considering leaving Greystead."

Giles abruptly lifted his gaze to stab Scowfield with a piercing stare. "No? How very peculiar."

"I fail to see why. William has no need to inform me of his every movement."

"Then I wonder where I got the notion you had some knowledge of Allendyle's whereabouts?" Pretending to consider the strange circumstance, Giles idly glanced toward the chessboard, his slender fingers moving to pull the ivory queen forward. "Ah . . . checkmate I believe."

The door opened, interrupting the tense atmosphere that filled the drawing room. Both gentlemen turned to regard the butler standing in the doorway.

"Dinner, my lord," he intoned.

"Thank you, Hudson," Scowfield said, clearly relieved by the servant's announcement. "Shall we go through, Carlton?"

"Certainly," Giles agreed, then, with a deliberate motion, kicked the pocket watch that he had earlier dropped to the carpet. "Hold a moment. What's this?" Bending down he picked up the watch he knew to be William

Allendyle's and held it up for his host to see. "This must be yours, Scowfield."

For a moment a blank look of puzzlement settled on Scowfield's dark countenance; then with the staunch composure that Giles could not help but admire, he held out his hand to firmly accept the proffered watch.

"Ah . . . yes. Thank you, Carlton. I must have dropped it last evening," he lied smoothly.

Any fear that his suspicion of Lord Scowfield stemmed more from jealousy of his familiar relationship with Roma than any substantial information was put to a swift end. He had effectively proved that this man was attempting to hide something surrounding William's disappearance.

"Unusual design," Giles commented in bland tones.

Scowfield gave him a stiff smile. "A family heirloom."

"Really?"

"Yes. Shall we go to dinner?"

Giles hesitated, wondering if he should press his momentary advantage. Then, deciding that he might frighten the man into committing a rash act they would both regret, he forced himself to swallow his impatience.

"After you, Scowfield."

Together they left the room and walked down the gallery to the vast dining room. With a deliberate effort, Giles adopted his most urban manner, turning the conversation to the latest political unrest confronting Parliament. Seemingly content to follow his guest's lead, Lord Scowfield added his own mild comments, unwittingly revealing a shrewd grasp of the current fractions within the government.

The dinner progressed without incident, and after sampling a fine port and viewing a collection of ancient coins set within a glass case, Giles at last took his leave. He was careful to time his departure only moments before the stroke of midnight, and making his adieus, he strode out of the house to where a groom patiently waited with his stallion. With casual ease, he swung up into the saddle and urged his horse back down the long, winding drive.

He kept the restless stallion at a steady pace, as if he had nothing more on his mind than reaching his bed at Rosehill, but his senses were on full alert for any hint that he was being watched or followed as he crossed the parkland. Reaching the gatehouse he continued for several more paces before slowing his mount and carefully searching the road behind him.

Eventually satisfied that his departure had not aroused undue interest, he slipped out of the saddle and moved to the darker shadows beside the road.

"Well?" he demanded, not bothering with any preliminaries.

Jameson stepped forward, the moonlight slanting across his sharp features.

"I have discovered nothing, my lord," he confessed in disgusted tones. "The servants are as tight lipped as one of them mummies out of Egypt. They won't pass on one word about their employer."

Giles couldn't help a small chuckle. "How grossly inconsiderate of them to be so loyal."

"I fear I have done nothing more than waste a bottle of gin."

Having unfortunately sampled the gin from the local inn, Giles was convinced the only waste was of a good bottle.

"My evening was hardly more profitable," he consoled the frustrated groom. "Lord Scowfield is proving to be as sly as a fox, and as difficult to corner."

"Did you find out nothing then?"

"I found out that Lord Scowfield knows more of William Allendyle's disappearance than he is willing to admit," Giles acknowledged, recalling the man's hasty claim to Allendyle's pocket watch. "In fact, I would bet my fortune he was directly involved."

Jameson arched a surprised brow at the stern accusation.

"What do you intend to do?"

Giles grimaced with exasperation. The same question

had burned through his mind since Lord Scowfield had revealed his hand.

"What can I do? I have no proof, no means of forcing him to tell the truth." He smacked a fist against his thigh. "Damn, but it is a frustrating tangle."

Sensing his employer's growing impatience, Jameson squared his shoulders with determination.

"Shall I poke around the estate and see if I can find anything amiss?"

Giles gave a swift shake of his head. "Not yet. I put a flea in Scowfield's ear. For the moment, let us sit back and see which way he jumps."

"Very good, my lord," Jameson conceded with obvious disappointment.

"You might, however, keep an eye on the inn." Giles offered instead. "If the mystery man happens to arrive, you can let me know as soon as possible."

The groom visibly brightened. "Of course."

With a wry smile, Giles turned and pulled himself back into the saddle. He was disappointed by the lack of tangible evidence, but he was convinced that he was at least a step closer to the truth. And one step was better than none.

"Now, I must return to Rosehill," he announced, his expression twisting with rueful amusement. "Lady Welford is impatiently awaiting my decision on whether she should choose to wear the gray tulle or the violet satin ball gown. A decision, I have discovered over the past few days, that carries profound complications and must be fully discussed and pondered with tedious care."

Blinking in mild surprise, Jameson watched as his employer urged the black stallion down the dark road.

He had always heard that love could make a gent a bit daffy.

Now he was certain of it.

Nineteen

"Roma, what the devil are you doing hiding yourself in this corner?" With a frown of exasperation, Claude halted beside his truant cousin. "Mama is nearly in a spasm looking for you."

With a tiny sigh, Roma realized that her momentary peace was at an end. She hadn't intentionally tried to hide from the roomful of guests her aunt had invited for the evening, but once she had drifted into the shadowed alcove, she had discovered that it was the perfect place to view the large saloon without being noticed.

"I am not hiding," she denied, the white lie slipping easily from her lips. "I was simply searching for a place in which I could stand without being trampled by the crowd."

Wry amusement replaced the irritation as Claude glanced around at the guests that mingled throughout the room.

"Lord, yes. Mama is of the old school that firmly believes the success of a party is only determined by how many times your toes are trodden upon. She refuses to accept the notion an evening's entertainment would be much more enjoyable with twenty comfortable guests rather than fifty miserable ones." Claude shrugged, his blue eyes lingering on the pallor of her features. "Is it only the crowd that is bothering you?"

Roma couldn't prevent a mocking smile. "What do you

think, Claude? My brother is mysteriously missing, I am engaged to a man who is little more than an annoying stranger and your mother has insisted on this party to introduce my pretend fiancé to the entire neighborhood. Should I be bothered?"

Claude gave a rueful chuckle. "All right, it was a ridiculous question."

"Indeed it was."

"But to be honest, cousin, I am so accustomed to seeing you face up to every problem that the sight of you hovering in this corner with that rather sick look on your face caught me off guard." He gave a self-conscious shrug. "I thought for a moment you might be jealous."

Roma instinctively stiffened at the ludicrous words, absolutely refusing to glance toward the tall, raven-haired man who had been surrounded by a circle of adoring women since the evening had begun.

"Jealous?" She lifted an auburn brow. "Pray, what would I have to be jealous of?"

"Well . . ." Claude blushed faintly beneath her steely gaze. "Whether it is pretend or not, Lord Carlton is your fiancé. Those girls should know better than to flirt with the man in such a shameful manner. Any well-refined lady would blush at such forward behavior."

With a tiny jolt of surprise, Roma realized that Claude's condemning words merely echoed the distaste that had smoldered in the back of her mind all evening. Of course, it had nothing to do with jealousy, she swiftly reassured herself. It was simply annoying to see well-brought-up girls behaving like common tarts just because a handsome and, at times, charming man had arrived in their secluded lives.

"I don't suppose you can fully blame them," she grudgingly conceded, her gaze overcoming her staunch command to stray toward the man she hadn't seen or spoken to for the past three days. As always the odd quiver of awareness flared through her body as she covertly studied the pure lines of his masculine profile and the exquisite fit of his elegant coat and pantaloons. There was little doubt that he easily surpassed every other male in the room, but forcing aside her very feminine appreciation for his decidedly male attributes, she instead concentrated on the charming smile he flashed with monotonous regularity at the bemused collection of women. "My fiancé seems to be going out of his way to encourage them."

Claude turned his head to follow her pointed glance. "He is only being polite, Roma."

She forced a small laugh, giving an indifferent toss of her head. "What do I care? He can flirt with whomever he chooses. In fact, it relieves me of the burden of pretending I find him anything but odious."

"Have the two of you had an argument?"

"When don't we argue?" she retorted, refusing to acknowledge the small flare of pain that accompanied the words. It wasn't her fault that the man had chosen to ignore her very existence for the past three days. Or that he preferred to treat her with taunting amusement rather than the practiced charm he was currently bestowing upon the giggling misses fresh from the schoolroom. "But to be honest, I have not clapped eyes on him for days, so for once we are not at daggers drawn. I can only assume he prefers the stimulating appeal of such obvious admirers."

Consumed by the sight of Giles lowering his raven head to catch the words of a diminutive blonde with vacant blue eyes and an overly exposed bosom, she missed her cousin's speculative glance at her unknowingly bitter words.

"I wonder what he has been up to," he murmured thoughtfully. "He certainly hasn't spent his time here. Perhaps he has been over to the Scowfield estate."

"At Freddie's?" His words managed to capture her interest and she turned to flash him a dubious frown. "What could he possibly be doing there?"

Claude shrugged. "I am not sure. He has, however,

taken an inordinate interest in Freddie. He has asked all manner of questions about his estate, his habits and even his taste in women. I found it decidedly odd to tell the truth."

No more odd than she did, Roma silently admitted. She would have sworn that Giles had taken a swift and unreasonable dislike toward Freddie. So why would he suddenly demand information that went well beyond idle curiosity?

Almost as if sensing her perplexed gaze, Giles suddenly raised his head from the chattering blonde, his vivid blue eyes abruptly narrowing as he studied her strained features that not even the vibrant curls or frothy golden gown could completely distract an onlooker from. Without a word, he detached himself from the group of fluttering damsels, and ignoring their pouts and imploring urges to remain, he firmly crossed the room to Roma's side.

"My dear, you look pale. Are you not feeling well?"

Ridiculously, it was the flare of sheer pleasure that raced through her at the genuine concern in his deep voice that made her rapidly retreat behind her familiar wall of antagonism.

"I feel perfectly fine." She tilted her chin to a defensive angle. "Besides, it is rather late to play the role of the devoted fiancé."

A raven brow arched at her petulant tone, and she suspected there was a mysterious glint of satisfaction deep in his eyes.

"Perhaps I have been rather remiss, but that is easily corrected." With a fluid movement he had her arm in a firm grasp. "A short turn around the terrace should reassure everyone that I am completely besotted with my intended."

A flurry of exquisite excitement raced up her arm at the touch of his warm fingers on her bare skin, and confused by the unexpected sensations, Roma found herself being escorted to the open French doors before she could form the instant protest that rose to her lips. But as they stepped into the blessedly cool night air, she managed to regain her shaken composure enough to send him a furious glare.

"There is no need for this absurd charade," she told him in a cold voice. "I was quite content to watch you dazzle the local schoolgirls with your wit and charm."

The husky male laugh she found so disarming mingled with the flower-scented breeze as he steered her toward the shadowed end of the terrace, his unnerving grip remaining on her arm even as they halted beside a marble bench.

"They at least appreciate my feeble attempts at flirtation. You, on the other hand, have remained remarkably immune. I can only hope that persistence will prove to be more effective than charisma."

She firmly hardened her heart against his nonsensical words. He was a shameless rake, and she knew that her continued disinterest in his masculine charms had pricked at his arrogant vanity. As a result, he was continually attempting to bait her with his outrageously suggestive words.

"Must you be so ridiculous? You know quite well I have no interest in a frivolous dalliance. You'll have to wile away your boredom with women more susceptible than myself."

"Frivolous dalliance?" His amusement only deepened at her sharp reprimand. "How can you label me as a libertine when I have willingly offered you my name and protection in the most honorable state of matrimony?"

Her heart jerked to a painful stop before lurching back into motion at an uneven pace. She was potently aware of his body heat that easily penetrated her thin muslin gown and the clean scent of his male skin. She was also disturbingly reminded of the captivating moments she had spent in his arms. The memories had haunted her dreams to the point that she feared she would never again close her eyes without seeing dark aquiline features and

brilliant blue eyes. Her unnerving reaction to his proximity made it impossible to treat his ludicrous words with
the disdain they deserved. Instead, she flashed him an
unconsciously alarmed glance.

"I wish you would not jest about our fictitious wedding," she complained. "It is difficult enough to endure
Aunt Clara's endless chatter without your taking such delight in roasting me."

"And what makes you so certain that I am roasting
you?" His mocking smile remained, but his tone was
oddly somber. "I have already told you, I believe we could
deal quite well together."

"And why would you want a marriage of "convenience?" she demanded with open suspicion. "You could
easily choose a woman with a title, a fortune and even
beauty. Why would you settle for someone like me?"

She thought she heard him heave an exasperated sigh,
but rather than pulling away in annoyance, he stepped
even closer, his fingers intimately stroking the sensitive
skin of her inner arm.

"Because you amuse me, Roma," he murmured softly.
"And more importantly because of this . . ."

Without warning, the raven head swooped downward
and the warm lips that had already created far too much
chaos in her life were once again closing over her parted
mouth in a plundering kiss that made her mind spin with
dizzying pleasure.

For days she had been attempting to convince herself
that the embraces she shared with this man could not be
as earth shaking as she allowed herself to imagine. A kiss
was a kiss, and it was simply her inexperience that made
his seem far more poignant and meaningful than they
were. But as her lips willingly melted beneath his persua-
sive mouth and she felt the irresistible wave of excitement
curl through her stomach, she was forced to acknowledge
this was no mere kiss.

How could it be when her entire body trembled with
the need to be held even closer to his lean frame? It did

not seem to matter that she was behaving in a completely shameless manner or that this man was a master at seduction. The only things that seemed important were the emotion storming through her and the completely unexplainable sensation that she was exactly where she belonged.

She gave a soft moan and as if he sensed her inability to resist the magical spell of his touch, his fingers tightened on her arms, slowly drawing her toward his broad chest.

"Roma . . ." He whispered against her mouth, his voice barely recognizable. "We must talk. There are so many things I need to explain to you—"

His words were abruptly cut off as the soft sound of approaching footsteps warned them that their privacy was about to come to an end, and with a muffled gasp, Roma pulled herself away from his clinging touch. Ignoring his soft curse and the frustrated fire that burned in those vivid eyes, she hastily raised a hand to absently push at her tumbled curls, unwittingly doing more damage than good. She felt a complete fool and could only hope that the darkness would hide the embarrassed color that rushed to her face.

"Roma, listen to me—"

"Not now," she hissed softly, feeling ridiculously close to tears as Claude appeared on the terrace, followed by what appeared to be a large horde of unknown guests.

"Giles . . . Oh, there you are." Claude breathed an audible sigh of relief as he caught sight of the two standing in the shadowed corner. "I believe that these . . . guests are here to see you."

Roma felt Giles stiffen at her side, but her gaze never left the lovely creature that detached herself from the group beside the door, looking ravishing in a low-cut satin gown that shimmered like pure silver in the moonlight.

"Giles, darling, I hope we are not intruding?" the woman purred, deliberately ignoring Roma as she floated across the terrace to lay a familiar hand on his arm. "We were on our way to my cousin's estate, and we simply could not pass by without paying a visit."

"Really?" Giles had abruptly retreated behind his mask of cool arrogance, seemingly unaware of the stunning brunette's provocative smile or the open invitation of her parted lips. "I have never known you to speak of any cousin who possesses an estate in the area. Certainly not one that could induce you to leave London at the height of the Season for a visit."

The lovely woman gave a dramatic sigh, ignoring the distinct frost in his tone.

"What do I care about London without you, Giles?" she demanded softly. "I have tired of this ridiculous argument. It is time we put the past behind us and continue on with our future."

Her tone was low enough to prevent the avid onlookers from overhearing the less than subtle words, but Roma could clearly understand every pleading syllable. A harsh, cutting pain tore through her heart as she realized that this beautiful woman was Giles's mistress. This was exactly the type of woman she would have pictured him choosing. Lovely, elegant and sensually sophisticated. Everything in fact that Roma was not, and for some ridiculous reason that only served to deepen the unexplainable anguish that rushed through her.

As if sensing her distress, Giles abruptly wrenched his arm free of the woman's clinging grasp, his dark features grim with displeasure.

"Lady Hoyet, I am afraid you have intruded on a private party given in honor of my fiancée. I think it is best if you and your guests continue on your way."

The woman gave a small gasp at his blunt words, her almond-shaped eyes suddenly shimmering with tears.

"You can not be so cruel, Giles. Do you truly intend to punish me by marrying this unsophisticated chit? She would only be miserable once you realize that you still love me. Can you not see this is all a mistake?"

"The only mistake is your being here, Lavania," Giles

gritted out, in his fury emanating static tension. "I suggest you leave before my desire to avoid creating a scene is overcome by my urge to physically throw you from this house."

"How unforgiving you are." She gave a delicate sniff, suddenly turning toward the silent Roma. "You should take careful note, my dear. Your soon-to-be husband can be a callous brute when he chooses. They say the streets of London are paved with the hearts he has broken; are you quite certain that you wish to be tied to such a man for the rest of your life?"

"That does it. You and your friends are leaving, Lady Hoyet. Make your good-byes."

Reaching out a hand, Giles grasped the woman's arm in a none-too-gentle grip, propelling her firmly away from the stunned Roma. There was a faint stir as the other elegantly attired people watched Giles approach, but one glance at his savage expression was enough to have them nervously shifting out of his path without a word.

Under any other circumstance Roma might have found their subdued retreat humorous. But at the moment she barely noted their hasty exit. Instead she found herself struggling to accept the horrid realization that had quite literally hit her like a slap in the face.

It couldn't be true. It was ridiculous, absurd, completely insane. But no matter how desperately she might attempt to convince herself she was merely reacting to the stresses of the situation, it was impossible to avoid the truth.

Somehow, in some way she had fallen in love with Lord Giles Carlton. That was the reason she had so mysteriously trusted him from the very start, and why she melted at his slightest touch. It was also the reason she had been torn with painful jealousy at the sight of his beautiful mistress.

Raising a shaky hand to the uneven beating of her heart, Roma gave a small shake of her head. She was a fool. An innocent child that hadn't seen the danger until it was far too late. And now the smug Roma Allendyle who had been quite certain she was too shrewd to ever open her heart to treacherous emotions was suffering the pangs of unrequited love.

"Roma, are you all right?"

With a reluctant blink, Roma forced the chaotic thoughts to the back of her mind, belatedly realizing that Claude had moved to stand beside her.

"Actually, I have developed the most shocking headache," she said, realizing that it would be futile to pretend nothing was wrong. "I think perhaps it would be best if I went home."

Claude was appropriately sympathetic. "I am sorry, Roma. I will go tell Mama and see you home."

"No." She gave a stubborn shake of her head. "Aunt Clara will need you here with the guests. I brought my groom with me, and it is only a short distance home. I will be fine."

"But, Roma—"

"Please, Claude." She eyed him in an unconsciously pleading manner. "I really would prefer to slip away unnoticed. I will make my apologies to your mother tomorrow."

Claude hesitated, then, sensing her determination, gave a reluctant nod of his head.

"Very well, but do not judge Giles too harshly, Roma. It was clear that the woman came here tonight to cause trouble. He at least deserves an opportunity to give you an explanation before you try and convict him."

Her smile was filled with self-mockery. "I have no right to judge him at all, Claude. He came here to help me find my brother, and if he chooses to have a dozen mistresses, then it truly is none of my concern. We would both do well to remember that important fact." She straightened her shoulders, refusing to display the pain that throbbed just below the surface. "Please tell Aunt Clara I am sorry her evening did not go as planned. Perhaps my next engagement will prove to be less distressing for everyone involved. Let us hope so."

Barely hiding the threatening tears, she slipped into the shadows surrounding the house. She had to get away before she broke down completely. And even though she realized her sudden disappearance would only fuel the gossip that was bound to occur, she knew it would be impossible to face Giles at the moment.

She needed time to reconcile herself to the startling revelations and, more importantly, to find the courage to face him without revealing the emotions that ran rampant through her heart. Of course, she wasn't sure there was enough time in the world to accomplish that difficult task.

Twenty

"Giles . . . You are hurting my arm."

The petulant wail did little more than harden the already grim expression on Giles's dark countenance as he half-led, half-dragged the reluctant woman toward her waiting carriage.

"Be relieved that it was your arm I chose to grab and not that lovely neck," he snarled in a low voice. "It was a definite temptation."

"Such passion." She gave a toss of her head, surrounding them in a cloud of cloying perfume. "Do you honestly imagine that milk-and-toast fiancée of yours will be woman enough to fulfill your insatiable needs?"

A surge of disgust rushed through Giles. It seemed impossible to believe that he had ever been attracted to this woman, or that he had once believed he could be satisfied with a relationship built solely on lust. Now he couldn't rid himself of her and her frivolous friends quickly enough.

"My needs are no longer your concern, Lavania," he informed her in icy tones. "And be assured, this is the last time you will attempt to embarrass me or my fiancée."

She gave a sharp laugh that didn't hide her bitterness. "Are you so certain she is still your fiancée, Giles?" she mocked. "She was looking distinctly uncertain when we left. Of course, no woman would like to think she is about to tie herself to a callous rake."

His grip tightened until she gave a small gasp. "I have no doubt you came here to create trouble, Lavania. And if I believed for a moment that I genuinely hurt you, then I might forgive you for coming here tonight. But this little display was no more than a vain need to revenge your pride. You are a shallow, selfish and grasping woman and, if you did manage to convince Roma that I am untrustworthy, then I will spend the rest of my life attempting to prove how wrong you are."

"Do not tell me you had the poor taste to fall in love with the chit?"

"Yes, I love her. And even though I am quite certain I do not deserve her, I am going to do everything possible to win her love in return."

A bleak, almost forlorn expression momentarily flitted across her beautiful features.

"I do not believe you. How could you possibly fall in love with a nobody without rank or fortune? You could have any woman in London."

"Roma possesses much more than mere rank or fortune," he informed her, unable to stir pity for the woman's brief regrets. She had long ago turned her back on love for the wealth and social position gained in a hollow marriage. "She has an unquenchable spirit and a generous nature that make every other woman I have encountered fade into insignificance."

"Please do not expect me to wish you well," Lavania retorted, her full lips twisted into a sneer.

"All I expect is that you treat Miss Allendyle with respect," he retorted, the warning in his tone unmistakable. "The next time you attempt to harm her, you will not be let off so easily."

She gave a disdainful sniff, but allowed Giles to bundle her into the waiting carriage without argument. Hopefully his warning would be enough, but Giles was fully prepared to do whatever was necessary to protect Roma from this woman's malicious nature. At the moment, however, he was more intent on ridding himself of the unwanted intruders so that he could return to Roma. He knew she was upset, not only because of Lavania's ill-timed entrance, but also because it followed on the heels of the consuming kiss that had left them both shaken. He had never intended things to get so out of hand; in fact, he hadn't meant to touch her again until he had confessed his love.

But the moonlight and the scent of her warm honey-suckle skin had effectively destroyed his stern discipline, and unable to resist temptation, he had given in to his burning need to taste the nectar of her soft lips. Her instant response had only inflamed the fires that smoldered whenever she was near, and before he'd known what was happening, he had discovered himself taking swift advantage of her unexpected vulnerability.

Now he had no doubt that she had scampered back behind her antagonistic shell of indifference. He could only hope she would at least be reasonable enough to listen to him. After tonight there would be no more games. He would tell her that he loved her and damn the consequences.

He was so anxious to return that he ignored Lavania's mocking farewell and even shoved aside one of the younger men who instantly paled at the thought of annoying such a famed marksman. He needn't have worried, however, as Giles strode past him without so much as a glance and, with a determined pace, circled the brightly lit house to return to the terrace.

But his desperate hope that Roma had chosen to wait for his return was instantly dashed as he crossed the garden to discover Claude standing alone in the shadows.

"Damn . . ." He heaved a sigh of exasperation, crossing toward the man who was clearly waiting to speak with him. "I suppose Roma has returned to the guests?"

"You suppose wrong," the young man surprised him by answering, his boyish face set in lines of accusation. "She decided it would be better if she slipped away quietly. And I must say I don't blame her. Whether your engagement is real or not, these people are Roma's friends and neighbors, and they believe you are her fiancé. How do you think she feels knowing that tomorrow they will all be discussing how you spent the entire evening flirting with every woman in the room, and to top it off, your mistress barged into the party and made a spectacle of herself? She is bound to be humiliated."

"I had no notion that Lady Hoyet would appear here tonight," he said, his tone unconsciously defensive. "And while I will freely admit that I am not, and never have been, a saint, I can assure you that I do not keep a fiancée and a mistress at the same time."

Claude gave an inelegant snort, clearly unimpressed "And what of your behavior tonight? You all but ignored Roma while you played the role of the callow flirt."

Giles responded with a restless shrug, the emotions boiling through his blood making it difficult to remain placidly standing on the terrace. He wanted to scream out his frustration or, better yet, gallop across to Greystead Manor and convince the exasperating woman once and for all that she needed him in her life. But he could do nothing but wait until the morning when he could decently make a proper call. Their relationship had strained the rules of convention enough without adding a midnight visit to his sins.

"If you must know the truth, I have avoided your cousin quite simply because she is far too shrewd not to guess that my emotions have become entangled."

There was a short pause; then a wide smile suddenly split the younger man's face.

"The devil you say. I had hoped the wind blew in that direction, but Roma was so adamant it was all no more than a sham I began to accept that she must be right."

"As far as she is concerned it is all a sham," Giles admitted, wry amusement at his self-made dilemma momentarily softening his grim features. "I have convinced her that she needs my help to locate her brother, but I seem remarkably inept at persuading her that our destinies lie together."

Claude's chuckle was filled with sympathetic understanding. "As I mentioned she can be annoyingly stubborn when she chooses."

"So I have noticed." He rolled his eyes at the understatement. "She is also sharp tongued, short tempered and thoroughly unpredictable. I have little doubt that any man foolish enough to take her on as his wife will find himself led on a merry dance. He will also be the most fortunate gentleman in the world."

"Well, if anyone can tame that willful cousin of mine it is you," Claude said. "Of course, we first must convince her . . ."

His relieved words trailed away as the sound of running footsteps echoed through the garden and both men turned to discover a man dodging through the rosebushes, his harsh breathing clearly audible as he rushed onto the terrace.

"My lord . . . you must come at once."

Puzzled by the intruder's bizarre behavior, Giles eyed him with wary suspicion, wondering if he were in his cups.

"Come? Come where?"

"Tomkins sent me," he panted, clearly exhausted from his long run.

Giles frowned. "Tomkins?"

"Miss Allendyle's groom."

A swift, all-consuming fear rushed through Giles as he realized that the man was speaking of the servant he had hired to keep a watch over Roma.

"Where is he? Has something happened?" Barely aware of his actions, he reached out to grasp the front of the man's uniform, nearly yanking him off his feet in his haste to discover what was wrong. "Is Roma hurt?"

"I do not know, my lord," the man stuttered, thoroughly intimidated by the wild-eyed nobleman. "We were taking the miss home when another carriage suddenly jumped into the road blocking the path. We didn't have no choice but to stop, it was that or turn the carriage over for sure . . ."

"Yes, yes . . . Just tell me what happened," Giles barked impatiently.

"I am trying to, sir. As I said, we had to come to a stop, and before we knew what was happening, a man suddenly leaped from the dark and pulled Miss Allendyle from the carriage."

Giles battled the mind-numbing panic that threatened to overwhelm his ability to think in a coherent manner.

"What man? Could you recognize him?"

"Not for certain, but . . ."—the man paused to swallow the lump of fear in his throat—"the crest on the carriage belonged to Lord Scowfield."

"Freddie?" Claude breathed in shock. "Good God, what the devil has gotten into him?"

Giles ignored the younger man's interruption, his concentration rigidly focused on discovering exactly what had become of Roma.

"What did he do once he had taken her from the carriage?"

"He forced her into his own carriage, and they took off. Tomkins is following them, but he sent me here to tell you what had happened."

"Good man." Giles loosened his hold on the shaken servant, his mind racing. At least Tomkins was in pursuit, and now he could join in the chase. Together they would save Roma. He had to believe that or go mad. "Do you know what direction they were taking?"

"The road that leads to the cove," he answered promptly.

"Very well . . ." He forced himself to pause and consider his options. It would do little good to rush about without some semblance of a plan. Roma's safety depended on his reacting in a sane and sensible manner. "Claude, I want you to go with this young man to the inn. My groom, Jameson, should be there, and hopefully

Jack Howe. I wrote and asked him to come. Tell them to meet me at the cove."

"But why should Scowfield abduct Roma—"

"Not now, Welford," Giles snapped. "Your cousin's safety depends upon how swiftly we can locate her."

The urgency in his voice must have communicated his leashed fear, for Claude gave a sharp nod of agreement.

"Let us go to the stables. That brute of a stallion of yours should have you caught up to those carriages before they go another mile."

Less than a quarter of an hour later Giles was galloping down the shadowed road, indifferent to the chill wind that whistled past his ears or the discomfort of riding in his tightly tailored evening gear. Instead, he desperately attempted to hold back the horrifying images of Roma hurt, perhaps even dead . . .

No, he wouldn't believe that, he told himself grimly, urging his horse to an even faster pace. He wouldn't accept that he could be too late. Even if Lord Scowfield was responsible for William Allendyle's disappearance as he suspected, that did not necessarily mean he intended to harm Roma. He might very well have planned this stunt to simply frighten her, or perhaps to warn her to halt her search for her brother.

But why would he take her to the cove? a taunting voice demanded from the back of his mind. And why risk abducting her in front of the servants when he was fully aware she rode unaccompanied every morning?

The questions pounded ruthlessly though his confused mind, plaguing him with a sense of urgency that made him toss aside all caution and plunge down the dark road at breakneck speed.

It seemed like an eternity, though he knew that it couldn't have been more than half an hour since he had left the Welford estate when he detected the distant sound of water breaking over the rocky coastline and knew that he was rapidly approaching the secluded cove. With a wary frown he slowed his weary mount, realizing that he should have caught up with the two carriages by now. Was he even farther behind than he had suspected? Or had the carriages pulled off the main road and taken one of the paths that crossed the numerous fields?

Seething with frustration, he narrowed his eyes, attempting to penetrate the heavy darkness as he slowly wound his way down the treacherous path to the crescent-shaped cove. He knew if they had turned off the road he didn't have a prayer of following them tonight. He could only hope that they were still somewhere ahead of him.

With instinctive caution, he edged his way onto the open beach, his initial glance almost missing the vague outline of a small boat at the edge of the water and the two forms that turned in startled surprise at his arrival. Looking for two large carriages, Giles was caught off guard by the sight of the men, and it wasn't until they swiftly headed toward him that he wondered if he might have stumbled into a dangerous situation.

Bringing the nervous stallion to an uneasy halt, he quickly considered his options, but even as he prepared to bolt to safety, the moon reemerged from behind a flimsy cloud and the unexpectedly familiar man nearest to him held up an urgent hand.

"Lord Carlton, hold a moment," Thomas Slater called, his tone commanding.

Startled by the unexpected encounter, Giles gazed down in puzzlement. "Mr. Slater, what brings you here?"

The man stopped next to the horse, tilting his head backward. "That is precisely the question I was about to ask you."

His words abruptly reminded Giles of what had brought him to the cove, and realizing that this man could be of considerable help, he forced himself to explain Roma's plight as concisely as possible.

The man listened in silence, but it was clear from his stiff stance that he was surprised they had discovered the traitor who had kidnapped William and even more surprised that Roma had now disappeared. As Giles finished, he gave a disbelieving shake of his head.

"A truly amazing tale, Lord Carlton," he said.

Rather taken back by the mockery he sensed below the casual words, Giles sent him a thunderous scowl.

"Amazing or not, Miss Allendyle is in danger. We must go in search of her."

"Unfortunately that is not possible."

"What do you mean?"

"Oh . . . I had fully intended to deal with the troublesome Miss Allendyle, but if what you say is true, then it seems someone has already taken care of one problem for me," Thomas Slater drawled. "And now I only have you to rid myself of."

Far too late Giles became aware that the second man had covertly moved to stand almost directly behind him. The initial sense of danger he had foolishly shoved aside returned full force, but not in time to save him from the obvious trap.

"What do you want, Slater?"

"Want?" The man gave a mocking laugh, the sound eerily echoing through the cove. "I want my very profitable business to continue. Do you know the money that can be made by selling the most trivial of information to the enemy? You see, unlike you, I was not born with the means to live the life I have always wanted, so I was forced to do what was necessary to achieve my goals. Unfortunately, my business sometimes includes dealing with overly curious individuals who poke their noses into things that are none of their concern. I have already taken care of William Allendyle. Now, Lord Carlton, I believe that you will have to join him at the bottom of the cove. A tragic waste, but quite necessary, I assure you." His smile was perfectly polite, but as his arm slowly rose, Giles saw moonlight glint off the barrel of his gun. "Now, if you would be so good as to dismount, we can get this unpleasant business behind us."

Twenty-one

"William . . . Oh my God, I knew you were alive, I knew it."

Roma threw herself at the man seated in the corner of the carriage with an enthusiasm that knocked him back into the cushions.

"I am alive and well as long as you do not strangle me to death, sister," William teased, his own arms wrapping about her tiny form despite his chiding words.

Half-laughing, half-sobbing she pulled back to absorb the familiar pale face and laughing green eyes that she had so desperately feared she might never see again.

"You have some explaining to do, William. I have been near Bedlam with worry, and then to have Freddie throw me in this carriage in such a manner—"

"I will explain all in good time, Roma, but now we must hurry," he said, holding her tight as Freddie jumped into the carriage with them and they took off with a violent jerk.

"Hurry? Where are we going?"

"To catch a traitor in the act," William said, his voice grim. "If my plan works, then the agents I contacted in London will be at the cove to personally witness Thomas Slater selling vital government information to the French."

Roma's already stunned mind became even more confused.

"Thomas Slater? But he is—or was—helping us search for you."

"I seriously doubt he spent much time searching for me, my love, not when he was quite certain I was safely lying at the bottom of the cove, which I no doubt would have been if it wasn't for Freddie."

Roma slowly shook her head, barely aware of the dangerously swaying carriage as they raced down the uneven road.

"I do not understand."

"It is all very simple, Roma." William tapped the end of her nose in an endearingly familiar gesture. "You were aware that I was working for the government as a courier. Thomas, in fact, was the first to approach me to offer me the opportunity. Our friendship and the need to occasionally pass on new instructions gave him the perfect excuse to stay at Greystead. No one suspected that it was no more than a cover so that he could meet with his own contact from France. A man who would stay at the inn and then sneak out to use a small boat to make his way to the cove. I didn't even sense that he was a double agent until I accidentally came across some papers he had left in his room. Like a fool I confronted him with his treachery, hoping I could convince him to turn back before it was too late. For my efforts I was efficiently knocked over the head and tossed into the cove."

Roma gasped, shuddering with horror at the duplicity of the man who had accepted their hospitality and pretended to be their friend.

"He was always so charming, even when I saw him in London. And all the time he thought he had managed to kill you . . ." Her voice broke as her stomach roiled with disbelieving disgust. "He must be completely evil."

"At least very desperate," William said, his tone filled with contempt. "But what he did not know was that Freddie had witnessed him tossing me unconscious into the cove, and as soon as he left, Freddie fished me out and took me to his estate."

Turning her head, Roma flashed the silent man a tearful smile. "How can we ever thank you?"

"All in a day's work, my dear."

William gave a chuckle. "It was a little more than that, Freddie. You see, he is also an agent for the government, and it was his plan to allow Thomas to think he had succeeded in getting rid of me. We hoped to keep track of his movements, and when he set up another rendezvous at the cove, we planned to reveal his treachery to the proper authorities. Unfortunately we had no notion he would wait so long to make contact with the French, or that you would be in any danger." His grip on her tiny waist abruptly tightened. "When I learned that you had stumbled across the papers I was supposed to deliver and that Thomas had decided to set a trap to scare you away from searching for me, I nearly gave up the whole notion. But Freddie offered to follow you and keep you out of trouble."

"A very trying task, I must say." Freddie gave a rueful chuckle "You proved to be decidedly elusive, and your extremely aggressive fiancé made me distinctly uneasy. I expected to find myself at quarters drawn every time I approached you."

Roma's cheeks flamed, and she was glad the darkness would hide her embarrassment from her brother's all too perceptive gaze.

"Giles . . . Lord Carlton very kindly offered to help me look for you, William."

"Really? And how is it that he became your fiancé without asking for my approval?" William demanded. "I am your legal guardian, and I warn you, my dear, I am very particular as to who can or can not become a member of this family."

"But, he isn't—I mean, we aren't . . ." She broke off in confusion, the distress in her tone clearly evident.

"Hush, Roma. I am merely roasting you," William said gently. "From what I know of Lord Carlton he is a fine man with a near legendary reputation for aiding his country in whatever capacity it might demand. He is also a man of honor, and whatever your relationship, I am quite sure you are in safe hands."

Roma's blush only deepened as she abruptly thrust aside all thoughts of the disturbing man. Her emotions were far too painful to deal with at the moment.

"So why did you see fit to kidnap me in such a fashion?" she demanded, hoping to shift the conversation back to the problem at hand.

"To be honest it wasn't planned," William confessed. "We intended to trap Thomas tonight, but we feared if he managed to elude us he might become dangerous enough to harm you. Freddie was going to Aunt Clara's party to keep an eye on you when we suddenly spied your carriage approaching. Since we didn't have time for a lengthy explanation we decided that it would be far easier to simply bring you along."

"Well, thank you very much." She gave a toss of her head. "I have no doubt I shall be covered with bruises on the morrow."

"Trust you to complain of bruises when we might very well have saved your life," William grumbled affectionately. "You never could be satisfied."

With a small cry she once more threw her arms about his neck, threatening to cut off his air supply despite her delicate appearance.

"I am satisfied now that I know you are alive. Oh, William, I was so terribly frightened that something horrible had happened to you."

William suffered her strangulation with brotherly indulgence, his own voice suspiciously husky with tears.

"You needn't concern yourself with that notion, Roma. I am much too stubborn to be taken away easily."

The tender scene was abruptly interrupted as the carriage lurched off the road and began a rocky trip over what seemed to be an uneven field.

"Goodness, what is happening?" Roma demanded, painfully bouncing across the seat.

"I have given instructions for the groom to lose your very persistent servants, and to find an isolated place where we can leave the carriage," Freddie explained, his arms spread wide to prevent him from being thrown from his own seat.

Gritting her teeth, Roma endured the painful ride in silence, but she couldn't prevent a small moan of relief when the carriage jerked to a sudden halt. She had no doubt that every muscle would be sore the next day and that the mere thought of sitting would make her cringe. Still, she forced her battered limbs to move as the two men swiftly climbed down from the carriage, stepping onto the overgrown field without a thought for her elegant gown.

The still night air seemed oppressively silent, and an unexplainable shiver of apprehension rushed down her spine. She had been too overwhelmed with joy at the sight of her brother to fully comprehend that the danger was not yet over, but as she joined the two men and the groom, who had efficiently dealt with the horses, she could not miss their somber expressions.

". . . I will not be left behind." Her brother was arguing softly, his tone familiar to Roma. It meant there was nothing that could be said or done to change his mind. "I have waited too long to confront Thomas Slater to wait here."

"And if he senses a trap or escapes before we can stop him?" Freddie demanded. "Then he will know you are still alive."

William shrugged. "It is too late to turn back now. Tonight is all or nothing. Of course, you will have to leave your groom behind to stay with Roma."

"Do not be absurd," she interrupted sharply, her voice remarkably like that of her brother. "You brought me this far. I fully intend to see the appalling man captured."

William heaved an exasperated sigh. "Roma, this is not the appropriate time for your stubborn courage. Thomas Slater is a dangerous criminal who has already proved how far he is willing to go to achieve his own ends. I will not allow you to go anywhere near him."

"It is not your choice to make," she hissed, her chin tilted to an aggressive angle. "And if you do leave me here I will only slip away and find you on my own."

"Roma—"

Freddie interrupted the bristling pair, his tone resigned. "We can not remain here arguing all night. Slater could be in the arms of Napoleon by the time we make our way to the cove."

William muttered a curse, running a distracted hand through his auburn hair. "Very well, but you stay out of sight and do exactly as I say. Is that understood, Roma?"

Her smile was the picture of innocence "Of course, William."

He threw up his hands in frustration, but there was no more argument as the two men turned to walk toward the nearby hill and she quietly trailed behind. Or at least, she attempted to be quiet. It proved to be a remarkably difficult task as the large stones jabbed easily through the thin soles of her slippers and the underbrush tore at the full skirts of her gown. More than once she was forced to bite her lip as she stumbled over the uneven ground, but she refused to complain or even ask them to slow their swift pace. She had demanded to be included in the dangerous mission, and she would ensure that she did not become a liability.

Concentrating solely on staying upright, she obstinately placed one foot in front of the other, winding her way around the sloping hill and then through the dense trees that fringed the edge of the cove. After what seemed to be an eternity, William raised his hand and they came to a halt behind a large bush.

Maintaining the required distance, Roma waited in growing anticipation for some sign the plan was going as expected, but when her brother suddenly stiffened and breathed out a disbelieving curse, she could stand the suspense no longer. Conveniently forgetting her promise, she moved to peer over William's shoulder, her gaze sweeping the seemingly empty cove until she spotted the trio of men standing a short distance from the line of trees. At first she merely noted that the man on the horse appeared to be in deep conversation with the man standing beside him; then something familiar about the set of the shoulders and the regal profile of the shadowy figure on horseback had her blood freezing with fear.

Giles . . .

She had no idea what he could possibly be doing at the cove. When she had left her aunt's house he had been surrounded by his mistress and her bevy of acquaintances. But at the moment, she had no interest in what had occurred to bring him to this place or how he had stumbled across Thomas Slater. All she could think of was that the man standing behind him held a large stick as if preparing to strike him, while Thomas held out his arm in a manner that could only mean he was pointing a gun directly at Giles's chest.

She absorbed the horrifying images in the space of a heartbeat, and just as swiftly she realized that Giles was completely defenseless. Thomas Slater, who had already attempted to murder her brother, was now on the verge of killing the man she loved more than life itself, and she knew she had to do something, anything to prevent the inevitable.

Not giving herself time to even consider the danger, she abruptly rushed from behind the bush, screaming with all her might as she struggled through the fine sand in an attempt to reach Giles's side. Her unexpected appearance had an explosive affect on the men before her, and with a jolt of surprise, Thomas Slater turned to watch her stumbling approach, the gun glinting in the moonlight as he instinctively pointed it in her direction.

Roma thought she heard someone yell, but she ignored everything but the aching need to save Giles from certain death. Battling her tattered skirt and the thick sand, she struggled forward, her breath catching in her throat as

Giles suddenly leaped from his horse and crashed on top of the distracted Slater. A gunshot pierced the night air and she cried out in fear, her wild gaze pinned to the two men rolling across the beach.

For a moment she was stunned into immobility; then, just as she realized that she was too faraway to help Giles, there was a rustle behind her and as if on some silent command, the entire beach filled with men, most in military uniforms, shouting and giving orders.

In the seething confusion, Roma dropped to her knees, the relief that Giles was indeed safe making her legs too weak to continue another step. Men rushed past her trembling form as they hurried to capture Thomas Slater and his accomplice, and she thought she glimpsed the familiar face of Jack Howe as he ran toward Giles with an anxious expression. But she couldn't move; in fact, she could barely think as the delayed shock quaked through her system.

Chaos reigned supreme for a time, and at first Roma barely noticed that her name was being shouted over and over. But as a large frame suddenly shoved its way through the milling soldiers, she glanced up to discover Giles charging toward her with savage intent.

Her sluggish heart gave an abrupt beat as she took in his bedraggled appearance, the love she had at last accepted singing through her in an intoxicating rush. He looked ludicrous with his elegant clothes half-ripped from his muscular body and his raven hair tousled across his forehead, but Roma was quite certain she had never seen a more wonderful sight. At least that was her thought until he drew close enough for her to read the fury etched across his stark features.

Her eyes grew wide as he halted in front of her, his hands reaching down to grasp her arms in a biting grip and jerk her roughly to her feet. Her gasp of pain went unnoticed, however, as he sharply shook her slight frame until it grew limp.

"Of all the loose-screw, dim-witted, idiotic things to

do," he shouted at the top of his lungs. "How you have
continued to live as long as you have is beyond my comprehension."

Thoroughly furious at his beastly attack, she glared at
him with raging disbelief.

"My life was doing quite well until you forced your way
into it, Lord Carlton," she stormed with a toss of her
head. "And now that my brother is safely home, you can
rid yourself of my annoying presence with a clear conscience."

He faltered, obviously surprised by her words. "Your
brother is alive?"

"Yes, Freddie has been hiding him at his estate. They
are the ones who set up this trap for Thomas Slater."

The vivid eyes rolled heavenward. "I might have
known. It appears your brother has the same knack for
risking my neck as you do. If I had any sense at all I
would get back on that horse and flee to London as swiftly
as possible."

"I have told you that you are free to leave," she said
stiffly, unaware of the misery that shimmered like a beacon in her eyes. "Perhaps you and Lady Hoyet can ride
back to London together."

He growled in the back of his throat, his features
abruptly softening as he gazed into her vulnerable expression.

"I said that is what I would do if I had any sense, but
that is something I haven't possessed since I spent the
night in a barn with a hazel-eyed sprite who bewitched
me to the point that I didn't even realize I had been
captured until far too late."

"I . . ." Her heart clenched at his rough voice, wanting
to believe he was sincere, but wary that she had somehow
mistaken his meaning. "You must be teasing. You are always furious with me."

He gave a rueful chuckle, his eyes filled with a blinding
tenderness that threatened to melt her lingering mistrust.

"Not always, my love, just when you frighten me half

to death, which seems to be all too often. When I saw
you running toward me tonight—" His voice abruptly
broke, and she found herself being hauled against his
wide chest in a sudden motion. "I love you, Roma. I love
you more than I thought possible, and it doesn't matter
what I have to do or how long it takes—I will make you
my wife. I absolutely refuse to live without you."

The arrogance in his voice was tempered by the flare
of painful uncertainty that rippled across his dark features, and with a surge of joy, Roma threw her arms about
his strong neck. She might not understand how such a
man could have fallen in love with her, but she had no
intention of wasting another moment on her long-held
insecurities or the vague fear that he might prefer a glam-
orous woman like his mistress. He had proved time and
time again that he was a man she could trust with both
her life and her heart.

"I suppose I have no choice, Lord Carlton," she teased
gently. "Besides, I have heard that marriages of convenience often work out quite well."

"I have a premonition that there will be nothing convenient about choosing you for my wife, Roma Allendyle,
but I wouldn't exchange you for a dozen demure debutantes. It seems I have a decided preference for fiery
sprites who are constantly stumbling into one scrape after
another."

"No more," she promised, her eyes shining with stunning emotion. "As Lady Carlton I will have my reputation
to think of, you know."

He gave a shake of his raven head. "The only thing
you have to think of is staying the same lovely, impetuous
woman I adore." He lowered his head to place demanding lips against her willing mouth, savoring her sweetness
before moving away with a tortured groan. "Especially if
your impetuous nature is enticed by the thought of a swift
marriage by special license rather than the more conventional wedding your aunt is planning."

The urgency in his husky voice was echoed in her pulsing blood, and with a provocative smile, she leaned even closer to his trembling form.

"Well, I have never been a conventional kind of woman . . ."

ABOUT THE AUTHOR

Debbie Raleigh lives with her family in Ewing, Missouri. *Lord Carlton's Courtship* is her first Regency romance and she is currently working on her second, *Lord Mumford's Minx,* which will be published in August 2000. Debbie will also have a short story in a regency collection, *Spring Kittens,* which will be published in March 2000. She loves to hear from readers and you may write to her c/o Zebra Books. Please include a self-addressed stamped envelope if you wish a response.

More Zebra Regency Romances

Merlin's Legacy

A Series From
Quinn Taylor Evans

__**Daughter of Fire** $5.50US/$7.00CAN
    0-8217-6052-1

__**Daughter of the Mist** $5.50US/$7.00CAN
    0-8217-6050-5

__**Daughter of Light** $5.50US/$7.00CAN
    0-8217-6051-3

__**Dawn of Camelot** $5.50US/$7.00CAN
    0-8217-6028-9

__**Shadows of Camelot** $5.50US/$7.00CAN
    0-8217-5760-1

Call toll free **1-888-345-BOOK** to order by phone or use this coupon to order by mail.

Name _____
Address _____
City _____ State _____ Zip _____
Please send me the books I have checked above.
I am enclosing $_____
Plus postage and handling* $_____
Sales tax (in New York and Tennessee) $_____
Total amount enclosed $_____
*Add $2.50 for the first book and $.50 for each additional book.
Send check or money order (no cash or CODs) to:
Kensington Publishing Corp., 850 Third Avenue, New York, NY 10022
Prices and Numbers subject to change without notice.
All orders subject to availability.
Check out our website at **www.kensingtonbooks.com**